A THUNDEROUS WHISPER

A THUNDEROUS WHISPER

CHRISTINA DIAZ GONZALEZ

ALFRED A. KNOPF

NEW YORK

Text copyright © 2012 by Christina Diaz Gonzalez

Jacket art copyright © 2012 by Ericka O'Rourke

Jacket photograph copyright © Denis Rouvre / Corbis Outline

All rights reserved. Published in the United States by Alfred A. Knopf, an imprint of Random House Children's Books, a division of Random House, Inc., New York.

Knopf, Borzoi Books, and the colophon are registered trademarks of Random House, Inc.

Visit us on the Web! randomhouse.com/kids

Educators and librarians, for a variety of teaching tools, visit us at randomhouse.com/teachers

Library of Congress Cataloging-in-Publication Data

Gonzalez, Christina Diaz.

A thunderous whisper / Christina Diaz Gonzalez.

p. cm.

"A Borzoi book"

Summary: Ani, a twelve-year-old Basque girl, and Mathias, a fourteen-year-old German Jew, become friends and then spies in the weeks leading up to the bombing of Guernica in April 1937.

ISBN 978-0-375-86929-7 (trade) — ISBN 978-0-375-96929-4 (lib. bdg.) — ISBN 978-0-375-98274-3 (ebook) — ISBN 978-0-375-87371-3 (pbk.)

1. Guernica (Spain)—History—Bombardment, 1937—Juvenile fiction.

[1. Guernica (Spain)—History—Bombardment, 1937—Fiction. 2. Spain—History—Civil War, 1936–1939—Campaigns—Fiction. 3. Jews—Fiction. 4. Spies—Fiction. 5. Friendship—Fiction.] I. Title.

PZ7.G5882Thu 2012

[Fic]—dc23

2011043445

The text of this book is set in 12-point Goudy Old Style.

Printed in the United States of America

October 2012

10 9 8 7 6 5 4 3 2 1

First Edition

To my husband and best friend . . . you are my lightning

A THUNDEROUS WHISPER

ONE

Invisible. Irrelevant. Just an insignificant twelve-year-old girl living in a war-torn country. At least that's what I'd been told.

And, really, no one ever seemed to notice me when they walked past the school's large courtyard. They only saw the other girls laughing and giggling in small clusters under the building's arches while the boys rushed out to challenge each other in a game of soccer or *pelota vasca*.

Rarely did anyone see the quiet, friendless souls . . . but we were there. Not really worthy of being picked on, we just came and went in silence. We rarely spoke to anyone, not even each other, although I could never remember why.

"Hey, you! Wait!" a voice called out from across the courtyard, near the steps that led to the cobblestone street below.

I had just walked through the school's main door when I saw Sabino, a boy from my class, waving. Immediately I turned to look back inside, certain that he must be calling someone else.

"No, you . . . Sardine Girl," he said. "Don't let the door close. I forgot our ball inside."

That's what I was called—Sardine Girl.

My father would say our family's clothes carried the scent of the sea, but that was just his fancy way of saying that we reeked of fish. It made sense since Papá had worked as a merchant seaman before joining the army and Mamá had always been a *sardinera*, selling the sardines that were the size of my feet, but stinkier, door to door. No wonder everything they owned, including me, smelled of fish.

I propped the door open with my right foot and stared as Sabino trotted toward me. He slowed down, and looking back at his friends, he pinched his nose.

They all laughed.

It wasn't that I was surprised at being ridiculed. . . . Usually, I just ignored it. But, on that particular day, the sun in a cloudless blue sky seemed to be signaling the arrival of spring, and I, like the weather, was ready for a change.

And so, taking a deep breath, I waited until Sabino was about four feet away, and then I moved my foot. *Kadunk!* The door reverberated, and I heard the latch click shut.

"*¡Idiota!*" he shouted as he pushed past me, pulling on the locked door.

"My name is *not* Sardine Girl," I muttered, my eyes never looking up from the ground.

❖　　❖　　❖

I followed the narrow cobblestone streets back toward my neighborhood, passing the shoe store, the fruit stand, and the people sitting at the small tables of the sidewalk cafés.

Glancing up, I could see a few women in the balconied apartments pulling in the day's laundry that had been hung out to dry.

I picked up my pace when I noticed that the large clock above the Plaza de los Fueros showed that it was already five-fifteen.

As I passed a few soldiers filtering into the local tavern, I couldn't help wishing Papá were also on leave from the front lines. He could be so close—the front lines being less than twenty kilometers away—and yet the distance seemed so great. He felt farther away than when he'd leave for months on a merchant ship. Of course, this time he might not return home.

Rounding the final corner, where the last city street ended and the dirt road into the countryside began, I heard the sound of squeaky wheels approaching. As I stepped to one side, I saw two brown oxen pulling a large, mostly empty, rickety cart. As one of the beasts passed by me, it briefly turned its head, its eyes meeting mine, then, after a loud snort, it looked away.

"You don't smell that great either," I mumbled.

The farmer, walking on the other side of the street, next to the larger ox, gave me a friendly nod before cracking the whip against the animal. I could see there was a bit of a bounce to the old man's step, which probably meant he had sold all his produce for a good price. At least someone was having a good day.

Actually, there were probably several people who were quite happy, as market days always brought an extra vigor to Guernica. Everyone in the region knew that Mondays in Guernica meant social events and jai alai games at the fronton after the market closed.

I loved Mondays too, but not because I wanted to socialize with anyone. No, for me this was the day that I didn't have to sell sardines with Mamá or do chores. It was the one evening when I was free to do whatever I liked. So I was headed to the place where my dreams and stories were born.

It was really just a large open field with a big oak tree, but it had always felt like my special place. The tree was ordinary, similar in size to the famous Guernica Tree in the heart of the city, I suppose, but this one had no long history behind it. It was only special and significant to Papá and me.

From the time I was a little girl, whenever Papá was in town, he'd bring me to that tree. We'd have picnics, and I'd listen to tales of his travels. During the last few years, Papá had insisted that I come up with my own stories, and he'd lie back under the tree and get lost in my world of princesses and magical creatures. He always listened to every word I said, as if I were reading from the Bible, and when I finished, he'd usually smile and say, "*Preciosa*, tell me another." And precious was how I felt.

I sighed. The last seven months of his being a soldier instead of a sailor had been like living on the edge of a crumbling cliff: any moment I feared that the land I stood on would give way. I couldn't wait for the stupid war to be over and for life to go back to how it used to be. Without my father, the only good part of my day was going to class, and that wasn't saying much. The only thing I liked about school was the books.

Walking up the mountainside, I clutched my sweater tighter to my chest as a cool breeze blew down the trail. Even in late March, on a beautiful afternoon, winter had not completely released its hold on northern Spain.

I had left the concrete and muted colors of the city behind and stepped onto a grassy patch of land. Here I could drink in the brilliance of the sky, the green and brown of the neighboring mountains, and dream and forget the world around me.

I thrust my hand into my skirt pocket, and my fingers rubbed the edge of the satin pouch buried inside. It had been Papá's gift to me before he left. A blue satin pouch made from the lining of his only suit. I grasped it and felt the small treasure it held. It was a reminder of all our days together.

And then I was there. The green grass surrounded the majestic oak, which stood tall, new leaves growing on its branches. The sun, slowly sinking toward the top of the mountains, cast an orange glow on everything and I knew I had about an hour to enjoy this before I'd have to head back.

I reached out and touched the warm, wrinkled bark, greeting it like an old friend. Settling into my favorite spot, where I could gaze at my city in the distance and still feel as if I were completely detached from it, I undid the leather strap around my schoolbooks and pulled out a thin notebook. I wanted to write a lighthearted story that I could send to Papá, something that would make him smile and forget, just for a moment, the ugliness of war.

Twirling the pencil that I always kept tucked inside the notebook, I stared at the shadows cast by some of Guernica's buildings. I tried imagining them turning into something wondrous, but everything that came to mind was sinister and frightening.

It still didn't seem fair that we were caught in Spain's stupid Civil War. The Basques had been living on the same piece of land since before records were kept, and now, just because we lived on what the world considered Spanish land, we'd been forced to pick a side. Neither group fighting really cared about the Basques, so I couldn't understand why it mattered, but a side had been chosen and now we must win to survive. I'd heard people say that losing the war would also mean losing everything it meant to be Basque.

I clenched the pencil so hard I could feel it begin to bend between my fingers. A little more and it would snap. I stopped and relaxed my hand. I couldn't dwell on the war anymore. . . . Papá deserved a good story. Closing my eyes, I hoped that my imagination would take over, but nothing happened.

It'd been the same the last few times I'd been to my tree. My thoughts would drift to the front lines, to the men dying and to the rumors that Hitler and his large German army were becoming more involved in the Civil War. It was bad enough that the country was tearing itself apart; now we had to fear that the Germans would help General Franco's side.

"Think about an island. About princesses," I commanded, squeezing my eyelids so tight that pink and blue spots appeared.

"Island princesses, huh?" a voice with a slight accent asked.

My eyes popped open, but the sunlight blinded me. All I could see was the silhouette of a person holding a large stick.

I shielded my face and braced myself for the attack.

TWO

"Didn't mean to scare you . . . at least not so much," the voice said with a slight chuckle.

My eyes adjusted to the light, and I saw that the figure was just a boy, not much older than me, with dark brown hair and even darker eyes. He was twirling a *makila*, a Basque walking stick.

"I wasn't afraid," I said, jumping up to face my newest tormentor. "More like . . . startled."

He tilted his head to the side as if sizing me up. "So, do you always talk to yourself?"

"No." I was already annoyed with this boy.

"Guess you only do that sometimes, huh?" he asked with a smirk.

I crossed my arms and gave him my best glare.

"Really? Is that supposed to be a menacing look?" He laughed, took off his beret, and stuck out his hand. "Let me start over. I'm Mathias. Nice to meet you."

I ignored his outstretched hand, choosing to raise a single eyebrow, a talent I'd inherited from my mother.

He kept his hand out. "C'mon. I just moved to Guernica."

"Figured that out myself," I muttered, hoping he would go away.

"Now what is *that* supposed to mean?" he asked, putting his beret back on and sticking his hand in his pocket.

I shrugged. "Nothing."

"What? Say it. I'm a big boy. . . . My feelings won't get hurt. It's my accent, right?" He shook his head. "Thought I'd gotten rid of it too. I was sure my Spanish was pretty good."

"No, it is." I sighed, as if the conversation were painful . . . which it was. "I just meant that lots of refugees have been moving to Guernica lately. Running away from the war and—"

"Listen, princess, my family doesn't run away," he corrected.

"Princess?" I gave him a sharp look.

"Weren't you muttering something about being a princess when I got here?"

"No. I mean yes." I rolled my eyes. "I wasn't talking about myself."

"Fine, if you say so." Mathias took a seat on the grass, gazed up the hillside, and then turned his attention back to me. "So, what's your name?"

The day had gone steadily downhill. Now I couldn't even enjoy my time alone.

I plopped down, defeated, and tucked my legs under my long skirt.

"Anetxu," I said, wondering why he was even talking to me.

"*Gesundheit!*" he replied with a grin.

"Huh? What?"

"It's German. . . . It means 'Bless you.' Like when you sneeze and go *achoo*. I said it because your name sounds—"

I could feel my shoulders tightening. "I get it. Very original."

"*Tranquila*, princess. I didn't mean any harm." He yanked on a long blade of grass and twirled it between his fingers. "So, you're from around here, right?"

"Mm-hm." I leaned against my tree and half closed my eyes, hoping he'd get the hint and leave.

"I thought as much. I've only been here a couple of weeks, but it isn't the worst place I've seen. Have you been to other cities?" he asked.

"Sure I have."

A sudden flash of interest ran across his face, and he sat up. "Really, which ones?" he asked.

"Bermeo," I declared, and immediately regretted it. I'd go there once in a while with Mamá to get the sardines from the fishermen, but it made Guernica look like a big city by comparison. Plus, the last thing I wanted to bring up was being Sardine Girl.

"Well, I haven't been there, but I don't think any place holds a candle to Berlin . . . except for maybe Barcelona."

"I like Guernica," I said.

"That's because you haven't been to other places."

"That's not it. You'd feel different if you were Basque."

"Ah, but you're wrong. I *am* Basque. My dad was born in San Sebastián, and that's as Basque as any town."

"So? That doesn't make *you* Basque."

Mathias took off his beret and ran his fingers through his dark hair as if thinking about what I'd just said. "Guess you have a point about that."

"Of course I do," I muttered. It felt like a small victory. . . . I just wasn't sure what I'd won.

Nothing else was said for a few moments and I thought about walking away, but I refused to give up my tree to the likes of him.

"Well, what do you think really makes someone Basque?" he asked.

I shrugged. This was getting to be worse than school. At least there I was mostly ignored.

"Think about it. If it's not where you're born, then is it what you speak?" He paused for a moment, then shook his head. "Nah, that can't be it. Anyone can learn a language. . . . I already know three, even if I can't understand much in Basque. There's got to be something else," he said.

"Does it really matter?" I asked, staring off at the horizon, pretending not to be curious about this boy. "If you're Basque, you just know it," I said.

"Hmph, typical of a girl," he said, tugging on another blade of grass and rolling it into a ball.

I turned to face him. "What does that mean?"

He leaned back on his hands and smiled. "Relax, princess. It's a fact that most girls don't like to think about complex things. Cooking and sewing are what they're suited for."

I narrowed my eyes and shot him a look, one that would certainly help us win the war if the army could turn it into a weapon. "You don't know what you're talking about. Boys are usually the ones who don't think." I could feel my blood boiling. "And don't call me princess . . . ever!"

For about a minute, neither of us said a word, and we didn't move either.

I watched a small smirk creep over his lips and realized I had never answered his question. "Your question isn't even that hard," I commented. "Being Basque has to do with your family history . . . where you come from."

He pinched his lips together, then shook his head. "Nah, that can't be it, because what would that make me? I'm Basque on my father's side, but German on my mom's."

I straightened up. "Your mother's German?" Suddenly his barely noticeable accent sounded much stronger, and the fact that he spoke several languages hinted at something much more dangerous.

Mathias nodded and grabbed at another patch of fresh grass. "Well, she used to be anyway."

I moved forward an inch or two. "*Used to be?* What do you mean . . . ? Is she, you know, dead?"

He looked up at me, his eyebrows slightly scrunched together. "Oh no. God no," he said, shaking his head vehemently. "There are new laws over in Germany that say if you're Jewish or part Jewish, you're no longer a German citizen. . . .

That's what I meant. They don't care anymore if you were born there or if your grandparents and great-grandparents were all born there."

"You're . . . *Jewish?*" I asked.

Mathias nodded.

I'd never met anyone who was Jewish before. All the people I knew, even the ones I really didn't know, were Catholic. I stared at him. He didn't look that different. But why was he talking to me?

"You ever been to Germany?" I asked.

"Of course I have," he answered, as if that were the most ridiculous question ever. "I may have been born in San Sebastián like my dad, but I grew up in Berlin. Most of my mom's family still lives there, but my parents and I have been moving around a lot these last few years. Lived in a bunch of different places."

"Like where?" I asked, thinking of all the places Papá used to describe. Maybe this would be what I'd write about in my letter to him.

Mathias looked away, seeming to conjure up an image in his head. "Barcelona, Paris, Madrid, but Berlin is still my favorite. It's beautiful there. Amazing architecture, food, history . . . It has to be one of the best places in the world."

"It can't be that great if your parents left," I answered.

He shrugged, and started to wipe away some of the dirt streaks on his pants.

I stayed quiet, waiting to see if our conversation was

finally over and he'd leave. I still didn't know why he was talking to me.

Turning his head to look at me again, he asked, "So, since you now know all about me, what would you say I am? Basque, German, or something else?"

My lips twitched. I resigned myself to the fact that he had no intention of leaving me alone. "You, Mathias— That's your name, right?"

He nodded.

"I say you are"—I thought for a moment, then smiled—"annoying."

His lips lifted up to form a half smirk, then a grin, which soon transformed into full-blown laughter. He was laughing as if I'd said the funniest thing he'd heard in a week.

It wasn't the effect I was going for, but his laugh was contagious, and I found myself smiling too.

After a few seconds, he caught his breath and lay back on his elbows. "I like you. You're a straight shooter," he said, staring at my face as if he were trying to decipher some secret code. "Can I ask you a question?"

"I don't think I could stop you," I said.

He tilted his head, ignoring my comment. "How come you don't have any friends?"

This was why I didn't like talking to people. I could have had a perfectly nice time by myself, but now he wanted me to explain *why* I was unpopular.

My hands twitched, and I almost got up. But if I left, then it'd be like surrendering my tree.

"Not that I'm one to talk," he continued. "I move around so much that it's sometimes hard to make friends."

I crossed my arms and tucked my hands underneath my armpits. "I have plenty of friends," I responded.

"Haven't seen you with any."

The hairs on the back of my neck stood up, and not because of the cool wind that was now blowing through the field. "You've been spying on me?" I couldn't forget that he was part German . . . or Jewish . . . or whatever.

"Not really spying." Mathias paused for a moment. "More like observing. I do that a lot."

I swallowed the lump in my throat and put aside any thought that this boy could pose a threat. "Hmph, sounds a lot like spying to me. You know what they do to spies, don't you?"

"Observing is not spying. And, yes, I know what happens to spies. They're lucky if they get shot."

That reminded me of the war and Papá. I wondered if Papá had ever met a German. I wasn't sure he'd approve of my talking to someone who was half-German. Then again, Papá was friends with a lot of people he'd met in his travels, so maybe it'd be all right with him.

"Hey, is everything okay?" Mathias asked after a few moments passed.

I nodded and felt my ponytail hook itself on a loose piece of bark. "Yeah, just thinking about stuff. My dad is fighting in the war." I carefully untangled my hair from the tree.

"Is he with the Itxasalde Battalion?" he asked.

I gave him a slight nod, but concentrated on tucking the

strands of hair that now dangled by my cheek back behind my ear.

Mathias kept probing. "So, is he a communist?"

I jerked my head up. "No! Not at all." I knew Papá hated what the communists were doing in other parts of Spain. I'd heard some horrific stories of priests and nuns being killed. "He just wants to protect our ways . . . to keep things how they've always been. Are *you* a communist?"

"Nope, don't think so." He shook his head.

"Good. Anyway, my father isn't really fighting. He helps in other ways. Works in the kitchen, I think."

"Oh, that's too bad. I'm sure that's not what he wanted to do when he joined."

"Hmph. I'd rather he be safe in a kitchen than out on the front lines. Soldiers need to eat too. Anyway, how'd you know the battalion's name?"

Mathias shrugged. "I've heard some of the men from town talking about it. Like I said, I watch and listen. You'd be surprised at how much you can learn when you're not busy talking."

I smiled. "So, I guess you're not learning much today."

The edges of Mathias's mouth twitched again before forming another big grin. "You can learn things by talking to people too." He swiveled around and leaned against the tree. "And what do you do when you're just sitting here?"

"Nothing much. Think up stories, daydream."

"About island princesses?"

"Huh? Oh, what I was saying when you sneaked up on me."

"I didn't sneak up on you. That's kind of hard to do with

this thing." He pointed to the *makila,* which lay on the ground next to him.

My eyes darted from the walking stick to his right leg. Something about how his pants draped wasn't right.

"Were you in an accident or something?" I asked, motioning to his leg.

He tugged on the pants, smoothing out the wrinkle by his calf. "Or something." For the first time, he didn't look at me.

Minutes passed and we settled into an uneasy quiet.

"So, you want to be an island princess?" Mathias finally asked, breaking the silence.

"Hmm? Oh no. That's just a story I made up a long time ago. I used to tell it to my father."

"You want to tell me?" he asked, staring straight out toward the horizon.

"No." I reached into my pocket, my fingers searching for the smoothness of the satin pouch.

The streetlamps of Guernica were already shining in the distance and the sky was growing darker by the second. It was time for me to head home.

I stood up and Mathias followed as I started to walk back toward town.

"Besides fairy tales, what other stories do you like?" he asked.

I shrugged. "Adventure, I guess. How 'bout you?"

He kicked a small rock that lay in the middle of the dirt road. "I'm not big into reading or hearing stories. I'd rather watch them."

"More observing?" I teased.

"Nah." He waved his hands in the air as if revealing an invisible sign. "I'm talking about films . . . Hollywood."

"Movies?"

Mathias nodded. "I get to see them because of my father's job."

"Is he *in* the movies?" An unintended excitement found its way into my voice.

"I wish. He's in charge of the new movie theater in town."

"Must be pretty rich." The words slipped out before I could stop them.

"Nah, not even close. He doesn't own the place; he just gets a theater started for the owners. Then we move to the next city."

I could see the paved road up ahead. We were now only a few blocks from my apartment. I wondered if he was going to follow me all the way home like a lost puppy.

"Have you seen a movie before?" Mathias asked.

"Um, sure." I hesitated. "Lots of times."

Mathias looked at me closely. "Really?"

I guess it was an obvious lie. "No."

Mathias perked up at my admission. "You want to go? I'm sure I can get you in. Father will make us clean the theater or something, but it'll be worth it."

The thought of seeing a movie was exciting. It was a luxury I'd never had or even thought of having. A chance to see a story come to life.

"That sounds good," I said, trying to be nonchalant.

"Yeah?" he asked, stopping to look at me.

His excitement was contagious. "Yeah," I answered with a smile.

"Perfect." He twirled the *makila* in one hand before using it to keep walking. "How about we meet there tomorrow?"

"Um." I had school, and Mamá expected me to help her sell the sardines in the evening.

"You don't want to?" Mathias asked.

"No. I mean yes . . . I want to go, but I have school. Don't you?"

Mathias shook his head. "Uh-uh. We're always moving around, and my mother used to be a teacher in Germany, so she teaches me at home."

"Oh." Although I didn't like school very much, it was better than being home all day. I also couldn't imagine Mamá being anyone's teacher. The only thing she'd ever taught me was how to remain quiet and make sure no one noticed me. During a war, I figured, that was pretty useful.

"Can't you miss the afternoon session?" Mathias asked.

"I suppose, but . . ." School was the least of my worries. Mamá would be the real problem. It'd have to be on a day when she didn't need me to work. "How about next Monday?"

We'd reached the city's first streetlamp, and under the glow of the light, I could see Mathias rub his chin. "No, the theater isn't open on Mondays. You sure you can't make it tomorrow?" He paused for a moment before continuing. "It'd be perfect because Father is giving a private screening at five and he'll let us watch from the back if we help with the cleaning before the bigwigs get there."

I mulled it over. I couldn't think how I'd manage it, but then again, how often would I have a chance like this? I bit my bottom lip.

"Don't worry," Mathias said. "We'll leave it for another day." He pointed toward the center of town with his *makila*. "I'm down that way."

"I'm over there." I glanced along the row of three-story buildings.

"See you around, then." He took a few steps toward the shadows of the narrow street, his *makila* making a tapping noise against the cobblestones.

It felt as if this were the end. I wouldn't see the movie or Mathias again.

"I'll meet you tomorrow!" I called out, surprised at the force in my own voice.

He spun around. "*¿De veras?*"

"Yes, really."

Mathias slapped the side of his leg. "Perfect!" he exclaimed. "Tomorrow it is. You're going to love it, princess." He waved before heading back toward town.

"My name is not Princess!" I called out.

"Oh, right. Sorry. See you tomorrow, Ani."

No one ever called me Ani either, but if I was going to have a friend, I supposed it really didn't matter what I was called. That's when I knew. A friendship, whether I wanted one or not, had been formed.

THREE

I opened the door to our dark apartment. The green velvet drapes over the window were closed, and the silence in the room confirmed that Mamá had not yet returned from her day of striking deals at the market.

Mondays always seemed to foretell my week. If Mamá sold all her sardines, she'd buy vegetables, eggs, and perhaps a piece of meat. If she didn't, we'd be eating mostly leftover salted sardines. Usually, it was somewhere in the middle, and we'd at least avoid eating fish for all our meals.

I flicked on the lights, stacked my two schoolbooks on top of the bench, and hung up my sweater. My reflection in the mirror by the door greeted me. I stared at my face as if my mother were the one seeing it.

How was I going to persuade her to let me go to the movies? For as long as I could remember, every day, after school, I'd been expected to work with her selling sardines. She would carry the basketful of sardines on her head, and I'd hold the scale and the brass weights used to weigh the fish.

"Ama, I have some wonderful news!" I said, clasping my hands together the way I'd seen the rich, proper ladies do in church. "I was invited to the movies."

I wrinkled my nose at the girl in the mirror, making the freckles that formed a bridge toward each cheek bunch together.

Saying something like that would never work. Mamá would be suspicious the moment I used the Basque word for "mother," even though she always called me *neska*, which was "girl" in Basque. When I was younger, I thought it was a nickname, like Papá calling me *preciosa*, but eventually I realized—"girl" was just a description, nothing more.

My mother was not going to be easy to convince. I thought of another approach.

"Mamá, wait until you hear what happened to me today!" I bounced up and down like a three-year-old.

Ugh! I shook my head. That would just annoy her. It annoyed me.

"Mamá, can I ask you for a favor?" My voice pleaded, and I tried my best to create pitiful eyes.

I stuck my tongue out at the reflection. Mamá would cut me off the moment I asked for something. She'd be telling me how we couldn't afford anything and how I was lucky to have shoes, because growing up as an orphan in Bermeo, she was always barefoot. Then she would say how all I did was take and never give back, how children shouldn't be heard unless spoken to, and on and on.

I rolled back my shoulders and lifted my head up high. "Mamá, I've been invited to the movies tomorrow afternoon. Isn't that wonderful?"

The door lock clicked.

Mamá was home.

I hurried toward the kitchen and tried to act busy.

"¡*Neska! ¿Neska?* Where are you?" Mamá draped her wool shawl over the empty hook next to my sweater.

"*Aquí, Mamá.* I'm right here." I wiped my hands on the back of my gray skirt.

"Don't just stand there. Come help me with this." She held out a brown paper bag.

I took a peek inside, happy to see that she hadn't come back with a basketful of sardines. There were three potatoes, some chickpeas, a few onions, and eggs.

"What? You thought there would be something new in there? Hmph!" She shook her head. "Always like your father, thinking life is going to give you more," she muttered.

I said nothing, but I secretly loved being compared to Papá . . . even if she hadn't meant it as a compliment.

I carried the brown bag into the kitchen and started to take out the week's worth of rationed groceries, which, a lifetime ago, might have been our food for the night.

"Wash and peel a potato. I'm making a soup with it," Mamá called from the bathroom.

"*Sí, señora,*" I said, slightly disappointed that we'd be having potato broth . . . again. I knew it was the best way to make a potato last for two days, but it still didn't soothe my grumbling stomach. I guess the sardines Mamá carried in her basket would have to do. . . . Not that I had any desire to eat another sardine ever again.

Mamá came into the kitchen and wrapped a white apron

around her long black skirt. "And no complaining about what I was able to bring home. We're lucky that I didn't give up being a *sardinera* when I married your father and I can help provide for this family. I don't want to hear that you're hungry for a piece of meat or—"

"I never say—"

She slammed the kitchen drawer shut and spun around. "Are you now calling me a liar?"

I shook my head so hard that I could feel my ponytail swing side to side. "No, Mamá. That's not what I meant."

"Hmph! It better not be what you meant." She turned back to the sink and began filling a pot with water. "An ungrateful child . . . Nothing worse," she muttered.

❖   ❖   ❖

Except for the occasional slurping of the soup or the crackling sound of the crusty bread being torn, dinner was silent. I knew it would be futile to ask to go to the movies. Mamá would think it was a waste of time—time that could be better spent earning money through sardine sales. As I cleaned the kitchen after dinner, I debated what to do.

Going to the movies might be selfish on my part—after all, Mamá always worked and never asked for a day off. But I always did what I was told, and rarely complained. Yet all I had to show for it was smelly clothes and zero friends. Plus, Papá would want me to go. And it wouldn't cost us a thing. . . . Mamá could make the sales by herself. She always said that having me there for the evening sales was better because people felt sorry for a mother and daughter having to work so hard, but one day wouldn't hurt. She'd say I was sick, and that might make people buy even more sardines. Yes, this could work. I just had to be convincing when I spoke.

I walked to the living room, where Mamá sat in one of the two wingback chairs that flanked the radio Papá had managed to get for us a few years back. I remembered sitting next to him, the two of us crowded into a chair made for one, listening to music or shows. Mamá would sit silently across from us doing her knitting or sewing.

I glanced at the empty chair. For the last seven months, by unspoken agreement, neither Mamá nor I had sat in that chair. . . . Papá was gone, but not forgotten.

Taking my spot on the footstool nearest to the radio, I watched as Mamá sewed a button onto one of her black long-sleeve blouses.

"¿Qué?" she asked, barely looking up at me.

I took a deep breath. "Um . . . Mamá, I was, um . . ."

"Spit it out, neska," she commanded, still concentrating on the button in her hand.

"Um, I was thinking that I shouldn't go to school tomorrow."

"Hmm." She didn't stop her sewing.

"Or make the rounds with you tomorrow evening . . ."

She paused and looked up at me. "Not go with me? You know we need every sale. Bad enough that your father still insists that you be at school and not work during the day." She shook her head. "What is this about?"

She was not going to simply let me go to the movies.

Mamá waited for me to answer, and when I remained silent, she resumed her sewing.

It had to be done. I swallowed hard and said, "I mean, um . . . I think . . . I, er . . . should see the doctor tomorrow."

Stabbing the needle into the blouse and setting it aside, she stared at me. "The doctor? Why? What's wrong?"

"Um, my head . . . and my stomach." I placed a hand on each. "I haven't been feeling well since this afternoon, and I'm feeling worse now."

"Well, you certainly ate like you were feeling fine." Mamá eyed me carefully.

"I didn't want to worry you," I answered.

"Hmph. I'm sure it's nothing. Just go to bed and you'll be better in the morning."

"Yes, ma'am," I said, getting up and walking toward my room, truly feeling sick to my stomach.

"*Neska*," she called out, "you know we don't have money for a doctor, so if you still feel bad in the morning, stay home and I'll sell the sardines myself . . . but only for tomorrow."

As I closed the door to my room, a smile crept across my face.

FOUR

I'd never really noticed how time went by slower when there was nothing to do. At first I'd stayed in bed, just in case Mamá came home after taking the train to Bermeo to get fresh sardines. After a while, when I was sure she wasn't returning, I sat in her chair and listened to the radio. Then I tried looking out the living room window, but our street was empty since most everyone who lived in this neighborhood worked in the factories on the other side of town. Finally, the wall clock showed it was a quarter to four and I could head out to meet Mathias.

Smoothing out the wrinkles in my brown dress, the one I usually wore on Sundays, I checked myself one last time in the mirror. The pretty white collar had yellowed a bit with time, but at least I didn't look like a *sardinera*. I sniffed my sleeve. I couldn't tell if it smelled, but I had to hope it wasn't as bad as my other clothes.

Before grabbing my dark blue sweater, I scribbled a

note saying I'd gone outside for some fresh air . . . just in case Mamá came home early. Then I set off for my day of extravagance.

The church bells of Santa María clanged four times as I ran down the cobblestoned streets around the Bank of Vizcaya. The movie theater, which had replaced an old dance hall, was up ahead, and I could see Mathias sitting on the building's front stoop, staring at his hands, his *makila* lying across his thighs.

I slowed down. Suddenly yesterday seemed like a long time ago. I wasn't sure what I was supposed to say to him. Perhaps he'd invited me out of pity. Or this was a prank of some kind. An overwhelming urge to turn around and go back home washed over me.

Something in the air must have told Mathias that I was near because he looked up just as I was about to leave. He waved me over, and, bracing himself on his *makila*, he stood.

"*Hola*," I said, not really looking at him as I approached the theater.

"Hi there!" he answered, taking a couple of steps toward me. "I'm glad you finally got here. Father wasn't thrilled with the idea of my having invited—"

"Oh, I—I can leave," I stammered. I could feel my face turning red. I knew I shouldn't have come. What a stupid girl I was!

"No, no." Mathias stuffed a hand into his pocket. "He's fine with it now. I told him we'd clean and sit quietly in the back. He liked the fact that I finally have a friend."

"Finally?" I asked.

"I mean here." Mathias waddled side to side as he walked up the two steps to the theater entrance and then propped open the door with his walking stick. "Let's go in. We need to start with the entrance, and then we'll brush the velvet on each seat to make it look new."

I walked past him into the theater lobby and stared at my surroundings. It was all so opulent. The brocaded wallpaper, the deep wine color of the cushioned bench in the corner, the large glass chandelier in the center of the room—and this was only the entrance. On the wall, behind a glass frame, hung a movie poster with a thin man wearing a tuxedo and a beautiful blond woman wearing a long gold dress. SOMBRERO DE COPA, with FRED ASTAIRE and GINGER ROGERS, was splashed across the sign, and in small letters underneath TOP HAT was written. I guessed that was the real name of the movie. Excitement was building in my chest, and the movie hadn't even started.

"Here." Mathias handed me a broom. "Start with this, and I'll clean the windows."

In a bit of a daze, I peeled my eyes away from the poster and began to sweep the floor. After a few minutes, I wondered if Mathias had invited me so he wouldn't have to do so much work. Perhaps his parents were like Mamá and he'd end up on the sore side of a belt if the place wasn't spotless. Maybe that's what had happened to his leg.

It didn't take long for us to finish cleaning the lobby and move into the main theater. The decor there wasn't quite as elegant, but I was still impressed by the fifteen rows of velvet seats that filled the large room. It was easy to see how this had once been a grand dance hall.

Voices from the lobby warned us that the group had arrived for the private showing.

"You almost done?" Mathias asked, dropping a wet rag into a bucket.

I had finished sweeping and was now working on cleaning the last row of theater seats. "Pretty much," I said as Mathias dimmed the lights.

"This way, ladies," a deep voice said as the door swung open.

"Mathias! Mathias!" the man called out. "Please make the room a bit brighter."

"Yes, Father."

As the lights came on again, I could see a tall man with broad shoulders and eyes just like Mathias's holding the door for everyone.

The first to enter were some ladies I recognized from church. They were the ones who always sat up front, wearing the latest fashions, and who covered their perfectly styled hairdos with fine lace mantillas in reverence of the Mass.

I slunk toward the back corner of the theater, hoping none of them recognized me as the *sardinera*'s daughter—or, worse, smelled me.

"Beatriz, why don't you and the other ladies sit together?" A tall, bearded man I knew to be Tomás Beltran, a high-ranking government official, made his way in front of the ladies. He gave his elbow to one of the women and walked her halfway down the aisle. "This will give you a perfect view . . . here in the middle."

"Of course, Tomás." The woman, wearing an emerald-green dress, motioned for the other ladies to follow, like a mother duck leading her young.

The other men stayed behind, near the theater's entrance, until Señor Beltran rejoined them. Mathias looked over at his father, then at me, and shrugged.

I sat down in the last seat, in the far back corner, and waited.

The women's voices carried through the theater, and I could hear them talking about the latest gossip. In contrast, the men were still huddled together, and their voices did not go above a hushed whisper.

A crackling and flicker of light on the huge screen interrupted the general chatter. Mathias dimmed the lights and silently made his way down the back row until he reached the seat next to me.

"Don't know why these women love this movie so much. . . . They've each seen *Top Hat* at least three times," he whispered, using the English name for the movie. "I think their husbands must be bored out of their minds."

I barely heard him because my eyes were fixed on the screen and music had filled the room. Within minutes I was swept away by the sight of Fred Astaire dancing and traveling through Europe. I gladly became absorbed into that world, forgetting everything except the subtitles on the screen and the images that accompanied them.

It felt like magic. A story come to life. Then a sudden stutter, flicker, and bright light jolted me into reality. The women began to talk casually among themselves as if this were a normal occurrence.

Mathias leaned over. "They're probably changing the reels," he whispered.

I nodded, half understanding what he meant.

"Hey, you want to go see the projection room? We can finish watching the movie from up there. Father might even need my help." He braced himself against the seat's armrests and stood up.

I glanced around, noticing that all the men had left. A small window above us was dimly lit, and I could see the light from the projector beaming through it, illuminating the entire theater. "Um, sure. If you think we can help," I said.

Mathias gave me a strange smile and led the way up some stairs. As we approached the semi-closed door, I heard voices arguing in Basque. Mathias raised a finger to his lips and inched toward the door.

Eavesdropping wasn't a good idea. It was a surefire way to get a beating. Mathias waved me over.

I shook my head and pointed back down the stairs. This was not what I had bargained for.

Mathias smiled, rolled his eyes, and waved me over again.

Realizing that he'd known what we might be getting into when he'd suggested coming up here, I mouthed a silent "No."

He mouthed back, "Don't. Be. Scared."

I was certainly not afraid, and to prove it, I climbed the

final step and stood toe to toe with him . . . my head not even reaching his shoulders.

"I can never understand what they're saying," he whispered. "You speak Basque, right? What are they talking about?"

The truth now dawned on me. He had invited me only because he needed a translator, not because we were going to be friends.

"Princess?"

I was about to tell him not to call me that when the voices from the other room became more heated, catching my attention. I listened for a moment.

"C'mon, tell me. We're in this together . . . you and me."

I sighed. Even if it wasn't real, it still felt nice to pretend to have a friend.

"They're talking about . . ." I paused to listen for a few more seconds, not sure if I was hearing correctly. "I think they said something about a German warship off the coast of Bilbao," I whispered. My eyes grew wider as I listened more intently to the flurry of voices arguing in the other room. "Someone is saying that the information they've been getting has been right so far and they need to just relay the message."

Mathias squeezed his hands around his walking stick. "Ha! I knew it," he whispered.

"Knew what?" I asked.

"Can't you tell?" Mathias's eyes gleamed.

"You mean . . . ?" I didn't want to finish the thought, but Mathias did.

He nodded, unable to contain the smile spreading across his face. "I think my father's a spy."

FIVE

The narrow hallway felt as if it were getting smaller by the second. The voices on the other side of the door were now all speaking at once, some in Spanish and others in Basque.

One voice rose above the others. "Capture the German ship? Are you insane? God help us if this makes things worse."

My skin prickled. I knew that voice. It was the same one I'd been listening to every Sunday since I was born. It was the parish priest, Padre Iñaki!

The other voices rose in protest.

Spies. Even people I never thought would be involved with the ugliness of war were plotting conspiracies. I studied Mathias's face. How could I be sure which side he was helping? How could they? His family was part German.

"What?" Mathias widened his eyes, as if I were the one whose father was involved in espionage.

I shrugged. "Nothing. I think we should go." I turned to

head back down the stairs. Adventure stories were one thing, but real life was something different.

Mathias pulled on my arm. "Just one more minute. Tell me what they're saying now."

"No!" I said, yanking my arm away from him. Unfortunately, I said it a little too loudly right when there was a lull in the conversation on the other side of the door.

Mathias grimaced.

Before we could take two steps, the door was flung open and hands grabbed the back of our collars.

I tried to get my balance, but I was already being lifted off my feet and tossed into the small room. Mathias fell down next to me, his *makila* still in the stairwell.

My heart pounded in my chest. I glanced at Mathias and then stared up at the men surrounding us.

"Mathias! Eavesdropping? You know better than that!" Mathias's father was red with rage. "I let you bring a friend to the theater and this is how you repay me?"

"I—I—I . . . ," Mathias stammered. "I mean, the movie stopped and we thought the reel might need to be changed and—"

"And you thought I would need your help? Really?" Mathias's father balled and unballed his fists, but glanced over at the film projector.

I wanted to run out of the room, pretend none of this had happened, but Mathias seemed to relish the fact that we'd been caught.

"Father, no, that's not it. . . . But now that we've heard what you were talking about, we can—"

"Don't say it, Mathias!" His father glared at him.

Padre Iñaki shook his head as he closed the door. "I feared this." He had Mathias's *makila* in his hands. "If children can sneak up on us, we've obviously not been careful enough."

A thin man with gray hair and a bushy mustache who'd been pacing back and forth in the tiny room raised a finger to his lips. "Padre, please," he said, silencing the priest. He then turned to face Mathias and me. "What did you two hear exactly?"

Mathias's father took a step to block the old man's intense gaze. "Federico, I'm sure they didn't hear anything. My son barely understands the Basque language, and, well, I don't even know this girl, but they are both just children, after all."

A short man whose large belly pushed at the buttons of his dark suit placed his hand on Mathias's father's shoulder and guided him away from us. He then turned around and squatted next to me. "We're not going to do anything to you," he said in a voice so calm that I couldn't believe he was sincere. "We won't even be upset, but I need you to tell me what you heard."

"*Nada*, nothing," I said, keeping my eyes on the ground. It was always better to fade into the background.

"They heard too much. I can tell," the man I knew to be Tomás Beltran said. He pointed a long, skinny finger at Mathias. "The boy, he may keep quiet—after all, he is your son—but the girl? She'll probably be gossiping with her friends by tomorrow afternoon, telling everyone that we're meeting here. Something has to be done!"

"We can help with whatever you're planning," Mathias offered.

I flashed an incredulous look at Mathias. Obviously, he and I had very different ways of handling the situation.

"Help? You've helped enough, young man!" Mathias's father spoke through clenched teeth.

"But, Father, listen." Mathias sat up a little taller. "We're involved now, and we won't tell anyone about the German ship or all of you meeting here. No one has to worry about us saying anything. . . . Neither of us has any friends in town."

A wave of embarrassment washed over me. It didn't matter that we were in serious trouble—that was something I didn't like to admit . . . even if it was true.

The potbellied man threw his hands in the air and stood up. "Hmph! Tomás is right. We can't continue like this. These visits already look suspicious . . . and Franco has informants everywhere. Imagine how this would be seen by my people at the bank. We're all supposed to be neutral parties. What happens if Franco wins? What happens to us then?"

Señor Beltran took one last look at us and then directed his comment to the group. "We need to talk . . . in private."

Mathias's father nodded. "There's a supply closet out in the hall. The children can wait in there."

"Good idea," Padre Iñaki said, handing Mathias his *makila* and opening the door to the hallway.

Mathias and I looked at each other.

"Go!" Mathias's father whispered.

As I was about to stand, Padre Iñaki knelt down on one knee, his black cassock draping around his ankles as he stared at me.

"Wait. You're Largazabalaga's daughter, aren't you?" he asked.

I nodded. "Yes, sir," I managed to whisper.

Padre Iñaki glanced back at the men and said, "Her father volunteered to go fight, even though he is . . . well, let's say he's not a young man."

The other men looked at each other in silence.

"He's the husband of the *sardinera*," Padre Iñaki added.

This caused a few knowing nods of recognition, although I doubted that men of their level in society associated with people like my family.

"So, you're the *sardinera*'s daughter?" Potbellied Man looked at me with new interest.

I gave him a slight nod.

"Hmm, that *is* interesting," he said, rubbing his bald head and glancing at the now very silent thin man with the gray mustache.

Mathias's father gave me a hand getting up and ushered me out the door to where Mathias was waiting.

As we stepped into the dark supply closet, Mathias shouted back to the men still in the projection room. "We can help with whatever you're doing. I know we can."

Mathias's father glared at him before quickly shutting the door, stranding us in total darkness.

Immediately we both pressed our ears against the door.

Just outside, I could hear one of the men saying something in Basque.

"I can't understand them. What are they saying?" Mathias whispered.

I listened closely, not wanting to miss any part of the conversation.

"Tell me," Mathias insisted, pulling his ear away from the door.

"Wait," I whispered.

I could hear the voices drifting back to the other room.

"They're talking about us," I said in a hushed voice.

"No? Really? I could've figured that out myself. What did they say exactly?"

"One of them said something about it being bad enough that they were using their wives as an excuse to come to the theater, hiding behind skirts."

"Uh-huh. What else?" Mathias asked. I turned to face him, and although I couldn't see him, I could sense him standing behind me, one arm propped against the wall of the small closet.

"They said the fight is doomed if it depends on children."

"Yes!" he exclaimed, and I heard him clasp his fist in excitement.

"Yes?" I asked.

"It means they're actually considering letting us help in the fight."

"What could we possibly do? We don't even know what *they're* really doing. I think we're in for a beating and nothing more."

The door opened suddenly, and Padre Iñaki motioned for us to join the others in the projection room.

Everyone in the room was silent and staring at us. The short, heavy man lifted up his monocle to inspect me a little closer. "This could work out very well. . . ."

"I still disagree." Mathias's father shook his head. "They're too young."

"I'm fourteen . . . almost old enough to fight," Mathias argued. "And Ani, she's . . ." He leaned over toward me. "How old are you?" he whispered.

"Uh, twelve. Thirteen in May," I answered.

"And Ani's almost thirteen," he declared. "We're not too young!"

Padre Iñaki smiled. "It does seem God may have set His hands in this."

My eyes went back and forth, watching each man's face as they reached some type of silent agreement.

"Joaquín." Padre Iñaki faced Mathias's father. "There would be little risk for them. It's obvious we can't continue to meet here."

"But my son, he has a bad leg. . . ."

"My leg is *not* a problem." Mathias clumsily took a step forward, shifting most of his weight onto his left leg.

"And you, young lady? This requires your cooperation. Are you willing to help too?" Señor Beltran gave me a cold, hard stare. "And not say a word to anyone?"

I stood motionless. This was not happening. I was supposed to be invisible.

"What do you want us to do?" Mathias asked, squaring his shoulders.

Señor Beltran completely ignored him, keeping his focus on me. He drew closer, and I could smell his mixture of soap and cologne. "You understand what we're doing, don't you? Why we are fighting."

I still said nothing. I couldn't.

"Good God, girl! Can't you speak?" he exclaimed.

Mathias gave me a jab in the ribs.

But before I could say anything, Potbellied Man called out, "Aren't you a true Basque?"

"Of course!" I said in a voice that came from deep inside me.

"Fine," Señor Beltran calmly said, resuming his politician's demeanor. "Then you understand that we must do everything we can to protect our way of life. If Franco and his army win, they'll strip us of who we are. They'll force us to be Spaniards instead of Basques. You wouldn't want that, would you?"

"No, of course not," I answered, taking a step back toward the door behind me.

"Ahem." The thin man cleared his throat, but his gaze was elsewhere, as if he didn't want anything to do with the conversation.

"Tomás, let me explain it to her." Padre Iñaki gently moved Señor Beltran out of the way and then took my hand. "You know that the Basque people have always been a proud, independent group."

I nodded, and he gave me a small smile.

"We've accepted Spain's rule as long as they accepted who we were. But that will change with Franco. All we've ever wanted was to be left alone, but that's not an option. We need to protect ourselves. Perhaps we've made a deal with the devil, but—"

"It's the devil we know!" shouted Potbellied Man.

Padre Iñaki rolled his eyes, but continued. "We just need to be prepared and help stop any attacks without appearing to be *involved*. Just in case."

"Just in case?" I asked.

"In case Franco wins," Señor Beltran explained.

"You'll help us, won't you? Make your father proud?" Padre Iñaki asked.

I wasn't sure what I was getting myself into, but I nodded.

"So, what do you want us to do? Infiltrate something?" Mathias asked.

"No, no. Nothing that dangerous." Padre Iñaki dropped my hand, and his smile grew wider. "We just need you two to be our . . . let's say, communications officers."

I glanced over to Mathias, and from the look on his face, he was as confused as I was. Mathias's father was quiet. His only reaction to the conversation was to constantly run his fingers through his hair.

Señor Beltran moved closer to Mathias's father. "Joaquín, when do you expect another message?"

"I'm not sure. I usually receive supplies early on Monday mornings. If there's information, it will come then." Mathias's father gave his hair another quick fingering. "I don't know about this new plan."

"It'll work perfectly," Potbellied Man proclaimed. "You just have the girl deliver the information with the sardines." He pointed over to me. "All of us will become loyal customers, buying at least a pound each. The boy can help her."

I could see their plan now. They would no longer need to meet at the theater if Mathias and I carried messages to them. I reached into my pocket and touched the smooth edge of the satin pouch Papá had given me.

"But what of the girl's mother? We'll need to ask her too," Padre Iñaki said.

"And if she says no, then what? More people who'll know what we're doing? Better to keep this among us." Señor Beltran looked at me again. "Girl, you'll need to deliver sardines to us on a regular basis, maybe every Tuesday. Even if there's no message, you'll have to come to our homes. . . . Can you do that?"

I swallowed hard and spoke. "I have to help Mamá on Tuesdays."

"Mondays," Mathias announced. "We can do it on Mondays." He turned to face me. "Instead of daydreams at your tree, we'll be living the story."

"That could work," muttered the thin man, who'd barely said a word.

"But what do I tell my mother?" I asked.

"Tell her we'll be paying a little extra or make something

up." Señor Beltran reached for his coat, as if the issue had been settled and it was time to leave. "You kids are always coming up with lies to tell your parents."

I thought about the story I'd told about being sick so I could come to the theater. It had been my first real lie, but clearly, it would not be my last.

SIX

Walking home that evening, with the sky turning purple, I felt as if I'd been pulled into a moving picture show and everything around me was part of a movie set. Nothing seemed real . . . not even me. It felt as if I were watching a version of myself walk by the storefronts and apartments of Guernica. The old women sitting on a bench near the town square, the pigeons that flew overhead, even the dirt that settled in the streets, all seemed posed. The only thing that kept reminding me that this day had not been a figment of my imagination was the sound of Mathias's voice.

"Once your mother agrees to it, then you should send me a message by hanging a handkerchief or something on your window," he said, his words finally making their way into my brain.

"What are you talking about?" I asked, looking over at him.

"You haven't been listening to me at all, have you?"

I shrugged.

"I was saying how you need to tell your mother that I can get you several wealthy clients on Mondays, but that we need to split the profits."

"Split the money? She's not going to like that."

"Well, I certainly wouldn't give you all the sardine money if they're my customers."

"You can't have customers if you don't have any sardines to sell," I countered.

"That's why we split the profits evenly. Plus, it's not as if my family has much money either. We'd like to have a little extra food every once in a while too."

"Hmph. Mamá's not going to be happy about getting just half."

"It's only fair, and I've seen your mother at the market-place. . . . She won't care as long as you're bringing in extra money. Anyway, why are you arguing? It's not like they're really our customers." He dropped his voice. "We're spies, remember?"

"More like couriers. Like those pigeons up there." I pointed to the birds sitting on the crumbling concrete edge of my building. "And, by the way, it wasn't very nice of you to trick me into going to the theater just so you could have someone translate for you."

"Trick you?" Mathias stopped walking as I pulled out a large key from my pocket. "I invited you because I thought we were becoming friends."

"Uh-huh." I was not going to be played for a fool twice.

"Okay, it helped that you could translate, but I could've

46

asked someone else. And now we get to do something important."

"Important?" I rolled my eyes. *"¡Por favor!"*

"No, seriously. We'll be making a difference. . . . We'll be heroes."

A hero. That wasn't insignificant. It wasn't a nothing. In fact, it was most definitely something. A big something.

I took a deep breath and put the thought aside. Mathias almost had me convinced . . . for a moment.

"I have to go in. It's nearly seven, and Mamá will be home soon."

"Okay, how early can you be here next Monday?"

"I'll come as soon as class lets out . . . a little after five." I glanced up at the window, thinking I'd seen the curtain move out of the corner of my eye. For a split second I worried that Mamá would be home, but she'd never be there this early. She would sell sardines until the streetlamps turned on.

"Perfect, I'll meet you then." Mathias turned and started walking back to the theater. "Don't forget the handkerchief," he called out.

"I won't! *Agur.*" I waved as he rounded the corner.

A small bubble of excitement rose in my chest, and I had to take a deep breath to push it back down. I couldn't allow myself to think that my world might change. Then again, I apparently now had a friend, we were spies, and one day, I might be a hero. The invisible bubble started to rise again, but this time I let it grow a bit. Could it be like in the movies, where anything was possible? Could I, the invisible, nothing girl of Guernica, actually matter?

I took the stairs two at a time until I reached the door of my apartment on the third floor. I was just about to slip the key into the lock when, as if sensing my hand, the door jerked open.

Mamá stood in the doorway, black leather belt clenched in her hand.

SEVEN

My heart stopped. If I could have shrunk into the cracks in the floorboards or melted into the peeling paint on the walls, I would have. Instead, I stood frozen as the black leather belt flew through the air, finding its mark: me. Instinctively, I grabbed my arm, already throbbing from where the belt had made contact.

"You worthless little liar!" Mamá yelled, dragging me into the apartment and kicking the door closed. She raised her arm to strike me again.

"No, Mamá. You don't understand." I shielded my face with my arms, but Mamá was swinging lower this time.

Crack! The belt stung my thigh.

"I understand plenty. And to think that I rushed through my route to come and check on you. You ungrateful child!"

She hit my other leg, this time with a backhanded swing.

"No, Mamá. I left you a note," I pleaded, trying in vain to block the quickening lashes to my arms and legs.

"*¡Mentirosa!* Liar!" *Crack! Crack!* "You think I didn't

49

see you with that boy? What did I do to deserve such a disgraceful, wretched child?" She topped off her question with her strongest swing yet, which wrapped the belt around my left ankle.

Somehow, in the middle of the whipping, I realized that for the first time I might actually deserve this punishment. I *had* lied. But Mamá's words were not biting through me as they usually did.

I was going to be a hero. I was more than a nothing.

"You are wrong, Mamá."

Something in the way I spoke made Mamá stop. Perhaps it was the fact that I said those words at all. I made the most of the brief reprieve.

"I left you the note because I was feeling better and wanted to go outside," I explained.

"Ha! And the boy? You just happened to run into him? You, a girl who's never had any friends." She dropped her belt-wielding hand just a bit. "I know what boys want with girls like you."

"No, Mamá. Mathias is a friend. *Just* a friend."

Mamá shook her head. "So pathetic . . . and naïve. As if a boy would really be friends with you."

The words stung my heart.

"He would! He is! In fact, he wants to work with me."

"Work with you?" Mamá raised a single eyebrow. "*¿Haciendo qué?* What could he possibly want to do with you?"

I took a step back, creating a larger gap between Mamá and me. "He wants to sell sardines."

"Sardines?" She scratched her cheek. "Well, that explains why he'd talk to you, but we don't need help. You and I manage fine on our own."

"No, he doesn't want to just help us. He knows people who'll buy sardines, and we can split the profits."

"Split? Well, that's certainly not a friend." She turned and walked to her room. I could hear her hanging the belt on the hook behind the door. "Sounds like a profiteer," she called out.

I breathed a sigh of relief. At least the lashing was over. And I couldn't expect Mamá to understand anything about having friends. . . . I'd never known her to have any of her own.

"Mamá, don't you think we could make some extra money? I'd work on Mondays so I wouldn't miss any of my deliveries with you," I said, following her to the kitchen.

Mamá spun around, almost causing me to run right into her. "Mondays! That would just take business away from me in the market." She shook her head. "You really don't think about things, do you, *neska*?"

I looked down at the floor. "I'm pretty sure these people never buy from you at the market." My voice was barely above a whisper. "That's why they want the deliveries." Pausing for a moment, I tried to think of something else to say. "Mathias knows these families because he runs errands for them. He'll have them buy sardines either from us or from another *sardinera*." Lying was much closer to storytelling than I'd imagined.

Mamá whirled around to face me. "Not that good-for-nothing, cheating Sonia? Is that who he's thinking of asking?"

I latched onto the idea. "Yes, that's who he mentioned as his second choice."

"Figures." Mamá grabbed two pot holders and pulled out a thick yellow omelet from the oven. I knew that most of the eggs she'd brought home yesterday and the leftover potatoes had been used to make it, although I couldn't imagine what would prompt her to cook a meal like that. She stared at me, then said, "Don't just stand there watching me work. Put a trivet on the table so I can set this down."

My heart fell. "*Sí, señora*," I said, not knowing how else to convince her about our plan. I'd been certain that losing sales to Sonia would make her say yes.

Mamá sliced the warm omelet into wedges, steam rising from each cut. "Who did you say his family is?"

"They're new in town. The Garcías." I rubbed my arm, which still stung. "His father works at the movie theater."

"Hmph." She looked up at me with an exasperated stare. "Plates, *neska*. We need plates. Do you think we eat like savages in this house?"

I dashed over to the dark wooden cabinet and pulled out two slightly chipped plates. I set them on the table and darted back to get the silverware, napkins, and glasses.

When I got back to the table, Mamá had placed a piece of bread and a thick wedge of the omelet on my plate. I could see the thin slices of potatoes layered inside. It had been a while since we'd had a meal like this.

As I devoured my dinner, Mamá spoke up again. "You're feeling better, hmm?"

I nodded, my mouth stuffed with the omelet.

"And this boy? Is he the reason you wore your best dress?"

I couldn't tell her about the movies. . . . That would lead to too many other questions. "Um, no. Not at all. I didn't know I'd even see him." Lying was becoming a bit easier. "I wore it because it was still clean from Sunday, and I knew I'd only be out for a little while," I explained.

Mamá raised a single eyebrow. "Don't know who you're trying to fool."

"Really." I took a sip of water. "It was a coincidence that I ran into him."

"Of course it was. How old is this boy?" she asked as she finished her own dinner.

"Um, fourteen, I think." I set my glass back on the table and waited. The fact that Mamá was still calm even though she didn't believe me was a good sign.

"Uh-huh." She pursed her lips. "I suppose even a *neska* like you will eventually draw a suitor or two."

"Oh no." I blushed at the idea. "It's not like that. Mathias is just my friend."

"You probably can't wait to leave me too," she muttered, wiping her mouth and tossing the napkin on her plate.

"Leave?"

Mamá stared at me from across the table. "Never mind that. I also saw that he's *cojo* . . . walks around with a limp. Is he sick or something? I won't be caring for a handicapped boy."

"He's not sick." I focused on the remaining speck of egg on my plate and tried to scoop it up with one of the fork tines so I wouldn't have to look at Mamá's reaction. "He just has a bad leg, that's all." I sneaked a glance over at her.

Her mouth twitched. She never had much compassion for the sick. . . . Then again, she had little sympathy for anyone.

"So I suppose you'll go with *el cojo* after school on Mondays to deliver the sardines? How many customers does he have, and how much do they want?"

"His name is Mathias, and his customers want about a pound each," I said, bringing the nearly empty fork to my mouth so I could savor the last morsel of the omelet. "I think he might have six or seven customers."

Mamá leaned back in her chair, thinking things over for a moment. "And you'll bring home *all* the money?"

This was it. I could feel the excitement rising inside me. "Yes, ma'am. I mean, I'll bring *our* share."

"Don't get smart with me or I'll give you another whipping." She pushed back her chair and took her plate to the sink.

"I'm sorry," I quickly answered, but butterflies were now filling up any empty space left in my stomach, and all I wanted to do was jump up and down to celebrate.

"If these new customers are wealthy, the two of you will probably look pitiful enough to them to even get you some nice tips." She looked at me over her shoulder as she put the dishes in the sink. "You have to bring that money home too. No keeping any of it for yourself, you hear me? I won't tolerate a thief."

"Yes, Mamá."

"And I better not find out that it's any of my customers from the market." Mamá took a bowl that had been drying on the kitchen counter and put it on the shelf above the sink.

I waited. I could sense how close I was to having my whole life change.

She walked to the table and picked up my empty plate, looking at me from head to toe. "Fine. We'll try it once with this boy. Next Monday I'll leave you some sardines before I go to the market." She shook her head and muttered, "This better be worth it."

I jumped up to hug her, but she took a step back. Instead of embracing, we stood there in the kitchen facing each other, neither of us moving.

A brief sigh escaped from Mamá's lips before she walked around me and headed toward her bedroom.

My excitement evaporated. It was clear some things would never change.

EIGHT

By Sunday morning, I was becoming genuinely concerned about my new life of espionage. I hadn't heard from Mathias, even though I'd hung my brightest neck scarf in the window on Wednesday to show him that Mamá had agreed to our idea. Maybe he'd changed his mind, or the real spies had decided not to trust a pair of kids.

I took a deep breath, inhaling the strong, woodsy-smelling incense that filled Santa María Church. Hearing the Latin prayers I had memorized as a little girl seemed to quiet my worries . . . at least temporarily.

"*Vámonos,*" Mamá whispered before the service was over. "We have a lot to do today." She genuflected at the end of the pew and headed toward the door.

I hesitated. I thought I'd have a chance to speak with Padre Iñaki after Mass, maybe get a sign that the plan was still on. A glance toward Mamá, standing with her hands on her hips by the side door in back, told me that there'd be no waiting around for Mass to finish.

I quickly made the sign of the cross and joined her.

"What took you so long? When I say go, I mean go." She pushed open the heavy door, and the morning sun was such a contrast from the darkened church that we both shielded our eyes.

"Yes, ma'am."

She shook her head. "No point spending time in there if you aren't paying attention."

I said nothing as we walked down the church steps.

"I bring you here, try to do right by your soul, and that's how you decide to thank me . . . by daydreaming. Your brother, God rest his soul, would never have been so distracted. He was focused . . . helpful to his mother."

I'd heard all this before. I could never live up to the brother who'd died before I was even born. I just nodded.

"He was too good. I didn't deserve a child like that," she said.

We continued to walk down the quiet street. I guessed Mamá thought I was the child she deserved. All I knew of my brother was what my father had told me. His name was Xavier, and he was a funny, outgoing boy who'd become sick while Mamá was pregnant with me. It always felt as if Mamá somehow blamed me for his death.

Before reaching the corner, Mamá abruptly stopped to look at me.

I searched her caramel-colored eyes. Somewhere in there was the girl Papá had fallen in love with. I could almost see that version of her in the wedding picture that hung in the living room. An eighteen-year-old with hope and excitement written all over her face standing next to a much older, but equally happy, man.

"Still so much like him . . . ," she said, slightly shaking her head.

I wasn't sure if we were talking about my dead brother or Papá.

Mamá's shoulders dropped for a moment, and her face softened. "During Mass, you were thinking of your father, weren't you?"

On any other Sunday, all my thoughts would've been with Papá. But today, I'd been thinking about me, Mathias, and our "special deliveries" . . . not that I expected too much to come of them.

I played with a loose button on my sweater. "Yes, I was thinking of him," I answered, not wanting to miss out on Mamá's kindness.

"Thought so." Mamá gently stroked my hair, her hand resting for a moment on my back. I wished it were more, that she would just wrap me up in her arms and hug me, but I was grateful for even this small bit of affection.

Ring, ring. A boy chimed his bike's bell as he sped by us. In his wake, I could sense Mamá's mood changing. She was being taken back to an earlier time, a time before I was born. I watched as the boy turned and disappeared down a side street.

Mamá sighed and pushed back her shoulders. "Stupid, really," she said. "The two of you . . . your father and you." Her voice cracked before regaining its normal strength. "Him for leaving, thinking he was going to make a difference, and you for worrying so much. Better to learn it now, *neska*. Nothing good comes from thinking you deserve more from this life than what it hands you. We're all insignificant. Just whispers in a loud world. Fifty years from now, no one will care if we even existed."

I stayed rooted to the sidewalk as Mamá made her way down the street. Instinctively, my fingers searched for the small promise of hope I held in the pouch Papá had given me. Mamá was wrong. I was not going to be insignificant . . . at least not anymore. Someday I would exist.

NINE

Monday afternoon arrived like any other day. I was still the girl in the back of the class, the one who walked home alone and spent most of her evenings delivering sardines with her mother. I was still an afterthought to most people, but now I was grateful for my invisibility. It could be a spy's best trait.

The moment the teacher dismissed the class, I bolted from my seat and practically sprinted home. Mamá had promised to leave me some sardines in the apartment, and I didn't want to be late for my new pseudo-career . . . even if I still wasn't sure whether that meant being a glorified courier or a spy. I just hoped the plan was still on. . . . I hadn't heard from Mathias, and I didn't want to have to explain any failure to Mamá.

As I rounded the corner, I spotted Mathias leaning against a lamppost. He was wearing a slightly wrinkled white shirt with the cuffs rolled up and gray pants held by brown suspenders. His clothes looked a little disheveled, almost as if he'd been working in someone's yard, although there were no yards in the city. For a moment, I had a vision of him spending his days sitting under my tree doing nothing, and a twinge of jealousy flared inside me.

Mathias gave his beret a slight tug and twirled his *makila* just the way Fred Astaire had done in the movie with his top hat and cane. He was trying to be so smooth and sophisticated, but instead, he dropped his walking stick and it rattled along the cobblestone street.

I doubled over laughing.

"*Mala*. You don't have to laugh so hard," he said, bending over to pick up the stick.

"I'm sorry. You just look so . . ."

He raised his eyebrows and tilted his head. "Dashing? Debonair?"

"Ridiculous!" I laughed again.

He rolled his eyes. "Girls," he said, smiling and shaking his head.

"I'll be right back. Mamá left the sardines in the apartment." I raced up the steps to the front door of the building.

"How much did your mother leave?" Mathias called out before I opened the door.

I looked back with the key in my hand. "I told her you had like six or seven rich customers."

"What?" he shouted. He made his way up the steps as quickly as he could. He dropped his voice to a whisper. "Didn't you count? There were only five men in that room besides my father."

I glanced around, just in case someone happened to pass

by. "Yeah, but aren't they paying us extra? Too much money might make Mamá suspicious, so I thought it'd be better to just say we had a few more customers."

He shook his head. "And you didn't think about keeping a few *pesetas* for yourself? C'mon, you can't be *that* honest."

I shrugged.

"An honest spy . . . I don't know about this," he muttered.

❖ ❖ ❖

"What's the exact address of our first delivery?" I asked as we walked toward the outskirts of town. We were now entering the area where all the big landowners had their chalets.

Mathias pulled out the sealed envelope from his vest pocket. "Twenty-Five Carretera San Bernardo." He held the envelope toward the sun and squinted.

"*Vale*, that means the house should be up a little further," I said, watching as he tilted the cream-colored envelope to different angles. "You've looked ten times. You're not going to be able to see what's inside."

"Yeah, I know. I wish my father had told me what he wrote, though."

"Fat chance." I shifted the weight of the oversized sardine basket in my arms. With only enough fish for six customers, there really was no need for such a large basket, but Mamá had only two sizes: big and huge. It was no wonder all the *sardineras* carried their loads on their heads.

Mathias put his free hand on the edge of the open basket. "Let me carry it for a while."

I pulled it away from him. "Don't worry. I got it," I said,

giving his leg and the *makila* a quick glance. "Plus, we're already here." I pointed at the path that led to the large two-story house.

"Wonder who owns this place?" Mathias asked, his eyes transfixed on the automobile that was parked by the side of the house.

"Tomás Beltran. He was the tall man with the beard."

"You sure? There's no name on here." He flipped the envelope over to double-check.

"Of course I am. Señor Beltran practically runs the city. He's always there with all the politicians whenever a president or leader comes to take the oath under the Guernica Tree. Everyone knows his house."

"Well, obviously not everyone," Mathias muttered.

As we walked closer to the large double doors at the front of the house, I couldn't help but notice how everything around me seemed to be coated with a layer of wealth. I even imagined the small statue in the fountain spilling out diamonds instead of water. Living here must be like living in a movie, I thought . . . a very rich movie.

"You know, I was thinking about the Guernica Tree." Mathias interrupted my dream. "I mean, when I lived in Bilbao—"

"You lived in Bilbao?" I asked.

"I told you, I've lived in a bunch of places. Anyway, when I lived there, I'd hear about the famous tree in the middle of Guernica where all the kings and rulers of Spain would come and promise to leave the Basques alone, but have you ever wondered why?"

"Why?" I asked, slowing down as we approached the front door.

"Yeah, why do the ceremony *under a tree?*"

I shrugged. "Guess 'cause it's just the way things have always been done. Don't you know Basque history?"

"Yeah, I know some of it." Mathias rapped on the door with its large iron knocker, then looked back at me. "I just think it's strange that they actually do it. C'mon, a tree, when the king of Spain is used to a palace?"

I thought about it for a moment, looking around at everything Señor Beltran owned. "All the money in the world can't make something significant. I mean, I'd rather have my tree than all the ones in some park. And mine doesn't have the tradition that the Guernica Tree has." I shifted the basket again to balance it on my right hip.

Mathias leaned on his *makila* and gave me a funny look. "*Your* tree? You mean the one out in the field? Who said it was yours?"

I shrugged. "I've been going to it since I was little."

"But you don't own it. Just because—"

A heavyset woman wearing a maid's uniform opened the door and glared at us. "Don't you two know anything?"

"We're here—" Mathias began to explain.

The old woman raised her hand to silence him. "¡*Basta!* Don't want to hear it. Deliveries go to the back. You don't come to the front door like an invited guest."

"Yes, ma'am." I turned to go around to the back.

She shook her head and looked at Mathias, her eyes

pausing at his walking stick. "Well, you're here now. The damage has been done. Let me see what you have."

I tilted the basket so she could see the sardines.

"Don't know what's possessed Señor Beltran to start eating sardines when he can eat anything he likes," she muttered, taking three of the fish and placing them on a sheet of newspaper that Mathias held out for her.

I glanced around her and into the foyer. I could see a small dark wooden table and a gold-crested mirror above it.

"Probably feels pity for the likes of you." She reached into her white apron pocket and took out several coins. "Here, he told me to give you this amount," she said, dropping the money into Mathias's palm. "Though it seems he's paying way too much for such a small amount of sardines. . . . Very strange."

"He's also buying some to be given to the poor." My eyes darted back to the old woman, and I smiled as innocently as I could. Who knew I was so good at this lying thing?

Mathias handed her the envelope with Señor Beltran's address on it. "This is for Señor Beltran too," he said.

"Yes, yes, *me lo imagine*. I didn't think it was a love letter for me." She scowled.

Mathias gave me a quick glance. "It's an invoice for the sardine deliveries made to the poor . . . and it's sealed."

"Now look here, boy, I don't know who raised you, but I know better than to open envelopes addressed to Señor Beltran. I'll give it to him just like I give him every other invoice and piece of mail that comes to this house."

"Yes, ma'am." Mathias gave her a slight nod and tugged on my sleeve, directing me to leave.

"Next time, use your brains and remember to come to the back door," the old woman called out. "Don't be such idiots!"

Mathias waved and kept walking.

I turned, immune to being called names, although a part of me had secretly hoped that things would somehow be different.

"And you, Sardine Girl, don't you think your boyfriend there should carry the basket instead of you? Not much of a gentleman, is he?"

I stopped and spun around.

"*¿Qué?*" the old woman challenged, but I had no response . . . though I wished I could let loose a tirade of insults about her wrinkled skin or tell her how we were more than what we appeared to be.

Realizing that I had nothing to say, the old woman dismissed us with a wave of her hand and closed the front door.

"*Estúpida,*" I muttered under my breath. I looked over at Mathias, who'd been watching with mild interest. "Ignore her," I said. "She doesn't understand that you can't do certain things because of . . . um, you know, the way you are."

I waited for Mathias to smile or thank me for understanding. Instead, his expression hardened into a glare. He turned and started walking back toward the main street.

"Hey, what's the matter?" I called out, shifting the basket to my other hip. "Wait up!"

Mathias didn't answer. He wouldn't even look at me; he just kept walking at a faster pace than before.

"Mathias?"

After a few minutes, the air between us was thick with resentment. "Are you mad because I came up with the story about giving the sardines to the poor?"

More silence from Mathias, and he was not slowing down.

"I thought she was getting suspicious and we needed a cover story. Aren't spies supposed to improvise and think on their feet? Don't get all upset just because you didn't think of it."

He froze in his tracks, his eyes blazing. "Of course that's not it. Unless you think 'the way I am' doesn't let me come up with stories too."

"What is *that* supposed to mean?" I asked, sensing that his seething anger was about to spill over into a full-fledged fight.

"You know what it means," he answered.

I put the basket down on the sidewalk and crossed my arms over my chest. "I was being nice."

"Well, I don't need you being nice or your pity." He leaned closer toward me. "In fact, I pity you."

"Me?" I took a step back.

"Yeah, you. A girl with no friends. That's really sad. That's the only reason I decided to talk to you."

"What?" I couldn't believe he was confirming my worst fear. "You mean when I was by my tree?" I grabbed at the long sleeves of my dress, trying to regain some control.

"There you go again. It's not *your* tree. You're just some stupid girl who daydreams by someone else's tree."

I wanted to run away and leave him behind. Do the deliveries by myself. But he had the envelopes, and so I did the only thing I could think of: I kicked him in his good leg.

"Ow!" he yelled, grabbing his shin. "Are you that much of an idiot?"

"Not as much as you," I replied, snatching up the basket and marching down the street.

When I reached the corner, I waited as a group of women passed by, each carrying a week's worth of rationed food. The usual chatter of voices was now being replaced more and more often with quiet sighs and the semi-defeated looks of people fighting for survival.

I stayed still, waiting to hear the *tik-tik-tik* of Mathias's *makila* hitting the pavement. I wasn't going to give him the satisfaction of turning around, but it was pointless to deliver the sardines without the envelopes.

After a minute or two, I glanced back, nervous that Mathias had left me behind and my career as a spy had already come to an end. I squinted, barely making out the shape of a boy sitting on a bench about a block and a half back, twirling a *makila* in front of him. I had walked the wrong way.

"Ugh," I grunted, heading over to him.

As I got closer to Mathias, I started thinking how it probably wasn't very smart to smack him on his one good leg . . . even if I was really mad. What if he was sitting because he couldn't walk or something?

"Glad to see you finally figured out we had to go this way," he said, standing up.

Obviously, my kicks weren't bone-breaking. "Guess we have to work together no matter what."

"Yep," he answered.

We walked in silence for about ten steps before I half-heartedly mumbled, "Sorry for kicking you."

Mathias gave me a look out of the corner of his eye. "Guess I kinda deserved it." I saw a sheepish smile cross his face. "It's been a while since someone booted me that hard."

We kept walking, not saying much else.

As we turned onto a street lined with several apartment buildings, Mathias spoke up again. "By the way, what I said about pitying you"—he turned his head to face me—"that wasn't true. There's nothing to pity about you."

My shoulders relaxed. The last remnants of my resentment toward him drifted away.

"I still don't understand why you got so mad," I said, glancing over at the address written on the envelope Mathias held in his hand.

He shrugged. "I don't like being treated like that."

"She was just a cranky old lady," I replied, adjusting my grip on the basket.

"Not her." He pointed to the top floor of a redbrick building. "That's our next stop." He paused to look at me. "I know enough to ignore people like that old woman. . . . I meant you."

"Me?"

Mathias sighed. "It's bad enough that other people see

me as different because of my leg. I didn't think you did." He shook his head. "I could've carried that basket."

The weight of his words landed on me like a pile of concrete. I knew that feeling. Always being seen as incompetent—less than what I was.

Mathias pressed a button next to the building's main door marked GOICOCHEA. "My father said he'll probably be home since he keeps bankers' hours."

"*Vale,*" I whispered, wishing I could say something to prove that I understood how I'd made him feel.

The main door buzzed, although no one had asked who we were.

"Let's go," Mathias said, pushing the glass door open.

"Hey, Mathias, you want to take the basket for a while? It is getting heavy," I said as we walked into the lobby.

"*¿Ahora?*" he asked, and pointed with his *makila* to the tall spiral staircase in the center of the room. "You want me to carry it *now*?" He chuckled. "You've carried it this far, I think I can wait until we come back down the four flights of stairs before I help."

I smiled. As usual, my timing was perfect.

TEN

We saved Padre Iñaki for our last delivery. It was a little after six-thirty when we approached the church rectory and knocked on the side door. Mathias had been carrying the basket with one hand and occasionally trying to balance it on his head. I'd offered to help carry it by holding up one side, but Mathias said we'd do it that way next week. . . . I knew he had something to prove. A young woman with long, dark hair opened the door and greeted us with a smile.

"¡*Las sardinas! ¡Qué bueno!*" she exclaimed. "Come in, come in. Go ahead and set that basket over by the sink." She ushered us into the kitchen, which was full of the heavenly aromas of onions, garlic, and spices melding together. "I'll be with you in a minute," she said, turning her attention back to the pot on the stove. "I have to finish this *sopa de ajo* or else dinner will be ruined."

"*Sí, señora*," I said, watching a little girl run into the room and hide behind the woman's long gray skirt.

"Oh, you can call me Lupe, and"—she pried the child away from her leg—"this is Carmita, my daughter."

Carmita sneaked a look at Mathias and me before burying her face in Lupe's skirt again.

"I'm Mathias, and that's—"

"Mami, *carga*," Carmita interrupted, raising her arms to be carried.

"Shhh," Lupe said to the little girl before wiping her hands on the apron in order to shake our hands. "*Un placer* to meet the two of you."

"Ma-a-ami!" Carmita tugged on Lupe's dress.

Ignoring her daughter's demands, Lupe turned back to the stove to stir the pot once more. "When Padre Iñaki told me that we were getting a few sardines to feed the homeless, I couldn't believe it. I don't know how that man stretches the little money we collect."

"Mami, up, up," Carmita pleaded, throwing her head back to look at her mother.

"Not now. *Mira*." Lupe pointed to some coins on a small silver platter. "You can help me by giving those to the pretty girl."

"No!" Carmita pouted. "*¡Carga!*" she demanded, jumping up and down with her little arms raised.

I cringed as I saw Lupe untie her apron. I'd seen Mamá do the same thing when I was young. Although, with me, it wouldn't have taken this long before I'd have been facing the back side of a wooden spoon.

"*Vamos*." Lupe bent down and picked the little girl up, tickling her tummy.

Carmita squealed with delight.

A sense of relief washed over me, and a huge smile spread across my face as Lupe carried her daughter to go look at the sardines.

"So, are you now doing deliveries without your mother?" Lupe asked, peering into the basket.

"Um, I . . . no . . . I mean, yes. . . ." I looked over at Mathias in a bit of a panic. My mind drew a blank. Was I supposed to say yes or no? Obviously, Lupe knew who I was. No clever story came to mind.

"Cat got your tongue, princess?" Mathias smiled, then directed himself to Lupe. "We're only doing this on Mondays since her mother's busy with the market. You're actually our final delivery." He raised the last of our envelopes in the air before placing it on the table. "This is for Padre Iñaki. Will you make sure he gets it?"

I shuffled my feet and stared at the ground, wishing I could slap my head for being such an idiot. All I had to say was the truth, and I'd almost blown it. Sometimes I needed to forget about making up a story.

Lupe nodded. "Of course. I'll give it to him as soon as he arrives." She gave me a quick glance before looking back at Mathias. "Princess, huh? That's sweet."

Mathias seemed confused for a moment, then his cheeks began to blaze as he realized that Lupe thought his nickname for me was a term of endearment. "Oh no. That's just Ani. I didn't mean—"

"Are you really a princess?" Carmita asked, staring at me as if I were some wondrous creature.

"No, sweetie, Ani is just a very pretty girl like you." Lupe readjusted the little girl on her hip as she tilted the large basket. "Oh my, are all these for us?"

"Um." I stole a quick glance at Mathias. I had already mentioned to Señor Beltran's maid that he was donating sardines to the poor. And all the other customers wanted only one or two fish, even if they paid for several more. This would fit our story.

Mathias gave me a shrug, picked up a little rag doll from the kitchen counter, and started tapping Carmita's arm with it.

"Oh no, it can't all be for us." Lupe shook her head. "We don't have nearly enough money for it. I didn't mean to put you on the spot. I just got confused because you mentioned we were the last ones."

I knew that the church would stretch the sardines to feed a lot of people, and we'd already been paid enough for my Mamá to be satisfied.

"No, you're right. They're all for the church. Some were donated," I said.

"Oh, how wonderful!" Lupe reached over to give both Mathias and me a hug—Carmita and her rag doll also getting sandwiched in.

"We need to get going," Mathias said, backing out of the group hug.

"Well, we'll definitely look forward to your visits on Mondays." Lupe smiled and gave my hand a gentle squeeze.

I walked out of that kitchen feeling warmer and lighter than I had . . . well, than I had in a long time.

"She was really nice," Mathias said as we strolled toward my apartment, which was only a few blocks from the church.

"Yeah, I'm glad we gave her all the sardines." I tossed around the empty basket, which Mathias had agreed I could carry again.

"What do you want to do now?" he asked as we approached the point in the street where the cobblestones ended and the dirt road that led out of town began.

I shrugged.

Mathias lifted his shirt up to his nose. "We're kind of smelly, and it's not that late." He looked up at the cloud-filled sky. It wouldn't be getting dark for at least another hour. "You want to air out? Go to the field?" He pointed down the road with his *makila*.

My nose couldn't register the odor of sardines on my clothes anymore, but I accepted the fact that we probably did smell. "By my tree?" I asked.

Mathias rolled his eyes. "It's not *your* tree, but yes . . . let's go there."

We started down the road, and I fell two steps behind Mathias just to mutter, "It *is* mine."

For most of our walk to the field, Mathias whistled a tune that sounded vaguely familiar. I kept trying to place the song, but, so far, all I knew was that it wasn't a church hymn or anything traditionally Basque. It was catchy, though, and the *tap-tap-tap* of his *makila* kept the beat.

It made for a nice accompaniment to what was turning out to be one of the best days of my life. I stared at the passing gray clouds overhead. Even without the sun shining, I felt warm inside. A part of me wanted to run as fast as I could, then dance and twirl around my oak tree. But I knew Mathias wouldn't be able to do it, and leaving him behind felt wrong.

The sound of trotting horse hooves made me turn around. An old farmer with white hair and a short beard was approaching us in his wagon.

"*Kaixo*, Mathias!" the old man called out, pulling on his horse's reins, slowing down right next to us.

"*Hola*, Garza." Mathias gave him a slight nod. "How's Julián? Is he feeling any better?"

"Little bit. Got him some more medicine here." He patted a small brown bag next to him. "You going up there now? Seems a bit late, but he does enjoy your visits." The old man's gaze went from Mathias to me. "Or do you have other plans?"

"We're just going out to the tree." Mathias looked over at me. "This is my friend Ani."

"Ah, nice to meet you, Ani. I've seen you out in the field by the tree many times with your father." He pointed to a small house, midway up the mountain. "My wife and I live up there."

Mathias leaned closer to me and whispered, "He owns this land . . . including *your* tree."

I glanced down at my shoes. "Nice to meet you too, Señor Garza. I'm sorry if we weren't supposed to be on your land."

The old man threw his head back and laughed. "Ay, *mija*. Your visits to that old tree are like a blue jay landing . . . always a welcome guest. And you can just call me Garza, everyone else does."

I smiled. *How had I never met this man?*

"I'll let you two young folks enjoy your free time." He snapped the reins and looked over at Mathias. "Will you be visiting Julián tomorrow?"

Mathias nodded and waved as the wagon wheels picked up the dust of the road and the old man headed home.

Just as I was about to ask who Julián was, Mathias leaned over with a sly smile. "Told you the tree wasn't yours."

ELEVEN

Sitting under the tree with a friend was different from being with Papá or being alone. The air felt charged with possible adventures . . . all of them real, not imaginary. Over the years, my tree had taken on the role of an old piece of furniture, like my bed . . . something familiar and comfortable. But now it was as if I'd put a different bedspread on it, making it new again.

"There." He pointed to the three small stacks of coins that were on the ground between us. "The first one covers what you said was the cost of the sardines, and the other two are our profit. I split it evenly, if you want to check."

"*Vale*, I believe you," I muttered, stroking the satin pouch in my pocket.

"What are you doing?" Mathias asked.

I whipped my hand out. "Nothing," I said.

"C'mon, what do you have in there? Is it a lucky charm or something? A rabbit's foot?"

"Ugh! No." I crinkled my nose at the idea of having an

actual rabbit's foot in my pocket. I reached in and pulled out the blue satin pouch to show him.

He scooted closer to me to see. "So, what's in it?" he asked.

I untied the little rope around the top and pulled out my secret treasure. "My father gave it to me."

"*¿Una bellota?* He gave you an acorn?"

"It's not just any acorn. It's the one we're going to plant together when the war is over so that I'll have my own tree."

Mathias smiled and tilted his head. "I was just bothering you about that whole not-your-tree thing."

"I know," I said, standing up for a moment to tuck the pouch back into my skirt pocket. "But this one holds a promise."

"What do you mean?"

"It's a long story . . . one I made up when I was younger." I sat down in front of him, excited to share one of my stories. "It's about a princess who's able to return home because of an acorn that—"

Mathias leaned back against the tree trunk. "Ha! You see? I knew you had royal blood in your veins. That's why I called you princess," he teased.

I gave him a scowl. "If you don't want to hear the story . . ."

He nudged me gently with his leg. "I'm just foolin'. Go on." He closed his eyes.

I stayed quiet.

A few seconds passed, and he opened one eye to look at me. "Aren't you going to tell me the story?"

"Nope. Not anymore I won't."

"Fine, it probably wasn't that good."

"Oh no, it was really good . . . but you'll never know."

He shook his head. "Girls," he muttered.

I stared up at the leaves overhead. "So, how do you know the Garzas?"

"Long story." He paused for a moment, relishing our switch in roles, but when I didn't react, he continued. "Garza and my grandfather fought together during the Great War. When we moved here, my father went to see him."

"That's it?" I asked.

"Um." He paused. "Yeah."

"Wow." I widened my eyes in fake surprise. "That *was* a long story."

"Funny." Mathias's gaze dropped down to his feet. "Thing is, when we got there, we found out his daughter and son-in-law had died and his grandson had polio. . . . They'd gotten it a while back during the epidemic in Madrid."

"Polio?" I grimaced. "Can't you catch that?"

Mathias shrugged. "He's not contagious anymore. Plus, it's not gonna hurt me anyway. . . . I already had it."

I looked over at his leg. "Is that why you use the *makila?*"

Mathias nodded. "The poor kid has it really bad, though. He can't walk at all."

"How old is he?" I asked, thinking about my brother who'd died.

"Seven. But don't get me wrong, he's plenty tough."

"It's nice that you visit him." I rolled on my stomach to watch a small black ant climb up and over one of the tree roots sticking out of the ground.

"Yeah, he gets bored living on a farm without other

kids around." Mathias took off his beret and ran his fingers through his dark hair. "Plus, I've been helping Garza around the farm."

"Doing what?"

"Anything . . . everything. His sons joined the war, so he doesn't have much help. Plus, I like the work."

I lifted my head to look at Mathias. "Farming?"

Mathias moved to lie flat on the ground. He stretched his arms over his head as if willing himself to get taller. "Yeah. Anything wrong with that?"

"No, just didn't think you liked that sort of thing. Thought you were all about being a spy . . . making a difference."

"There are lots of ways to make a difference. Garza says I'm a natural farmer."

"What else does Garza tell you?" I teased.

"He tells me stories and stuff that might come in handy one day. Besides, I could be a spy and use being a farmer as my cover."

I propped my head on one hand. "What kind of stories?"

"Mostly war stories. Tips on how to be a good soldier. Like remembering to breathe and listen before firing your gun because you can aim better when you know which direction the enemy is shooting from. Also to never run in a straight line because zigzagging targets are much harder to hit."

"Sounds pretty obvious."

"Well, of course." He rolled his eyes at me. "Good advice usually is. But the one thing he says I should always remember is, if under attack, find a foxhole and stay there . . . especially if there's a bombing run."

"Bombing? Hmph, I don't think that'll really happen." I stuck out my finger and watched a little ant crawl up and over it, continuing on the path set by the other ants. "Look how many false alarms we have every week. Lots of people don't even go to the shelters anymore when they hear the bells and sirens."

"That's because they take things for granted. My father makes us go down to the shelter near the theater every single time."

"Well, my mother says that when your time is up, it's up. She keeps on selling . . . siren or no siren. Plus, what could anyone really want to destroy here . . . the Guernica Tree? What kind of commander wastes bombs on an oak?"

Mathias shrugged. "Still. You never know."

"I think boys just like to talk about war," I said.

Mathias closed his eyes again and laid his head back. "That's because there's always a war to talk about, princess. Always."

TWELVE

The school day seemed to drag on longer than normal. All I could think of was that there was an exciting world outside and that suddenly I was a part of it.

I stared at the pages of my book, not really reading the words. The jarring sound of the school bell and the rustling of the students getting up from their desks snapped me back to the world at hand. My usual routine of having to meet Mamá in front of our building to help with the sardine sales could explain why I was never in a rush to get out the door.

As I trudged along the school's courtyard, my thoughts kept wandering to all the "what if" scenarios that working with the spies might bring. *What if we messed up and lost a letter? What if we got caught? What if—*

"Hey, princess! Over here!" a voice called out.

Usually I kept my eyes fixed on the ground, but the voice made me look up.

"*¡Aquí!*" It was Mathias, standing by the archway closest

to the front steps. He was waving his *makila* in the air, try-ing to get my attention.

My first instinct was to run over to him, but then I re-membered where we were. School. Other kids were around. And he had just said "princess," not "Sardine Girl." This would not be good.

I casually walked over, looking around to see if any-one noticed. "What are you doing here?" I asked in a hushed voice.

"Father wants us to make more deliveries . . . on Fridays as well as Mondays. Can you do it?"

I glanced behind me. There still wasn't anyone pay-ing attention to me . . . as usual. "I don't know. Mamá was happy with the money I brought home last night, but I don't think she'll let me skip a day of working with her." I glanced up at the clock at the top of the school building. It was five after five. "In fact, she's expecting me now. I have to get going."

Mathias stayed put. "She'll make extra money by selling on her own and having you make deliveries with me. Your mother will say yes if you just explain it to her."

I shook my head. "You don't know my mother." Out of the corner of my eye, I saw some boys on the other side of the courtyard cluster together.

"Ani, it's important." Mathias clasped his hands together as if in prayer. "Please," he pleaded. "Father says there's a lot of activity. He might even clue me in to what's going on, but first we have to do this. We can do them real fast, in an hour or so. I have to be home before sunset for Shabbat anyway, so you can meet up with your mom after we're done. C'mon, I already told him we would."

"You should've talked to me before agreeing to it," I said, glancing over his shoulder just in time to see one boy point his finger our way. I looked back at Mathias. "And what's Shabbat anyway?"

"Jewish day of rest and prayer. You've never heard of it?"

I shook my head, watching as a few boys began to cross the courtyard.

"On Fridays before sundown, Mother lights candles, and we have a special dinner. When we were in Berlin, I'd even go to synagogue with my grandparents and— Are you even listening to me?"

"Let's talk about this somewhere else." I put my hand on Mathias's elbow, trying to usher him away from the school and the boys who were now making a beeline toward us.

"Why? What's the rush? And you still haven't told me if you'll even do the Friday deliveries."

"Fine, I'll figure something out and do them." I tugged on his shirtsleeve with a greater sense of urgency. "Let's just go."

"What has you—" He turned around to follow my gaze.

"*Mira, mira.* Sardine Girl has herself a boyfriend!" a voice exclaimed.

Sabino, the school bully, was now only a few feet away from us, with the rest of the boys huddled behind him.

"Ha!" He pointed to Mathias's *makila.* "And he's *un*

cojo. Can't even walk straight. . . . Isn't that just perfect?" Sabino called back to his friends, who had stopped to watch.

I pulled on Mathias's suspender. "*Vámonos.* Let's just go," I said, knowing that Sabino was not someone you messed around with. It was better to ignore and be ignored.

"You have a problem?" Mathias squared his shoulders and thrust out his chest as Sabino got within a few feet of us.

Sabino laughed while everyone in the courtyard stopped to stare. By now, he and Mathias stood only a few inches apart. "No problem here, my brother," he announced in a loud voice. "Just surprised to see Sardine Girl with someone."

"Don't call her that," Mathias said in a voice deeper than his own.

Sabino laughed. "Why not? That's what she is. . . . Can't you *smell* that I'm right? She's just plain old Sardine Girl."

I pulled at Mathias again. "Forget it. Let's go."

Mathias pushed away my hand. "I said not to call her that!" His eyes narrowed as he stared at Sabino.

"Fine, tough guy." Sabino forced another chuckle. "If you like Sardine Girl, I don't mind. Guess there's no accounting for taste"—he pinched his nose and looked to the crowd—"or smell."

Laughter broke out all around.

That's when Mathias did it. In a split second, he let go of his *makila* and drove his fist forward, landing it squarely on the side of Sabino's jaw.

A hush fell over the schoolyard as Sabino staggered back a step. I waited for him to unleash his fury on Mathias, but instead his eyes glazed over, his knees buckled, and he dropped to the ground.

"*¿Alguien más?*" Mathias asked, looking at the boys in the crowd, his fists ready for a fight.

No one stepped forward.

In fact, people started walking away and turning their backs on the whole scene while a couple of boys dragged Sabino off.

"Just go," an older boy who had rushed over told Mathias. "No one needs any more trouble from the likes of you."

"Trouble from us?" I couldn't believe what I was hearing. "*Eres un idiota,*" I muttered, shaking my head. "You have no idea what really goes on here."

The boy just shrugged and tried to break up the crowd.

"*Vamos,*" I said to Mathias as I bent down to pick up his *makila*. "I think you proved your point."

"Good," he said, rubbing his knuckles for a moment. He had a smug look as he whispered, "Guess my dad was right."

"About what?"

He clenched and unclenched his hand, trying to stretch out his fingers. "He always says that the one who punches first punches last."

A smile spread across my face as I realized we were truly friends. I held out the *makila* for him. "Sabino had it coming. But I have to admit, I didn't know you could hit like that."

Mathias took the walking stick, and we headed out of the schoolyard. "Yeah, well, the truth is, I'm pretty sure I only had one punch in me."

I gave him a little nudge with my elbow. "Don't worry. With a fist like that, that's all you'll ever need."

THIRTEEN

A bird screeched overhead. I glanced up as it circled once before landing on the corner of my building. I could see the twigs from its nest sticking up, and I imagined baby birds greeting their mother with open beaks. One day soon those birds would be old enough to fly, and then *bam!* Their mother would kick them out of the nest. Fly or fall . . . no in-between.

"*¿Qué tú haces?* Looking into that gray sky, waiting for the world to end?"

I turned my attention back to the cobblestone street to see Mamá standing next to me with the large basket on her head. "No. I'm just—"

"Doesn't matter. We have work to do. Are you ready to go?" She thrust the brass scale and weights into my hands.

For two days I'd been waiting for the right moment to ask Mamá about doing the Friday deliveries with Mathias, but there never seemed to be a good time. Lately, she'd been in a fouler mood than usual. Always complaining about the refugees escaping the front lines and flooding into Guernica or about the failures of the government that got us into this Civil War mess. I had to be extra careful to stay out of her way while I was home just to avoid the belt.

At least school wasn't bad. At first I was worried that there'd be some kind of fallout from the Mathias-Sabino fight, but it had all been relatively normal. There were whispers and a few fingers pointed in my direction, but I think Sabino took more grief about it than I did.

"*Vámonos, neska.* The main streets are filling up with riff-raff from every other neighboring city, and it's going to be tougher to make our sales."

I followed her down the street. "But won't some of them buy sardines? Maybe become our customers?" There had to be a way to put her in a better mood.

She turned quickly around, never losing the balance of the basket that was perched on the small rag atop her head. "*No seas tonta.*" She pursed her lips as if she couldn't believe I was her daughter. "You can't be that ignorant." She reached up to shift the basket. "Those people won't buy anything. They're living on handouts. Running from the front lines and coming here. If anything, we might get a few of them trying to steal the sardines. So walk faster and watch our things. We need every *peseta* we can get."

"*Sí, señora,*" I replied, walking alongside her.

This was it. Things weren't going to get better. I had to speak up. With a deep breath, I took the plunge. "Mamá, I know how we can make some more money."

She didn't break her stride nor cast a glance my way.

I continued. "Mathias says his customers want deliveries twice a week—Mondays and Fridays. I can do those deliveries while you do the normal sales and we'll both be making money."

"Hmph, sounds like sardines are becoming more fashionable." She paused and placed the basket on the ground. "Or the rich are becoming more like us poor folks."

"I guess," I muttered, not wanting to press her for an answer.

She wiped her face with her shirtsleeve and stretched her back. I'd just joined her, but she'd been selling all day.

Those few seconds seemed to last forever. Finally she spoke up. "Guaranteed sales are always a good thing," she said, almost talking to herself instead of me. Her lips twitched back and forth before she gave me a slight nod. "Fine, I'll do the Friday rounds on my own. After all, before you were born, *neska*, I always did them by myself." She heaved the basket back up to her head. "Never expected you to stay with me for too long," she said before resuming her walk down the street, yelling in Basque and Spanish, "*¡Sardina frescue! ¡Sardina fresca!*"

I guess baby birds weren't the only ones learning to leave their nests.

As we rounded a corner, strong winds whipped around Mamá's billowing black skirt, puffing it out like a parachute. Even though we hadn't made any sales, I wore a silly grin on my face, knowing that I'd soon have another day of deliveries with Mathias.

"*¡Señora! ¡Señora!*" someone from behind us called out.

Mamá and I turned around, thinking we were about to make a sale.

It was the postman, carrying his gray sack across his body and waving an envelope. *"¡Una carta!"* he shouted.

"A letter?" In one quick motion, Mamá removed the basket from her head and dropped it on the ground. She ran over because we both knew who it would be from.

I picked up the large basket, which sat in the middle of the street, struggled a bit with its weight, and waddled over to join Mamá, who had already torn open the envelope.

"It's from Papá?"

Mamá nodded without looking at me. She was completely immersed in what Papá had written.

After a minute or so, I saw her eyes begin to glisten with tears that would never be allowed to fall.

Her shoulders sagged and she sighed. "The fool," she whispered, thrusting the paper toward me and grabbing the basket.

I walked and read the letter at the same time.

Papá wrote that he was safe, but that he was being re-assigned from his job in the kitchen to actually fighting on the front lines. Apparently, some of the injured were being sent to prepare the food, and those who were still healthy like him were being sent to battle.

I stopped reading for a moment as I crossed the street. Mamá never once looked back to see if I was still there.

I returned to Papá's letter. He said that he was fighting to protect us and his homeland, and that he'd do his best to come back in one piece. He asked that Mamá and I take care of each other and never forget how much he loved us. At the bottom of the letter, he'd drawn a picture of our oak tree.

I stopped walking. My heart and thoughts wanted to soar into the sky, catch the April breeze, and float until they found Papá.

Why did he leave us? Weren't we more important than this stupid war? How could he risk his life when I needed him so much?

Fear and pain stewed into anger.

"¡*Neska!*" Mamá called out.

I clenched my fist and crinkled the letter. I wasn't sure if I was mad at Mamá for thinking Papá was a fool, or at Papá and myself for being foolish enough to think we could make a difference.

By eight-thirty the streets had grown dark and we were headed home. Long shadows cast out whenever we walked near the lampposts, and although we'd sold almost all the sardines, our mood could not have been more grim.

Mamá and I didn't speak, because nothing needed to be said. We both knew where our lives were headed, and it was a road that we'd apparently travel without Papá.

As we got closer to our building, I saw the familiar silhouette of a boy with his *makila*.

I sighed. I definitely didn't want to hear any of Mathias's talk about war or doing something important. I just wanted to be left alone.

"*Kaixo, Ani. Arratsalde on, señora,*" Mathias said when we were only a few feet from him.

My eyebrows scrunched together at the sound of him speaking in Basque.

Mamá lifted an eyebrow and looked him up and down. "Do I know you?" Mamá asked him in Spanish, then, staring at his walking stick, realized who he was. "You're the boy with the customers, right?"

"*Sí, señora.*" He stuck out his hand. "I'm Mathias García."

"Hmph." Mamá ignored his outstretched hand. "Make sure you split the profits evenly. *Neska* over there may not catch on, but I will," she said, and with that, she stepped around him and continued down the street, carrying the nearly empty basket.

"Why are you speaking in Basque?" I asked. "It won't impress Mamá, if that's what you're thinking."

Mathias shrugged. "Worth a shot. Thought it might help with the Friday deliveries."

"She already said yes," I mumbled as we started walking.

"Great! I knew you'd convince her."

I didn't look at him.

Mathias picked up his pace so he could walk backward and face me. "So, the other day, after I saw you at the school, I hung around outside one of the cafés listening to some of the old men. Turns out Franco's trying to form a blockade of the ports. Even laying mines and stuff. Our side's been finding them, though."

"Hmph. Our side," I muttered, my mind still on Papá's letter.

"I wonder if that's the type of information we're delivering.

Stuff about the blockade, or maybe it's about the ground troops."

I shrugged. The idea that the war was this thrilling for him turned my stomach.

The excitement in Mathias's voice was unrelenting. "If only we could read one of those letters." He stopped for a moment. "I bet we could really help if we knew what to be on the lookout for."

I kept walking, not bothering to look back. "Yeah, sure," I said in a voice that he could still hear even though I was several steps ahead. "Because we're really going to make a difference. Pfft."

I heard the familiar tap of the *makila* as Mathias caught up with me. "What's eating you? You're acting like you don't care about what we're doing."

I spun around and spat, "What we're doing? We've delivered *one* message. Something a carrier pigeon could do. So, yeah, I guess I really don't care."

Mathias took a step back. "I'm not sure what's gotten into you, but we *are* making a difference."

"If that's what you want to believe, fine. I'll do the deliveries because we need the money, but I just want this war to be over. It doesn't matter who wins or what Hitler or Franco does."

"Wow, princess." Mathias shook his head. "That's a ridiculous thing to say . . . no matter what's eating you."

I shrugged off his comment. "Maybe so, but it's true." I paused. "And don't call me princess."

He gave a long whistle. "You are in one bad mood."

I glanced up to see Mamá standing by our window looking down at us. "Mamá's waiting. I've got to go."

"Fine. See you on Friday?"

"I guess." I plodded up the steps of my building. "Not that
it really matters," I muttered.

"You're wrong, prin— I mean Ani," Mathias called out as
I started to go inside. "There's something in the air. Something is going to happen. . . . I can feel it!"

FOURTEEN

School dragged on as never before. Everything seemed so pointless. I wished I hadn't pretended to be sick, because now I felt like I really needed to stay in bed.

All day long, I'd been convincing myself that I didn't want to see Mathias or do the Friday deliveries, but as I walked home and saw him on the front stoop, a sliver of anticipation crept back into my chest. Quickly I pushed it away. I had to remember that I was nothing more than the daughter of the *sardinera*.

"Hurry up!" Mathias waved me over.

I kept my slow stride.

He tapped his foot, waiting for me to get closer.

"The sardines are upstairs. I'll go get them." I spoke with no emotion.

"No, wait." He gave me a slightly wicked smile. "I've got an idea. Can I go up with you?"

I stared at him. It was completely wrong to allow a boy into our apartment without Mamá being home.

"Are you crazy? There's no—"

He pulled out an envelope and showed it to me. "Look, the back flap isn't completely sealed. If we steam it, it'll probably come unglued and we can see what's inside."

I took the envelope and flipped it over in my hands.

Mathias nudged me. "C'mon. You know you're as curious as I am."

I shook my head. "I can't let you up. Mamá would kill me."

"Fine, then you steam it open. Just promise not to read it until you come back down."

I hesitated. What if I messed it up?

"I just hold it over boiling water?" I asked.

"Yes, but don't get it too close, because then the paper will get soggy. And hurry. I've got to be home before sundown or my mother will kill me."

The envelope seemed to get heavier. "What if we can't get it closed again?"

"Take a look." He pointed to the back flap. "Part of it never sealed, so we can lick it closed. Plus, if you steam it right, the glue will get tacky and we can just press it down."

I pulled out the key and took a few steps toward the door. I glanced around. No one was watching. "Fine, come up and do it."

In an instant Mathias was by the door. "This is going to be good!"

Waiting for the water to boil, I wondered what we could possibly do with any information we might learn.

"This is pretty stupid," I said just as the first of the bubbles rose from the black pot.

"Why? No one has to find out that we know. And if we understand what's going on, we can keep our eyes open for things."

I didn't want to be involved any more than I already was. I'd survive this war by doing what I did best: being invisible. "I'm just doing this because it's the quickest way to finish up the deliveries and get my share of the money."

Mathias rolled his eyes. "So you told me yesterday." The water began to boil, and Mathias held the envelope several inches above the pot. "I don't know why you're acting this way." He paused. "It's not like you."

"You don't even know me."

Mathias ignored my statement, concentrating on keeping the sealed part of the envelope close to the rising steam.

"See," he said, his eyes not even blinking. "It's already loosening up. Get me a knife."

I opened the drawer next to me and handed him the sharpest one.

He slid the blade under the open end, toward the now loosely glued side. The flap lifted easily, without even a crinkle.

"Pretty good, huh?" He was obviously pleased with himself.

"What does it say?" I asked, leaning over his shoulder as he unfolded the letter.

Mathias shook his head. "It's written in Basque. You read it."

I scanned the short letter. "I understand the words, but they don't make much sense."

"Just tell me what it says. Maybe we can figure it out."

I read the letter twice before translating it into Spanish.

"It starts by talking about a party and how it will be a wonderful event. Says that now that the party has been moved from Madrid to Bilbao, they'll need to look at the guest list again." I paused to stare at Mathias. "This is about a party? When Bilbao has barely any food and people are starving?"

He shook his head. "*Party* must be a code. Maybe Madrid isn't their only focus in the fighting. . . . Keep reading."

I looked down at the paper. "It says that their first guest has already arrived in Bilbao but that he had great difficulty getting there because of the storm coming from the west. To avoid future storms, the other British guests are advised to stay in France for a few days. But then they should take the same road that their first guest took."

"Hmm."

"Hmm? We're couriers announcing the arrival of some British people in Bilbao. This is what's so important?"

"I'm not sure the letter refers to people."

"Whatever . . . It isn't that important, and neither are we." I folded the letter back into the envelope.

"No, just hear me out. If someone found the letter, it might not seem important. But what if the guests are ships?"

"Ships?" I rolled my eyes.

"Yeah. Listen, I heard my father talking about a British merchant ship that had to be protected by the Brits' navy because some of Franco's destroyers wanted to stop it from going to Bilbao. It was in the newspaper."

"The Brits? They're not helping end this war, so who needs them?"

"Ani! Without those British ships bringing food and supplies into Bilbao, a lot of people would starve. Guernica might do okay because there are so many farmers and fishermen around here, but other cities are in real trouble. It's not only about this place."

I shrugged off his comment and gave him back the envelope.

"Actually, I've got to hand it to Franco. It's a pretty good plan 'cause starving people usually can't fight." Mathias flipped the envelope over and licked it closed. "If Franco's guys can maintain a blockade long enough, they'll be able to just waltz in and take over. Genius."

"Genius would be to have this war end now," I said, grabbing the basket of sardines Mamá had left next to the partially open window. She always kept them there so they'd stay as cool and fresh as possible. There was never a doubt as to where the *sardinera* lived.

"Done!" Mathias showed off the perfectly sealed envelope. "You ready?"

I was already out the door.

FIFTEEN

Making my way down to the first floor, I could hear Mathias's *makila* tapping on each stair behind me. The sound bothered me. His breathing irritated me. Everything about him right now was a nuisance.

"Hurry up!" I called back before stopping in midstride.

I recognized the tone in my voice. The arch of my shoulders as I carried the basket down the stairs was also familiar. I could even imagine the look on my face. I was turning into Mamá.

"What's the matter? Why'd you stop?" he asked.

I glanced at him. He wanted so much to make a difference, to be involved. Just like Papá . . . just like me.

We were all fools.

"Hey, is this about the deliveries? You're not getting scared we'll get caught or something?" Mathias whispered.

"No." I waited a moment longer on the staircase, then I rolled back my shoulders. "Let's just go. The sooner we start, the sooner we finish."

All the way to Señor Beltran's home, we walked in silence.

Once there, we went around to the back and made our delivery, and then we continued to the next stop. That's how the next three stops went. Nothing eventful. In fact, the silence made it just like walking with Mamá. The only difference was that we were carrying the basket of sardines together.

As the church's cupola came into view, Mathias dropped his side of the basket. A few sardines tumbled out, flopping onto the street. "I can't take it anymore." He stared at me as if I was supposed to say something. "What *is* the problem?"

"Nothing," I answered, bending down to pick up the spilled sardines.

Mathias slapped the basket's rim with his *makila*. "No! You've been acting weird since yesterday. Something's up."

I stayed still, waiting to be ignored.

"Tell me," he demanded. "We're friends, aren't we?"

From my crouched position, down by the basket, I answered, "I don't have friends."

"Do you really and truly want me to leave you alone, then?" he asked, and I could hear the anger and frustration behind his words. "Because I can definitely do that. You can go back to being by yourself."

I swallowed the lump that had formed in my throat. I could feel my nose twitching as I tried to hold back the emotions climbing their way to the surface. Seconds later, a single tear ran down my cheek.

"Aw, shoot! Don't cry." He put his hand on my arm. "You

don't have to tell me anything if you don't want to. We'll finish this last delivery and go home."

I quickly wiped the stray tear away and declared, "I'm not crying. I never cry."

Mathias looked confused. "Okay."

My knees felt wobbly, so I turned to sit on a nearby stoop. Mathias followed my lead.

After a minute of not saying anything, I took a deep breath and slowly let it out. "Papá is fighting on the front lines," I said softly.

"Uh-huh, but you knew that."

"No, I mean really fighting. He won't be working in the kitchen, he'll actually be in battle." I let out a shaky breath. "I always thought that since he was older, they wouldn't make him fight. Even though the army needed volunteers, Mamá thought they'd take one look at him and send him home."

"How old *is* he?" Mathias asked.

"Does it matter? The point is, no one comes back from the front lines."

Mathias looked down. "Some will."

"I just have this feeling that Papá won't. That I won't see or hear from him ever again." The thought I'd feared, the one I didn't want to face, was finally put into words. Another tear threatened to trickle out. I rubbed my eye before it could escape. "Then I'll really be alone," I whispered.

"You'll still have your mother," he offered.

I shot him a look.

Mathias smiled. "You'll still have me." He gave me a nudge.

I looked into his eyes . . . then punched him lightly in the arm. It was all I could think of doing.

"What was that for?" he asked, rubbing the spot where I'd hit him, although I was certain it hadn't hurt.

"For being my friend," I said with a slight smile. "A very good friend."

He knocked his knees against mine. "We'll always be friends."

"And spy partners," I added with a smirk.

"Finally! I caught you filthy spies!" a voice from behind us exclaimed.

Before I could turn or stand, a hand grabbed the back of my shirt collar and dragged me up.

My heart beat so hard that I thought it would bruise my ribs.

Mathias jumped up, getting between me and the man who'd grabbed me. "Let her go!" Mathias demanded.

The man was hefty, with light brown hair and a thin mustache. He pushed me back and then twisted the front of Mathias's shirt as he pulled him closer. "Go ahead and fess up. I know spies when I see them!"

Thoughts sprinted through my head. Mathias still had the last envelope. What if he searched us? What excuse could we give? Maybe we could say that we just found the envelope or that we saw someone drop it. I started to build a story about a tall stranger in an overcoat who dropped it as he walked by us. We couldn't see his face because his hat was pulled down low. I could do this. I'd read enough stories to come up with my own.

"No, we're not spies. We were just following this tall man wearing an overcoat who dropped . . ."

Our attacker glanced at me before turning his attention back to Mathias. "Don't deny it!" he said, shaking Mathias by the shirt. "Did Crespo send you? Thinks I'm seeing his girl-friend again?" His eyes had narrowed into little slits.

Mathias was already pulling back his fist when the man's comment clicked in my head. We hadn't been caught . . . not yet. He didn't even know about the envelope.

"Yes, Crespo sent us," I blurted out, holding back Math-ias's arm. "But we didn't see anything. We've never done this before, and"—I used the line that I'd always hated hearing—"we're just kids."

The man released his grip on Mathias's shirt. "Hmph. Of course you didn't see anything! Nothing to see."

I squeezed Mathias's arm and widened my eyes at him, hoping he'd get the message to play along.

"But don't tell me this is the first time," the man contin-ued, standing so close to us that I could smell the cigarettes he'd smoked. "I know when I'm being watched."

"No, really. Maybe someone else was doing it before, but you caught us right away," I said, giving him my most inno-cent look.

Mathias straightened his shirt and added, "You're just too smart for us."

I winced. Too much . . .

The man looked at the two of us and shook his head. "Stupid kids." He put on his beret, tugged it low over his fore-head, and shoved past us. As he started down the street, he looked back and yelled, "You make sure to tell Crespo that if he was a real man, he'd confront me himself and not send sniveling children to spy!"

"I'll make sure to tell him!" I said with relief-filled laughter bubbling over my words.

Our would-be attacker paused, clenched his fist, and glared at us.

I glanced over at Mathias, wondering if we'd have to make a run for it.

The man then stuffed his hands in his coat pockets. "No-good kids," he muttered before walking away.

Mathias and I remained quiet until he rounded the corner, and then, the moment he was out of sight, we broke into hysterical laughter.

SIXTEEN

During the next two weeks, Mathias and I continued making our deliveries, but we weren't able to open any other messages. The envelopes were now sealed and taped, so either someone realized that we had opened and resealed one of them or Mathias's father was being extra cautious. Regardless, we now kept our ears open for any information about the British or about merchant ships that were trying to get to Bilbao. The newspaper reported that more ships were being confronted in international waters by Franco's destroyers, but so far they were still safe as long as there were escorts from the British navy. The problem was, once they got within three miles, it was up to the Basques to provide safe passage, and there were mines along the way.

"*Neska!* Don't go too far. I'll need your help carrying the fish back to the train station." Mamá turned back to the wiry old fisherman who was haggling with her over the cost of his catch.

We'd come together to Mamá's hometown of Bermeo to

108

get the sardines. It was a short trip by train that Mamá made several times a week, but on that Thursday morning she had insisted I help her because she wanted to get a larger order. In the past few days, with more refugees escaping the front lines and flooding into Guernica, our sardine sales had risen. Mamá still complained about all the people, but she did so a little less forcefully, and I didn't dare say I'd been right about the increase in business.

I looked out at the calm waters of the port and the small boats that dotted the horizon. The morning sun coated everything around me in a golden light, and for a moment it seemed as if I were somewhere else. Somewhere peaceful and serene and not in the middle of a civil war.

"*Come basuras.*" A man stumbled along the pier, pushing aside anyone in his way. "That's right, I think you're all eating garbage." He pointed a finger toward a small group of fishermen and shouted, "*Todos creen que se van hacer de dinero.* You believe you'll actually be able to provide for your families doing this type of work day after long day. Ha!" He smirked as he walked past me and then pounded his chest. "I'll show all of you. *¡Yo soy el que va a salir de aquí!* I'll be the one who actually gets out of this godforsaken place!"

With those words, he promptly collapsed right by my feet.

I took a quick hop backward in case he decided to grab at my ankles.

"*Vamos,* Guillermo." A man wearing clothes that looked almost like rags came to help the man stand up. "Let's get you home. You're obviously drunk."

No one else seemed to be paying attention to what was happening. They were all too busy with their fish to be bothered with what was going on inches away from me.

"Raúl," the drunk man said as he slumped down again, "you're my only ffffriend." Guillermo slurred his words. "Don't hate me."

Raúl glanced toward me and gave me a look, as if apologizing for his friend's behavior.

"*De veras*," Guillermo continued as Raúl tried to pull him up again. "I had no choice. This ssstupid war will be over sssssoon enough anyway. Thissss was my chaaance." He spun around in Raúl's arms. "My one chance!" he shouted to no one in particular.

"*Sí, sí.*" Raúl humored his friend. "You did what you had to do." He looked around the pier. "Where's my— Ughhh! I must've left my bag on the boat." Propping Guillermo against a piling, he grabbed his friend's face, forcing the drunkard to look at him. "Stay here," he commanded. Then, turning to me, he said, "Don't let him stumble into the water. I'll be right back."

Before I could respond that there was no way I could stop a grown man, Raúl was running down the pier.

Guillermo stared at me with glassy eyes. "You understand, don't you?" he asked.

I nodded, glancing around, hoping that someone else would come by so I could leave.

"Look at them." He pointed back to some of the fishermen. "Don't even have shoes. I want more. . . . I deserve more."

I said nothing and kept looking around.

"Right?" Guillermo asked.

"Yes. Of course," I answered, facing him again.

He leaned back against the piling, a look of vindication washing over him. "That's right." He stumbled one step toward me and lowered his voice. "Waaant to hear a sssecret?" he asked.

I shook my head as he leaned back against the piling.

"Suuure you do."

"No, not really." I didn't want to think about what a man like this would consider confidential.

"It's the war that makes usss do these things," he mumbled, scratching his unshaven cheek. "Besssidesss, those ships would've been sssstopped one way or another. Who cares iffff one more makes it to those ffffancy people in Bilbao? It wasss my turn to make sssome money from thisss war business. Plusss, they were being all sssneaky about it . . . coming in from Fraaance."

I straightened up. This wasn't just drunk-man talk. "Wait, what? *Señor*, what do you mean . . . exactly?"

"*¿Señor?*" He smirked and stood upright. "You think I'm the type to be called *señor?*" He stared at me, then inched closer so that I could now smell the overpowering stench of alcohol, fish, and who knows what else. His face got very serious, and he whispered, "You just be careful tomorrow, little one. There'll be potatoes flying through the air."

The idea of flying potatoes must have struck him as quite funny because he started to laugh right in my face. My eyes watered with the vile smell and I almost pinched my nose, but I kept staring at him . . . trying to understand what he was saying.

He stopped laughing and gave me a serious look. "Potatoes flying over the sssseven sssseas." He clapped his hands together. *"Boom!"*

"An explosion?" I asked, hoping to make sense of his words.

Guillermo held up his finger. "Just one. One really big one. The price to pay for a better life." He burped as he said those last words. "Why should I care about those money-grubbing Brits?"

My jaw dropped and I inched back. "You—you're going to set off a bomb?" I stammered.

"Me?" He pointed at himself as if I might be speaking to someone else. "No, no. I wouldn't do sssomething like that." He started to slur his words again.

He had my undivided attention. "But you just said—"

"All I did was pass on some information that I happened to come across. Can't help what other people do with the secrets that I overhear, right?" He smiled, showing off a couple of gaps between his yellowing teeth.

Time seemed to stall as I took in everything the drunk man had said. I studied his face to see if this was some sort of prank.

"Flying potatoes over the sssseven sssseas, flying potatoes over the sssseven sssseas," Guillermo sang, oblivious to everything else around him.

"Sorry I took so long." Raúl interrupted my thoughts and grabbed Guillermo's arm, putting it around his shoulder. He looked back at me as he propped up his friend. "You're a good kid. Thanks for watching him."

Guillermo's eyes had a glazed look, and he smiled at his friend. "You ffforgive me, right, Raúl?" he slurred.

"Of course, of course." The two of them stumbled as Raúl tried to walk with the off-balance Guillermo.

Guillermo turned back to look at me and put a finger to his mouth. "Remember, shhh."

SEVENTEEN

The screeching of the train's wheels announced our arrival back at Guernica's station. The short trip from Bermeo hadn't given me much time to decide what I should do, but I knew I had to do something. Even if the drunkard was talking nonsense, I couldn't take the chance. People might die.

I had to find Mathias.

Pushing my way around a few people, I walked toward the train door, waiting for it to open.

"Really, *neska*? Where is your head today?" Mamá pointed to the basket I'd left behind.

By the time I went back and got it, most of the people were off the train and Mamá was waiting for me outside on the platform.

"Took long enough," she muttered, avoiding the crowd by going around the main building.

I waddled after her. "I'm sorry." I readjusted my grip on the rim of the basket. "It's heavier than usual."

Mamá balanced her oversized basket perfectly on her head, the brass scale hanging off a loop on her belt. "Don't complain, *neska*. More sardines mean more sales. More sales mean more food. What you need to do is carry it like I do."

I nodded, but kept mine pressed against my stomach. I feared that carrying it the way Mamá and the other *sardineras* did would seal my fate as one of them forever.

"Now give me the weights for the scale." She held out her hand, and I gave her the small brass pieces. "If you hurry up and drop off the basket at home, you'll still be able to make it to your precious school before the afternoon session starts."

"*Sí, señora*," I said, moving as quickly as possible but still struggling with the basket.

Mamá pursed her lips. "Carry it that way and it'll take you twice as long, *neska*." She was already halfway down the street, carrying her own, heavier load with ease. "You decide what's important."

I sighed and lifted the basket on top of my head, balancing it with both hands. I was definitely able to walk a little faster. With every step, I repeated, "I am not Sardine Girl. I am not Sardine Girl."

The day felt warm for mid-April, and the combination of the quick pace, heavy basket, and fear that someone might spot me made me feel even hotter. Sweat trickled down my back. I had to make it just two more blocks without being noticed, but that was getting harder as more people filled the streets. It was a little past noon, and I'd already decided to skip all my afternoon classes in order to find Mathias. We had to tell his father what I'd heard.

Then, when I was just a few steps away from my building, I heard those dreaded words.

"Hey, Sardine Girl! Over here!"

I spun around, causing the basket to wobble dangerously, and spotted the face I least wanted to see . . . Sabino.

EIGHTEEN

He sprinted toward me. "My oh my." He smirked. "Guess your school days are over, huh, Sardine Girl?"

"Get out of here, Sabino," I said through clenched teeth.

"Ooh, it talks. All these years I thought you were mute."

"You're not worth the breath it takes to talk to you." I balanced the basket with one hand and pulled out my house key.

From behind Sabino a woman in a pretty blue dress waved at me. "*Gracias*," she called out as she got closer. "Thank you for waiting."

She looked up at the basket still on my head and then at Sabino. "Sabi, didn't you tell her how much I needed?"

He shuffled his feet. "Um, we hadn't gotten to that yet."

She shook her head and smiled at me. "My son—what am I supposed to do with him? Always sweet-talking the pretty girls." She pinched his cheek and pointed up to the basket. "I'll take six of your largest sardines, please."

Sabino . . . sweet-talking *me*? I almost laughed out loud at how clueless this woman was.

"Is there a problem?" she asked.

Mamá would never let me pass up a chance to make a sale. That would be equivalent to sacrilege.

"No, no problem." I pulled the basket off my head and placed it by my feet. "I just don't have my scale because I was taking these home to be sold later. But I can estimate how much each one weighs and give you a price . . . if you like."

"No need. I always buy them at the market on Mondays, so I know how much six should cost." She peered into the basket. "So, these are very fresh, right?"

"Yes, just caught this morning," I answered, searching for the largest of the sardines and putting them on the ground next to me.

"Here you go. Will this do?" She showed me the coins in the palm of her hand.

It was exactly what I would've charged. Mamá would be happy about this sale. "Yes, that's perfect," I said, picking up two of the six fish and handing them to her.

"But aren't you going to wrap them up?" she asked.

"Oh, I . . ." My unexpected sale was slipping away.

"Of course not. . . . You just said these were to be sold later." She looked around. "No problem. Poochie, be a good son to your pregnant mother and untuck your shirt. You can make a little cradle with it and carry them for me until we get home." She gave me a wink and patted her small belly. "Have to satisfy these cravings!"

"But I'll stink like sardines all day!" Sabino complained, already untucking his shirt for me to place the fish on.

"Not at all," I said in an exaggerated tone. "You'll just smell like the sea."

"That's the right attitude," his mother said as she ruffled his hair.

Sabino glared at me.

I smiled.

As they walked away, I yelled, "See you later, Poochie!"

The days of Sabino calling me Sardine Girl were over.

Within five minutes, I'd dropped off the basket of sardines and was back outside with only one thought: find Mathias.

I raced through the familiar streets of Guernica, my feet barely touching the cobblestones as I dodged people strolling home for lunch. Soon I found myself under the theater's marquee, which listed *La Fuga de Tarzan* as the new movie that was playing. I took a deep breath and rang the bell by the side entrance. Even though the theater was closed at this hour, I hoped Mathias would be home helping his father or having lunch with his family.

I waited a few seconds before ringing the bell two more times. Someone had to be home.

The door creaked open just enough for me to see a woman's face looking down at me.

"*¿Sí?* Can I help you?" she asked in an accented voice, still standing behind the partially closed door.

"Um, is Mathias home?"

"No, I'm sorry." She took a step out into the open, and I could see that she was a tall, slender woman. She wore a simple flowered dress with buttons down the front, a black sweater, and an apron wrapped around her waist. "Are you . . . Ani?" she asked.

I nodded.

She smiled and took my hand in hers. She gave it a small squeeze and introduced herself. "I'm Mathias's mother. It's wonderful to finally meet you."

"Nice to meet you too, ma'am." I gave her a quick smile. "Do you know where he is?"

Mathias's mother didn't seem to pick up on my urgency. "He speaks very highly of you, and it's nice to see him with a friend. Moving around so much . . . makes me worry, you know?"

Unconsciously, I had started to tap my fingers against my thigh. I glanced down and stopped myself. I didn't want to be rude, but I was wasting valuable time. "Um, yes. He's a good friend. Do you—"

"Would you like to come in and wait for him?" She fidgeted with the sleeves of her sweater. "I'd love some company. It's so rare for me to go out these days."

I shuffled my feet. "Maybe another day. I just need to find Mathias right away. It's important. Can you tell me where he is?"

She stiffened up a little.

"Oh! Of course. He's at the Garza farm." She got closer to me and lowered her voice. "Is everything . . . okay?"

"Um . . ." I stared at her, not quite sure if she knew that her husband was a spy. "It's nothing . . . really," I said, playing it safe . . . just in case.

"Well, then, I hope you'll visit another day." She waved me off.

As I took a step back and started to turn, she said, "Remind Mathias not to stay out too late. I want to eat early since his father's out of town."

Her words stopped me in my tracks.

Mathias's father was gone? I thought Mathias would go with me to talk to his dad. Who would we tell now?

NINETEEN

I had run at full force halfway up the mountain, but now I was slowing down. The cool air was coming in and out of my lungs in short little pants. I bent over to take a deep breath before starting another sprint to the Garza farm.

As I straightened up, a figure caught my eye. The silhouette of a boy walking with a *makila* toward one of the fields farther up the mountain. From the way he took each step, I knew it had to be Mathias.

"Mathias! Mathias!" I yelled, waving my hands over my head.

I saw him lift his *makila* in response. He then turned and walked away from me.

"No!" I yelled. "Come back!"

With a sudden burst of energy, I raced up the mountain path. I was almost there when I saw Mathias coming back to meet me. When we got closer, I could see the worried look plastered across his face. "What are you doing here? Don't you have school?" he asked. "Is something wrong?"

I shook my head but had to pause for a moment to catch my breath. "Mamá . . . she had me go with her to Bermeo and . . ."

"Oh." His shoulders relaxed. "I thought something had happened. I told Garza that I had to leave early." He started walking down the mountain again. "Well, guess I'm done now. . . . Want to hang out by the tree?"

"No." I pulled him by the elbow to make him stop, my heartbeat finally slowing down. "Something did happen."

Mathias eyed me and then smiled. "You got some information, didn't you?"

I nodded, but had to wait for the cascading thoughts in my head to settle down.

"So, tell me!" he begged, unable to wait any longer.

"I think something might happen. . . . I mean, he wasn't very clear about things, but—"

"He who?"

I took a breath. "This drunk guy in Bermeo who said—"

"A drunk guy?" Mathias scrunched his eyebrows. "Doesn't sound too reliable."

"I know, but he said certain things . . . made me believe that . . ."

Mathias scratched his head. "What kind of things?"

"He talked about a ship coming from France that wouldn't be making it to Bilbao because of an explosion."

"Explosion?" Mathias cocked his head to the side. "Wait, you think he wants to bomb it?"

I could tell by Mathias's reaction that he thought this might be important information. "Not him personally, but he may have given information about a ship to Franco's men."

"Franco's men? Why do you think that?"

"Because he was mumbling stuff about a payoff even if it meant some Brits got hurt. He'd been stumbling around the pier yelling about getting what he deserved, and then he'd ask his friend to forgive him."

"Forgive him?"

"Mm-hm. His friend pretty much ignored him, but when his friend left for a minute, he started talking to me."

"Talking to you?"

I put my hands on my hips. "Could you stop repeating everything I say?"

"I'm not doing that." He paused for a moment. "Did he say anything else? Think of his exact words."

I felt as if the entire scene in Bermeo were being re-played in my head like a movie. "He muttered something about the Brits being money-hungry and that there'd be flying potatoes—"

"Flying pota—" Mathias clapped his hand over his mouth, realizing that he was about to repeat what I'd just said. "Sorry," he mumbled. "And his friend didn't say anything about all this?"

"No, his friend wasn't there for any of it. I was stuck watching him . . . making sure he didn't fall into the water and drown. That's when he told me."

Mathias bit at the corner of his fingernail. "You don't think he was just playing with you?"

I shrugged. "I think he was too drunk to lie, but I can't be sure."

Mathias's lips twitched back and forth. "We should tell my father, but if he asks how we know about the ships, we'll just say it's because of what's been in the newspaper. We don't mention opening the envelope, all right?"

I nodded. "But we need to tell someone else; your dad isn't home. Your mom said he's gone until tomorrow."

"Wait . . . you were going to tell him without me?"

"*Por favor*, don't be stupid. I went there looking for you. And don't worry, I didn't tell your mom anything." I stared at him, seeing the wheels turn in his brain. He was putting together the pieces just like I had. "Mathias, you think this could be real too, don't you?"

Mathias didn't say anything but let out a deep sigh. "I don't know . . . maybe. But we do need to tell someone . . . just in case. Any suggestions?"

I'd been thinking of this ever since I'd left Mathias's mother. Of all the men in the spy ring, there was only one I felt I knew. Only one I trusted.

"Okay, c'mon." I pulled on his shirtsleeve. "We have to go to church."

TWENTY

I banged on the rectory door. No one had answered when we'd politely knocked a few seconds earlier. I thought Padre Iñaki would be at the church, but finding the place empty, we'd run over to the rectory, hoping he was having a late lunch at home.

"No one's here," Mathias said, stating the obvious.

I banged on the door once more and turned to face him. "Fine, now what?"

Mathias tapped his finger against his *makila*. "Maybe . . . we stop the ambush ourselves."

"You and me?" The idea was ludicrous.

"Why not?" A slight smile snuck across his face. "Think about what the guy told you. Did he say when or where it was going to happen?"

Leaning against the door of the rectory, I went over the conversation again in my head . . . word for word. "He never said when it was happening, just that it'd all be over tomorrow."

"Uh-huh." Mathias started tapping his *makila* against the cobblestones. I knew he could see himself saving the day. "So it's probably happening tonight, right?"

"Yeah, I guess, but he never said where it would happen or which ship would get hit. And unless you know how to get in touch with the ships over in France—"

Mathias stared at me. His tapping was now a fast drumbeat. "But you said the people were Brits. So it's a British ship in France."

I widened my eyes and straightened up. "*Do* you know how to get in touch with those ships?"

His tapping suddenly stopped. He dropped his eyes, and his shoulders slumped. "No," he muttered.

I fell back against the door. "Well, we need to tell someone who does. Maybe—"

"Mathias! Ani!"

We both looked toward the entrance of the narrow alleyway to see Lupe walking with a large bag in her hands. Carmita was already racing toward us.

I crouched down and opened my arms. Carmita jumped into them. Visiting her was the closest thing to having a little sister I'd ever experienced.

"And what brings the two of you here on a Thursday afternoon?" Lupe glanced around. "No sardines . . . so is this just a friendly visit?"

"Actually, we're looking for Padre Iñaki," Mathias explained as I stopped twirling Carmita around and set her back on the ground.

"Well, he's out visiting the sick. Maybe I can help? Unless it's a question of faith." Her eyes twinkled. "That I leave to him."

A dizzy Carmita stumbled as I got closer to Lupe.

I bit my bottom lip. "Um, I don't think . . ."

Lupe tilted her head and gave us a sideways stare. "You two are up to something. I can tell."

"No, it's nothing," I said quickly. "Just a question."

With a slight smirk, Lupe nodded. "Suuure, if you say so."

Carmita tugged on Mathias's sleeve. "Come!" she demanded. "¡Ven!"

"No, really, Lupe. Nothing's going on," I said as Carmita pulled me toward the rectory.

She smiled knowingly. "I understand. Secrets are meant to be kept." She shifted the bag in her hands. "You can try to catch Padre Iñaki tonight around eight. He should be back by then."

Carmita was now leaning back, using all her weight to pull Mathias and me closer to the rectory. "Come on. We can play hide-and-seek."

Mathias bent down to be at eye level with Carmita, forcing her to let go of us. "Not today, Carmita. We've got to go. We're in a hurry." He clasped her hands in his. "We'll play next time. Promise."

"Why?" she whined. "Don't you want to play?" Carmita asked, looking up at me.

Lupe put her hand on her daughter's shoulder and steered her away from us. "Not today, little one. Plus, I need your help putting away some of these things. There might even be a special treat for you if you do a good job."

"*¿Dulce?*" Carmita asked, her eyes getting large with excitement at the thought of something sweet to eat.

"Maybe . . ." Lupe gave me a wink as she pulled out her key. "But say goodbye to our friends first."

"*¡Adiós!*" Carmita shouted as Lupe opened the door and the two of them disappeared.

Mathias and I turned away from the rectory and refocused on the problem of what to do next.

"So, should we walk over to the bank?" Mathias pointed to the left with his *makila*. "It's close by and we could wait for Señor Goicochea there. I'm sure he'll be back when he's done with lunch."

I took a deep breath and thought about it for a second. "I'd rather tell someone else."

Mathias scrunched his eyebrows. "Why?"

"There's something"—I shrugged—"I don't know . . . strange about him. I don't trust him too much."

"Hmph. Seemed nice enough to me. Always giving us a piece of hard candy when we make his deliveries."

"I think that's part of the problem. Felt like he was buying us somehow."

"Candy won't buy us," Mathias muttered.

"Yeah, but he doesn't know that. People sell each other out for less."

"True. So who do you think we should trust?"

I thought about it for a moment. "How about Señor Beltran? I used to hear my dad say nice things about him."

Mathias shrugged. "Sure. He seems to be calling a lot of the shots anyway."

I pinched my lips together and stared at the people returning to work after lunch. "The only catch will be getting him to pay attention to what some kids have to say."

"Oh, he'll listen." Mathias eyed the crowd and then looked back at me. "We'll make sure of it."

TWENTY-ONE

"Is Señor Beltran here or not?" Mathias asked the old woman, his voice rising with frustration.

"I already told you two to be on your way. Now go!" The gray-haired maid scowled at us and started to close the door.

"We just need to speak to him for a minute," I pleaded for the third time while Mathias pushed against the door with both hands. "He'll want to see us."

The door swung open, almost causing Mathias to fall into the foyer of the home.

"See you? Ha!" The old woman threw her head back for a moment, then fixed her narrow eyes on us. "A couple of scrawny kids show up—at the front door, no less—and expect an important man like Señor Beltran to speak with them? Just the thought of it!" She pointed a bony finger at us. "I don't know what kind of game you two are playing, but—"

"Señor Beltran!" Mathias yelled at the top of his lungs.

"Stop that." The woman gave a quick glance up the flight

of stairs before looking back at me. "He's not here. Should've told you that earlier . . . so just go."

Mathias shouted again, and I joined in. "Señor Beltran!" we screamed in unison.

Panic crossed the old woman's face. "What are you doing? Stop that!" She tried forcing us out, but Mathias shouldered his way farther into the room.

We both kept yelling.

"Please!" The old woman grabbed Mathias's *makila*. Wrenching it out of his hands, she used it as a bat to make us move back.

"What is going on?" a gruff voice called from somewhere inside.

"Perdóneme, señor." The old woman turned her attention to someone behind the door. "It's these horrid children. I tried to send them away because I knew you were resting, but—"

I pushed my way into the house while the old woman was distracted. "Señor Beltran, we need to speak to you!"

The moment our eyes met, Señor Beltran could clearly tell something was going on.

"Matilde, let me see what they want and I'll send them on their way," he said.

"But I . . ." Matilde's eyes darted from Señor Beltran to us and back again.

Señor Beltran lifted up a finger to silence the old woman. "Just go make some coffee and bring it to me in the study."

She nodded, glared at us as if we were the devil's own children, then disappeared toward the back of the house.

The moment she was out of earshot, Señor Beltran's

placid expression changed to a mixture of concern and anger. "This better be good," he said in a low voice.

"It is. Tell him." Mathias pushed me forward.

"Well, the thing is," I mumbled, "I heard, um—"

"Speak clearly, girl. Keep your voice low, but just spit it out."

"*Sí, señor*." I took a deep breath. "I was in Bermeo this morning, and this fisherman was telling me about an explosion that was going to happen—"

"An explosion? Why would someone talk to *you* about this?"

"Well, he wasn't actually in his right mind," Mathias explained.

"You were there too?" Señor Beltran quizzed Mathias.

"Um, no. But I—"

Señor Beltran lifted his hand. "Then you don't have anything to say." He faced me again. "Continue."

"Mathias is right. The man wasn't in his right mind when he was talking to me. . . . He was drunk."

"You came here, made a scene by yelling at the top of your lungs, to tell me the ramblings of a drunkard?" He shook his head in disbelief. "I knew involving children in all of this was a mistake."

"No, you don't understand. He was very convincing. He mentioned the Brits and their ships in France. And an attack on one of them trying to get to Bilbao."

"I'm sure he was very believable," Señor Beltran said in a condescending tone, then looked at Mathias. "I'm guessing your father didn't believe you either?"

"My father won't be home until tomorrow."

"And Padre Iñaki is gone too," I added.

"So, I'm your third choice, huh?" He sighed. "Listen, I'm glad you're trying to help, but what this drunkard fears has been in all the newspapers today. Everyone knows that it'd be a devastating setback if a merchant ship were attacked in our waters, especially if it somehow makes it through Franco's blockade, but that's not going to happen."

"But what if—"

"What if what? Franco's blockade won't hold up if the British navy keeps escorting the ships through international waters, and we're taking care of the rest. Don't get caught up in the rambling delusions of a drunk." Señor Beltran turned his back to us. "Now, if you can see your way out . . . I have work to do."

"What if he was telling the truth and he really does know something?" Mathias grabbed Señor Beltran by the arm. "I think—"

Señor Beltran stopped Mathias in midsentence. "Young man, your involvement is limited to just sardine deliveries . . . not thinking!"

There was an icy staredown between the two of them until Mathias slipped his hand off of Señor Beltran's suit jacket. "Please, just listen to her story . . . for one more minute," he said in a pleading voice.

"Fine." Señor Beltran pulled out his pocket watch by its chain and checked the time. "You have one minute. Tell me exactly what the drunkard said about this explosion. Did he say when or where it was going to happen? Did he say a ship's name?"

I looked down at the floor, squirming with the realization of how little I had to offer.

Señor Beltran tapped his foot. "I really don't have time for this."

"We just thought . . . I mean, I was worried because he said there'd be a big explosion." Then I spit it all out in one long burst. "He said the Brits were greedy and the people in Bilbao could go without supplies for a little bit, and that this was his one chance to make money and that it was just one little piece of information that he'd sold. . . ."

I watched Señor Beltran sigh and look down at his watch again, but that didn't stop me.

"He talked about it all being over tomorrow and to be careful because there'd be potatoes all over the seven seas and—"

Señor Beltran was shaking his head, but then he froze. "Wait, did you just say the *Seven Seas*?"

I nodded.

"He specifically said *Seven Seas*?" Señor Beltran bent his head and got closer to me. "Not that there would be potatoes scattered across the ocean or something like that?"

"No. He said *seven seas*. Why?"

Señor Beltran straightened up and thought for a minute. His smug expression had turned serious.

"The *Seven Seas* is the name of a British ship that is carrying food—namely, potatoes—through a back channel into Bilbao tonight. It'll be the first ship to come through since Franco sent out his warships. No one is supposed to know

about that ship. We've also got some . . . let's just say important items on board."

"Oh." Then I realized what he was saying. "*Oh!*"

Mathias nudged me. "I knew this was important," he
whispered.

I rolled my eyes. He hadn't believed me at first either.

"This does change things." Señor Beltran began to pace
around the small foyer. He continued to speak, but it was
more as if he were talking to himself than to us. "If he made
reference to the ship's name . . . well, not many people know
that. And you said he sold this information to someone?"

"Yes, sir."

"A drunken man's guilty conscience isn't much to rely
on, but still . . ." He walked toward the back of the room.
"Matilde, forget the coffee. I'll be in my study, and I don't
want to be disturbed." He looked back at us. "The children
are leaving!"

"So, we did get good information?" I asked.

"Yes. Yes, you did." Señor Beltran put a hand on each of
our backs and guided us to the door. "Now the two of you
have to go. If you hear of anything else, you come find me."

Before we could say another word, the door was shut and
locked behind us.

TWENTY-TWO

The next morning all I could think about was the ships trying to make it to Bilbao. Had the *Seven Seas* reached port? Was there an attack or explosion? Had we actually prevented it?

It was impossible to concentrate in class. Listening to the teacher go on and on about math equations when a war was being fought a few kilometers away . . . it all seemed ridiculous.

The clanging bells of Santa María caught my attention. The war had found a way to sneak into the school. Like trained sheep, everyone in the classroom quickly walked toward the front of the room and lined up by the door. There was no mistaking what this was. . . . The constant ringing of church bells and the distant wail of the factory siren could mean only one thing: air raid.

At least the possibility of one.

My heart beat faster. So far there hadn't been a real attack, but after the bombing of the Basque city of Durango a few weeks earlier, the threat seemed much more real.

I stood and followed the rest of the students as our teachers rushed us down the stairs to where a storage area beneath the building had been turned into a bomb shelter.

"Stay together and go toward the back," one teacher shouted as other people joined us in the room.

I glanced around at the low, curved ceiling lit by a single lightbulb hanging in the middle of the room and felt the dampness of the concrete walls rub against me. It was enough to make anyone's skin crawl.

Within a minute, the room was full and the air began to feel thick. I could still hear the warning bells ringing outside, and then the sound became almost imperceptible as the door was closed.

The teachers and students gathered together at the back, and everyone else who'd come seeking refuge stood closer to the entrance. As we waited for the all clear, two elderly men, who both looked to be over eighty years old, stood near the center of the room whispering to each other, and one of them broke out laughing . . . the sound bouncing off the walls.

As their voices became more excited and their conversation grew louder, I heard words like *ship* and *blockade* reverberate through the cavelike room.

Keeping my back to the men, I inched closer until there was only about a foot separating us and I could hear their conversation clearly.

"It went along the river all the way to Bilbao. Heard it

avoided the open sea because there was going to be an attack of some sort against it."

"Nothing like getting some good intelligence to stop those scoundrels. Especially now that they say Franco has Moroccan mercenaries on the front lines. . . . Those soldiers . . ."

I leaned back to hear more. Why had they paused? I wanted to turn around but didn't want to be obvious.

"Keep hearing that those Moors are looking for young schoolgirls to become their slaves . . . do all the cooking and cleaning. Then, when they can't work anymore, they cut out their hearts and give them to their animals."

I swallowed the large lump that had formed in my throat.

"Yes, pretty little girls . . . like this one!" A hand clamped down on my shoulder.

A small scream erupted from deep inside me.

The two old men started laughing again as every head turned toward us.

I spun around, realizing that they'd been making up the whole story.

My eyes narrowed, and I glared at them. "That's not very funny," I said as I heard snickering behind me.

The taller of the two men tilted his head, and like an old grandfather reproaching a young child, he wagged his finger at me. "Well, it's not very nice to eavesdrop on Alejandro and me."

I glanced down at my shoes. There wasn't much I could say to that.

Alejandro, wearing a broad-brimmed hat instead of the typical beret, spoke up. His chuckling had finally started to wane. "But we really shouldn't have scared you." He paused and tapped my chin. "Especially since you must be scared enough during these warning alarms."

Looking up at the two of them, I gave a slight smile. "Sorry, I just wanted to hear more about what was happening with the war."

"Is your father fighting?" Alejandro asked.

I nodded.

"I figured," he said. "Good man, I'm sure." He looked at the concrete ceiling a few inches above his head. "If only *we* were a little younger . . . ," he muttered wistfully.

The bells rang out again, giving the all clear, and everyone started to head out. I put my hand on the old man's forearm to keep him from leaving. "Could you tell me what you were saying about the ships? You said one of them came up the river?"

"Ah, yes. Everyone was talking about it over at the café." Alejandro elbowed his friend. "Franco can't stop us with his silly blockade, right, Gustavo?"

"Never!" the tall man proclaimed proudly, pounding his chest with his fist so hard that it caused him to go into a coughing fit.

"Go get some water!" Alejandro directed as the tall man pushed his way through the crowd that was already funneling out the door.

"Is he okay?" I asked.

"Oh, sure. We're just a pair of *viejos*." He reached into his jacket and pulled out a pack of cigarettes. "Comes with age." He tapped a cigarette out. "Now, you wanted to know about the ships, right?"

I nodded as several students walked around us, trying to get out of the bomb shelter.

"Ships are the lifeblood of this area . . . especially during wartime. Gustavo and I were both seamen. . . . We should know." The old man pulled out a silver lighter and with shaking hands lit his cigarette.

I was about to tell him that Papá was a seaman too, but he continued talking.

"I'm telling you, our soldiers and people in Bilbao will get their food and supplies. Between Basque smarts and British muscle, those merchant ships will make it through . . . every time!" He pounded his chest, creating his own small bout of coughing.

As he regained his breath and took a drag on the cigarette, I asked, "Do you know the name of the ship that got through last night?"

He blew out a ring of smoke and started toward the door. I was the last one left standing in the room.

"Of course. Everyone knows the name of the ship that broke Franco's blockade: the *Seven Seas*."

TWENTY-THREE

I couldn't wait to tell Mathias the news. We *had* made a difference! The *Seven Seas* got through okay. It must have changed its route or something.

Since most of lunchtime had been wasted on the air-raid warning, I had to wait until after class to find Mathias. Luckily, I didn't have to search long. I spotted him standing right outside the school's courtyard.

"Did you hear?" I called out, taking the steps two at a time. "The *Seven Seas*—"

"I know." He gave me what looked like a painful smile. "But—"

"But nothing. We did it!" I said, twirling around.

"Yes, but . . ." He glanced back, taking note of who was there with us. "That's this morning's news," he said. "C'mon." He turned away from me. "Let's walk and talk."

It didn't take a genius to realize that whatever he had to say . . . it wasn't good.

"Did something happen to the ship?" I asked.

"No." Mathias looked around at the other students walking by.

"So, what's going on?" I asked, stopping at the corner.

"Keep walking," Mathias said over his shoulder.

"What's the hurry? Why aren't you celebrating?"

Mathias didn't break his stride, and I had to hustle to catch up to him. "Why—"

Mathias lifted up his hand as we passed by the bank. "I'll tell you in a minute."

We didn't say a word for another block. "Mathias, no one else is here. What happened?"

He looked both ways and behind us to make sure we were alone. "There's a spy in the group."

"Um, yeah. They're all spies. That's the point."

"No," he interrupted. "You don't understand. There's a spy for Franco in the group. A double agent."

"Wha— How do you know?"

"Father told me. The reason he was gone yesterday. He got some information. . . ." Mathias paused as a middle-aged woman passed by and went into one of the neighboring apartment buildings. When he was sure she was gone and the street was clear again, Mathias continued. "He verified that someone's been reporting to Franco."

"Wait, so who's the double agent?" I whispered.

Mathias shrugged. "Father wouldn't tell me, but I think we might know."

My eyes widened. "Señor Goicochea?"

"Didn't you say he was strange?"

I slowly nodded. "But I didn't think he . . . So, now what happens?"

Mathias took off his beret and twisted it in his hands. "That's the worst part." He ran his fingers through his hair. "Mother says we're not safe here anymore. We've been 'compromised,' and—"

"Hold on. Your mother knows about all the spy business?" I asked.

"Yeah." Mathias put his beret back on and guided me toward an empty bench in the plaza. Within minutes the place would probably come alive with people strolling and socializing, but for the moment it was relatively quiet. He leaned closer to me. "Seems she always knew. . . . Father just didn't want her to know that I'd gotten involved too. She wasn't happy about that."

"Huh." I thought about my visit with her. She didn't seem like a spy's wife. Then again, that was probably a good thing.

"Anyway, she says it's time for us to move."

"Move!" I exclaimed. Then, looking around, I dropped my voice. "Move?" I repeated. "Where?"

Mathias shrugged and leaned back. "They were talking about it when I left. Maybe Madrid, but who knows? I think they're telling people that we have a sick relative we need to help."

"So that's it?" I searched his face for the answer I wanted to hear. "You just leave?"

Mathias sighed and stared up at the sky. "It's not like I want to go. They know I want to stay, but Father says the front lines are starting to falter. We might have had to make a quick exit no matter what."

I thought about what he was saying. If things were getting too dangerous for a family of spies, then . . . "Wait. What about me?"

"You?" he asked, looking back at me.

My stomach felt as if a lead weight had been dropped in it. "Yeah. Haven't I been 'compromised'? What happens if Guernica falls and Franco's men come in? Won't I be considered a spy? Anyone think of that?"

"Father says no one will care that either of us helped. He even tried telling Mother that. But he did say that he can help get you and your mom out too."

I'd never thought about leaving Guernica before. This was my home. . . . It would always be my home. I shook my head. "I can't leave."

Mathias turned toward me, eagerness in his face. "But you could go to Madrid . . . with us."

"You don't even know if that's where you'll go." I thought about telling Mamá that we had to move. It would probably be safer to take my chances with Franco's soldiers. "Anyway, if you think your mother was unhappy about you being involved with spies, think of how mine would react. She doesn't believe in getting involved. She'd kill me if she knew."

Mathias slumped back. "I'm sorry I got you into this."

"I'm not," I answered. And I meant it.

"You may not regret it now, but you might later."

"Nope. Never." People were starting to come into the plaza, and the pigeons were already taking their positions, knowing bread crumbs would soon be thrown their way. "We should go start our deliveries."

"All right. But think about leaving. It might be a good idea," Mathias said, standing up and holding out a hand to me.

Telling Mamá news like this could never be a good idea.

As we walked toward my street, Mathias pushed a loose rock out of the way with his *makila*. "Strange to think that these will probably be our final deliveries."

I stopped walking. "Today? You won't even be here through Monday?"

Mathias shrugged. "When my parents say go, it's go."

I was suddenly realizing what all this really meant. There'd be no more making a difference, no more extra money, and worst of all, no more friend.

TWENTY-FOUR

"There has to be something we can do. C'mon, think!" I commanded as Mathias and I walked along the narrow street, each holding one side of the large basket of sardines.

"There's nothing . . . trust me. I've been through this before." He stopped to look at me. "I used to argue, but now"—he paused—"I understand. It's all part of the job."

"A rotten part," I muttered.

"Yeah. I just hope we go back to Germany. Now that I know what Father really does, I think he'll let me help."

"Planning to take over the family business?" I teased, a gentle wind blowing down the street as we left the last row of businesses and headed toward the wider avenues that led to the rich side of town.

"I've got to. People like you and me, we've got to stand up to evil. It's who we are."

"Mm-hm," I muttered. The truth was, I'd never thought of standing up to anything or anyone until I met Mathias.

"But why head back to Germany? There's plenty of evil here. Things are bad everywhere."

Mathias's face twitched. "Yeah, but you have no idea how bad things are getting there. Imagine living in a place that hates you for just being born."

"I don't think people over there would *hate* you—"

Mathias stopped abruptly, almost making me lose my grip on the basket. "Yes! Yes, they do!" he said, almost arguing with me. "My grandfather was sick last month, and he couldn't even get a doctor to help him because they made it illegal to treat Jews. Like we were lepers or something."

"That's only a few stupid people," I said, pulling on the basket again so we'd continue walking up the tree-lined path to Señor Beltran's house.

"You'd be amazed how many people don't care what's happening to us." He shook his head. "Jews can't vote anymore, and we're not allowed to have certain businesses. Heck, if we lived in Germany, we probably wouldn't even be friends. You being a Catholic girl and me being Jewish. And you can forget about a girl like you ever growing up to marry someone like me—that's illegal too. They'd put us in jail for that. And what they've been doing to anyone who speaks out . . ."

Mathias kept talking, but I was having a hard time concentrating on whatever else he was saying. One word in particular had become lodged in my brain.

"Are you even listening to me?" He rolled his eyes. "I swear, why do I bother telling you this stuff?" he said.

"I *am* listening. It's horrible what Hitler is doing over there, but people will come to their senses and things will go

148

back to normal." I paused for a moment. I'd never thought of Mathias as anything but a friend. "What did you mean about getting married? You mean us?"

"Huh?" Mathias gave me a puzzled look and then let out a long sigh. "I was trying to make a point. I'm not saying we'd really get married."

I gave the basket a slight push with my hip, which caused it to bump his side. "You'd better not be saying something stupid like that."

He took a step and shifted his weight to keep his balance. "I just said I wasn't."

"Better not," I added, grabbing the basket so I now carried it by myself. I finally had a friend. . . . I didn't want it all to be ruined.

"I said I wasn't." He placed both hands on his *makila* and stopped to stare at me. "How much clearer do I have to be? I don't want to marry you."

"Good!" I shot back, walking up the steps to Señor Beltran's back door.

"Fine," he said, still standing a few feet behind me.

I had just set down the basket and knocked on the door when I turned back to face him, hands on my hips. "Wait. Why wouldn't you want to marry me?" I asked as the door behind me creaked open.

Mathias threw back his head and let out a big "Ughhh! Girls!"

I smiled. That was better.

TWENTY-FIVE

We didn't mention the end of our deliveries to anyone except Lupe. She didn't seem to care that much about not getting the sardines; it was the idea of not seeing us that really disappointed her.

"Mondays and Fridays just won't be the same without the two of you," Lupe said, not taking her eyes off the bubbling pot in front of her.

"Again, again!" demanded Carmita when Mathias stopped bouncing her on his lap.

"*¿Caballito otra vez?*" Mathias faked his surprise. "How many times are you going to go for a pony ride?"

"Lots and lots!" Carmita squealed as Mathias bounced her up and down on his knees again.

"I'll still come by whenever I can." I placed what I knew would be our final envelope on the kitchen table.

"And maybe I'll come back in the summer to work at the Garza farm. I can—"

"You didn't tell me that," I said, interrupting him. "You'd really come back?"

Mathias shrugged. "Maybe." He tickled Carmita in the ribs. "Will you remember me in a couple of months?"

Carmita giggled, then bobbed her head up and down.

"Ani, *búscame*. Look for me," she commanded, jumping off Mathias's lap. She ran over to Lupe and tried to duck behind her mother's long skirt for a game of hide-and-seek.

"*Ya, Carmita.*" Lupe pulled her out by the arm. "Our friends probably have other places to go."

"Not before I see them!" Padre Iñaki walked into the kitchen, and Carmita made a beeline for him.

He reached down and picked up the little girl.

"So, I'm guessing your father already talked to you?" he asked Mathias.

"Yes, sir. He said he'd already spoken to everyone and that you'd understand."

"Of course. Family is hard to deny. I can understand how a sick relative would need help. We'll certainly miss you"—he glanced over at me—"and what the two of you have been doing."

I gave him a small smile. It was strange not to tell a priest the whole truth, but I guess there was no real way to know who the double agent was.

"Yes, these sardine deliveries have been a godsend," Lupe said, taking Carmita from Padre Iñaki.

"Well, I wanted to talk to you about that, Ani." Padre Iñaki put a hand on my back and guided me to the corner of the kitchen. "I've spoken to our benefactors, and they'd still like to donate sardines and have some delivered to their homes, just not as many. Maybe every two weeks? Starting in a couple of weeks." Padre Iñaki gave me a look. "You can manage this on your own, right?"

Should I keep doing this even though there was a double agent? Mathias thought we were meant to fight evil. . . . Was this the way I'd do it? On my own?

I slowly nodded, but more doubts were creeping into my thoughts. Maybe I should follow Mathias's other advice and just tell Mamá. Plus, who would give me the messages to deliver, and where would I pick them up?

As if reading my mind, Padre Iñaki added, "It will all work out. You'll start your deliveries at Señor Beltran's house and go from there . . . ¿entiendes?"

I could tell things had already been discussed and decided. I would do it for now. . . . I could always change my mind later. "Sí, I understand."

"Well, this is good news: sardines and visits from you." Lupe squeezed my cheeks and smiled. "Things are a bit less dire."

My eyes avoided Lupe's because I knew that things were most certainly *not* getting better.

She walked over to Mathias and leaned Carmita toward him. "Say goodbye to Mathias, Carmita. He's leaving on a trip with his parents."

Carmita gave Mathias a big, slobbery kiss on the cheek. "*Adiós*, Mati. Have fun," she said.

Mathias and I exchanged a quick glance. There was nothing fun about any of this.

TWENTY-SIX

A strong breeze ruffled the leaves of the tree-lined street and whipped around a few loose strands of my hair. Mathias and I were aimlessly walking, neither of us saying a word. I reached into my pocket and pulled out the satin pouch Papá had given me. Tugging at the soft braided rope that kept the acorn inside, I flipped the bag over to let the seed tumble out. Rolling it in my palm, I thought about how people kept leaving me behind. First my father, now Mathias. Perhaps it was time I moved on too. . . . I could tell Mamá everything, and we could leave town before it was too late.

I sighed.

There was no way Mamá would leave, and all I'd get for my trouble was a serious beating. It would also be the end of my making a difference.

"Think it'll really grow one day?" Mathias asked.

"Huh?" I glanced down at the acorn in my hand. "Oh, I hope so."

Mathias pointed to an empty bench, and we headed toward it. "Where would you plant it?"

"I don't know." I squeezed the acorn before putting it back in its pouch and taking a seat. "I always thought I'd plant it somewhere in Garza's field."

"I'm sure Garza would let you." Mathias sat down next to me. "I can ask him if you want."

"Yeah. Guess that would be good."

We didn't say much more after that.

Sunset was approaching, and I knew Mathias had to be home for Shabbat. Over the course of the last few weeks, I'd learned a lot about him and how his parents worked to balance the fact that his mom was Jewish and his dad was Catholic. Shabbat dinner was something that they always tried to have, even though Mathias had been late a couple of times.

"Guess you need to head home," I said, wishing there were something else to talk about. But Mathias would be gone in a few days, and that was all either of us was thinking about.

"Yeah, guess so."

I decided to walk back with him. As we strolled past the darkened shopwindows and the noisy taverns, I felt a heavy veil of sadness weighing on my shoulders.

"I wish you didn't have to go," I said in a quiet voice as the last streaks of sunlight colored the sky in pink and purple hues.

"I know." Mathias stepped off the sidewalk to let a family carrying suitcases walk by. "But there's not much choice. We all have to make sacrifices."

"Still don't like it."

"Yeah, me neither." He bit at one of his fingernails, then analyzed all the others. "You're the best friend I've had . . . well, in a long time." His gaze fixed on the cuticles of his left hand.

"Thanks," I said, shuffling my feet and finally kicking a loose pebble into the street. "You're my best friend too." My voice cracked a little as I spoke.

We reverted to a heavy silence until we reached the front of his apartment building.

"Enough!" Mathias broke the gloomy spell. He shook himself out like a dog drying off. "No more of this depressing stuff. In the movies the leading man doesn't act all mopey when things don't go his way. We need to have some fun . . . do something. What do you think?"

"Um, okay." I paused, thinking about the movie I'd seen and how much had changed since that day. "I'll take your word about the movies, though. . . . I only saw the first half."

"You're right. . . . I forgot! You never finished seeing it."

"Nope, but that's okay," I said, knowing that half a movie was better than no movie at all.

Mathias tossed his *makila* from one hand to the other. "So that's what we'll do. Come over and I'll have my father give us our own showing. That way you'll get to see a whole movie."

I shook my head, but smiled at the thought. "I can't. You know I have to do the deliveries with Mamá tomorrow. But it was a nice thought." I looked up to see his mother at the window. She waved at me.

Mathias glanced up too and signaled for her to give him one more minute. "I have to go in, but . . . Wait, I have an idea. Why don't you have your mother come too? She can have lunch with my family, and then we'll all watch the movie."

"Ha," I chuckled. "That might work if I had anyone else's mother."

"No, we can do this. What if we do it on Sunday? You don't make deliveries after church, right?"

"No." I mulled the idea over. "I'm just not sure. You haven't even asked your parents. You're leaving in a few days, and they may not want to—"

"It'll be fine. I know it." He stepped closer to me. "My parents feel guilty about making me move. Why do you think Mother isn't out here pulling me inside for Shabbat dinner? I know they'll say yes. C'mon. Ask your mother."

"But you know how she is. . . ."

"So?" he said, his eyes twinkling with the possibility.

I shook my head. "She'll probably just say no."

Mathias gave me a half smile and leaned on his *makila*. "But she might say yes."

I thought about it for a few more seconds.

He folded his arms like a little boy ready to pout. "Do you not *want* to come over?"

"No, no. I didn't say that." I just didn't know if I wanted Mamá to go with me.

"Then let me handle my parents and you deal with yours, *vale*?"

I let out a short sigh. "*Vale*. Okay. I'll ask Mamá. No promises, though."

"Fine, but you have to ask."

"Yes, I will." I spun him around and pushed him toward the door. "But get inside before your mother gets angry."

"Fine," he answered. "I'll expect you on Sunday."

The shadows of the night were already growing longer, and I turned to head home myself. A permanent smile had replaced the sadness from a few minutes earlier.

Lunch and a movie with Mathias on Sunday. There was still some fun to be had.

As I reached the lamppost on the corner of the street, I heard the sound of a window opening, and from the darkness Mathias yelled, "Don't forget to ask your mother!"

Mamá. This night was still not over.

TWENTY-SEVEN

I stared at the wrinkles that darted from the corners of Mamá's dark brown eyes. *Would I look like her when I was old?* I'd never really given it much thought, but now I wondered. Maybe she had been like me when she was young. Had there been a time when she wanted to be something else? Maybe I should tell her about leaving. . . . It could be a chance to start over . . . for both of us.

"*¿Qué?*" Mamá asked, lifting her eyes to meet mine. "What are you staring at?"

"*Nada,* nothing," I answered.

"Hmph, you're acting different today. Something happen during your deliveries?" Mamá tore off a piece of bread and ran it along her plate, letting it sop up whatever sauce was left.

"Um, well, actually, there was—"

"You put the money you earned in the drawer, right?" she asked, wiping her mouth with the napkin.

"*Sí, señora.* In the box, by the Bible in the top drawer."

She stood and took her plate over to the sink. "Don't forget that I know how much money is in there at all times."

I rolled my eyes since her back was to me. "I'd never take anything without permission."

"It's just a reminder," she answered. "Were you saying something about what happened today?"

"Mathias's family is moving next week."

Mamá didn't turn around. "Oh," she said, not sounding too interested.

"We'd made a bunch of plans, and I thought—"

"No point in crying over what's done." Mamá paused for a moment, holding the plate under the running water. "You'll keep his customers, right?"

"Kind of. The customers cut back their orders too. They only want deliveries once every two weeks."

Mamá threw the sponge into the sink. "¡Qué cosa! We need the extra money now more than ever!"

I stayed quiet. Perhaps the timing wasn't right to ask about the movies or mention moving.

"Well, we'll just have to go out and try to do more sales every day. No more of this easy living for you. We'll even work Sunday morning if we have to."

"Um, about Sunday . . ." I picked at the edge of the napkin that rested on my lap.

"Let me guess. . . . You don't want to work?" she said, still not bothering to turn around to look at me.

"No. I mean yes, um, just not this Sunday." I twisted the napkin edge. "Mathias invited us to have lunch with his family."

Now Mamá turned around. "Why? Aren't they moving? What's the point?"

"To thank us for helping sell the sardines. We'll also get to see a movie at the theater."

Mamá shut off the faucet and wiped her hands on a cloth lying by the sink. I could see her thinking about it. "*El cine*, huh?"

I nodded. "Can we go?"

Mamá didn't move or say anything. A chance to watch a movie was tempting for anyone . . . even her.

"I suppose . . . it would be the polite thing to do."

I smiled. Seeing Mamá be gracious might be better than the movie.

"Mathias and I can also make some plans for when he comes back in the summer," I said as Mamá walked out of the kitchen. "Maybe sell some more sardines," I added for good measure.

She paused right outside the doorway and glanced back at me. "Summer? Ha! Once that boy leaves, he won't come back. Best that you realize early on that people always leave. Look at your brother, and now your father. Can't get too attached or else you won't survive."

"No, that's not what'll happen. We'll see each other again. . . . He told me so."

Mamá walked away, shaking her head. "Eventually you'll learn, *neska*. We all do."

TWENTY-EIGHT

All day Saturday Mamá and I walked the streets of Guernica trying to make as many sales as we could. We didn't stop even when the air-raid warning sounded. As usual, Mamá regarded it as a false alarm, and she continued her calls of "¡Sardinas, saaardiiiinas!" over the sound of sirens and church bells. So far, she'd always been right, but it felt as if we were tempting fate.

And then, in what seemed like the blink of an eye, it was Sunday afternoon, and Mamá and I were walking toward the theater after Mass.

"¿Me veo bien? I look fine, ¿verdad?" Mamá asked me as some of the more refined women from church crossed the street in front of us.

"Of course you do." I'd noticed Mamá sniffing her sleeve during Mass, probably wondering if her nicest white blouse, the one with the lace trim on the collar and cuffs, smelled just like all the rest of her clothes.

"You said they don't put on airs, right? Because you know

I can't tolerate self-righteous people." Mamá tugged on her brown skirt, adjusting the waist, as we walked by one of the crowded cafés.

"No, his parents are very nice. They both speak Spanish and—"

"Spanish?" She stopped in the middle of the sidewalk, causing a few people to maneuver around us. "Why wouldn't they be speaking Spanish? Don't tell me they're foreigners?"

I looked down at my feet, regretting having said anything. It would have been better for Mamá to have realized that after she met them.

"Oh my Lord! An afternoon of stinkin' foreigners telling me how superior they are! Well, I'll tell them exactly where they can—"

"Mamá, please," I begged, my stomach already churning. "Don't talk like that."

"What?" She pursed her lips. "You think I'll embarrass you?"

"No," I whispered. "I just want to have a good time today."

"Hmpf." Mamá rolled her eyes and said nothing else.

As we continued walking, past storefronts that had heavy sandbags stacked along their doorways, I thought of how the war now surrounded us. It could come from Franco's soldiers breaking through the front lines or from the Germans flying above us. That's when I realized Mamá still didn't know Mathias's mother was German. Things could get very ugly during lunch.

I needed to say something. Make sure Mamá didn't insult his family.

We were walking across the town's center plaza, where the pigeons and people all gathered, which meant that Mathias's apartment was around the corner. A few more seconds and we'd be there.

I glanced at Mamá's profile as she stared across the street at the theater. There was no more time to come up with the right words, the right approach. . . . I had to tell her.

"Mamá, there's something you should know. Mathias—"

"I'm not going in," Mamá declared, cutting me off. She looked down at her well-worn shoes. In a low voice, she said, "I don't fit in here."

For a moment, a huge weight lifted off my shoulders; then I saw Mamá's face. For the first time, she looked defeated.

I glanced up at the window above the theater. Mathias's mother stood by the open curtains watching us.

Thoughts swirled in my head. I didn't want to go and have Mamá cause a scene, but she also deserved to see a movie once in her life. "Mamá, they're good people and, look . . . she's already seen us."

"I don't know what I was thinking," Mamá shook her head. "This isn't me."

"But we can't just leave. We have to tell them something."

Mamá sighed. After a few seconds, she simply said, "You should go."

"Mamá, I—"

"No," she said forcefully. "I've made up my mind. I won't go in. You can." She cupped my chin with her hand and stared straight into my eyes. "*Neska*, you don't need to have my life."

"But we can both have a new life," I blurted out.

"What?"

I knew I had to tell her. Let her make the choice. Perhaps we could start over in Madrid. "Mathias's family . . . they offered to help us move, too. If we want, we can go somewhere else . . . away from here. Papa can join us later."

"Run away? From Guernica? Leave the place where I last saw your brother, God rest his soul." She quickly made the sign of the cross. "All because of a silly war? Never!" Mamá rolled back her shoulders. "If Franco's troops come in, so be it. We'll sell sardines to them." She shook her head. "I suppose I shouldn't be too surprised to hear you say this."

"No, I only meant—"

"You certainly aren't the same girl you used to be." The slightest hint of a smile seemed to cross her face before quickly disappearing. "Which isn't necessarily a bad thing. At least you've become a somewhat stronger creature."

"I, um, uh . . . ," I stammered, unsure of what I should do or say next.

"I knew this moment would come." She turned me around so I'd face the theater. "I've seen you changing over the last few weeks. It's time for you to make your own decisions, Anetxu." She tucked a loose strand of hair behind my ear before giving me a nudge forward. "Just don't depend on anyone . . . become who *you* need to be. It has to be what you want because, in the end, we're all left alone."

And with that she turned to walk back home.

At first, I didn't move. Mamá's words seemed to echo in

my brain. The fact that she had called me by my name high-lighted that this was no ordinary conversation.

I thought about chasing after her and telling her that I didn't care about seeing the movie. That selling sardines was going to be my life, too . . . but that would be a lie.

Plus, for the first time, I felt Mamá wanted something different for me.

Mathias flung open the front door to his building and ran across the street. "Where's your mother?" he asked.

"It's just me." I looked at the street filling with other people, but for me it seemed empty. "She couldn't stay."

"But you're not going . . . are you?" he asked.

"Well," I bit my lip, still unsure of what I should do. I didn't want Mamá to feel alone.

"You have to stay," he said. "I leave in two days."

"I can still meet you tomorrow out by the tree. No deliveries, right?"

"No, no deliveries tomorrow." He looked back toward his apartment. "But what about today? The movies and my parents. Our plans." His eyebrows scrunched together, trying to make sense of the situation.

Mamá had told me to make my own decisions. Not her choices . . . mine. I didn't want to live like she did. I was already making a difference, and even without Mathias, my days of delivering secret messages weren't going to be completely over.

"C'mon." Mathias took my hand. "You can deliver sardines any other day," he said, walking me across the street and to his front door.

He was right, I could always help Mamá later. She'd see that I hadn't abandoned her.

But as I stepped over the threshold of the building and the door closed behind us, a feeling of sadness, laced with touches of excitement, pinched at my heart.

Sardine Girl was gone.

TWENTY-NINE

The next day I looked at the school clock at least a hundred times. Even though there weren't any deliveries to be made, Mamá had agreed that I could spend the afternoon with Mathias and not help her at the market. I think she knew that I would've gone to see him no matter what and I'd have been willing to accept a beating for it.

The sound of the bell dismissing us from class was like the pistol at the start of a race. I rushed out of the school-yard and down the crowded streets, weaving around people and carts. Mathias and I had agreed to meet by my tree, and I wasn't going to let anyone slow me down. Every minute counted.

I turned onto the dirt road that led to the countryside, kicking up lots of dust on my way to the tree because I refused to slow down.

Then it hit me. I paused to catch my breath. I wouldn't be

able to enjoy a regular day by my tree with Mathias. Were we going to pretend that this was any other day? He was leaving the very next day. I knew I wouldn't cry, but I really wasn't going to laugh either. It felt as if a gaping hole had opened up in my chest.

I thrust my hand into my pocket and felt for the satin pouch.

"Ani!" Mathias waved his *makila* in the air. He was already walking toward me across the field.

I smiled, refusing to believe that this would be goodbye forever.

"Hi, Mathi—" I stopped midword because in the distance the church bells had begun to ring.

I could feel every one of my senses go on high alert.

Mathias, who was now next to me, scanned the horizon and then looked back at me. "You think . . . ?"

I stood still. We both knew that the nonstop clanging of church bells could signal an incoming attack. I waited for the factory sirens to start wailing.

We searched the sky again.

"I don't see anything," he said as the sirens joined the chorus of bells. "You think it's another false alarm?"

"Probably. Maybe we should go home or to a shelter," I suggested, not wanting to tempt fate as Mamá so often did. "Just until they give the all clear."

"There's no time for that. We can go up to the Garza farmhouse. That's closer." Mathias started walking up the mountain path.

A flock of birds heading in from the coast caught my eye. Then I focused. . . . Those were no birds.

"Mathias, look!" I pointed to what was clearly a group of planes coming our way.

"I see them! We have to go!" Mathias grabbed my hand and started a hobbling dash toward a ditch that someone had converted into a makeshift foxhole by placing sandbags around the edge.

"The tree. They won't see us there. It'll be a better place to hide," I suggested.

"We won't make it," he said, pushing me into the dirt pit.

Moments later, a plane whizzed by, heading straight for Guernica. It was flying so low I could see swastikas on its wings and tail.

"They're German," I whispered. "But they wouldn't . . . I mean, why? We're just a little market town to them."

Mathias didn't answer. I looked over and saw him gripping his *makila* so tightly that his knuckles were turning white. A few mumbled words were all I heard before the roar of several more planes drowned out everything.

Then there was silence. For several minutes neither of us moved, barely daring to breathe, but the eerie quiet proved to be too much. The planes had come, and as far as we could tell, they had gone without doing anything.

I let out a deep breath. "They were just scaring us."

Mathias slowly nodded and stood up. "Way to wrap up my stay in Guernica, huh?" he said, holding out his hand to help me up.

Both of us crawled out of the ditch, and although I'd been petrified a few moments earlier, a sense of giddiness seemed to overtake me. "Now you have to come back in the summer. Guernica must be pretty important if Hitler wants to see what we're doing."

"Yeah, Guernica . . . the great military base of women, children, and homeless refugees," Mathias teased.

I put my hands on my hips. "*Oye*, you don't have to be cruel."

"Wait a minute, you just said the same thing!"

"Yeah, but I'm from here. I can make fun of my own town."

Mathias rolled his eyes and shook his head. "I can never win," he muttered.

I smiled. "Want to go back to the tree?" I asked, my heart beginning to settle down from all the excitement.

"Sure."

As we walked back toward the field, the church bells started sounding again.

"Think that's the all clear?" Mathias asked.

"Must be." I took out my satin pouch and thought about Papá.

"Strange how the planes were flying so low. . . . It was like they wanted everyone to see them."

"Probably just to scare us." I wondered if that's what it was like being on the front lines . . . always being afraid.

"But why bother? They had to know everyone would run to the bomb shelters." Mathias stopped, his expression changing. "Why are those bells still ringing?"

I shrugged, and as I lifted my head up to the sky, several dots came into view. The planes were back, but this time flying much higher.

"Mathias . . . ," I whispered, pointing up.

"I see them too," he said. "This is bad."

A high-pitched whistling noise filled the air and then a loud *boom* rocked the ground. Smoke, or maybe it was dust, started rising from a spot along the mountainside.

Wait, I thought. *The mountainside? There are only farmhouses there.*

Another high-pitched sound made me cover my ears, and then a wave of energy pushed me backward to the ground. Mathias and I both clambered to stand up again as the ground beneath us continued to tremble.

We were now halfway between the tree and the ditch, in the middle of the field. We needed to run . . . somewhere.

I could hear more bombs being dropped in the distance . . . in Guernica. A pungent smell had begun to fill the air, like burning fuel or gunpowder, but different.

There was no doubt. We were under attack.

The sound of planes grew louder. They were coming our way again.

"Foxholes are best. Garza always says that," Mathias mumbled, still not moving.

I nodded, grabbed Mathias's hand, and ran, almost dragging Mathias behind me, but I wouldn't let go no matter how he stumbled. The sounds of things exploding filled the air. Most were in the distance, but I could see smoke scattered along the mountainside too.

At the edge of the road, we both jumped into the ditch and waited. As we huddled close together, Mathias put his hand over my head as if to protect me. I turned to look at him. His eyes said it all.

This was the end.

THIRTY

The bombers came and came again. High-pitched whistling noises made it seem as if the sky itself were screaming out in pain. The wind carried the acrid smell of fuel and destruction over our hole in the ground as more death fell from above.

Mathias and I didn't move from that ditch for what felt like hours. There was nothing to do, nowhere to go. We waited while an eerie silence crept over the land. My heart pounded with the hope that it was over and the growing fear that it would never end.

I wanted to say something, but there weren't words for what I was thinking, what I was feeling. I reached out and gripped Mathias's hand as hard as I could. At least we were together.

A few seconds later, we heard voices yelling in the field.

"Someone's coming!" I said, reaching up over the edge of the ditch to see who it was. Mathias tossed his *makila* over the top and climbed out after me.

In the distance I could see several people running away

from the smoldering city. They were yelling and screaming at each other to keep going. Guernica was burning.

"I need to go. My mother—" I couldn't finish the sentence. "We need to help."

Mathias grabbed my hand. "Wait. It might not be over."

I saw a woman running across the field with a little boy. "The bombers are gone, Mathias. It has to be over."

"Not yet. Garza always said foxholes—"

I shook free from his hold. "Garza isn't here, and this isn't really a foxhole," I argued. "It's just a ditch with some sandbags."

"Close enough," Mathias said, not moving an inch.

"Look! People are leaving the bomb shelters." I pointed to the dots in the distance scurrying out of town. "We can go." I walked forward, expecting him to follow.

Mathias looked up at the sky.

"C'mon!" I yelled, but stopped walking, sensing that Mathias wasn't following me. I glanced back and saw him frozen, his eyes still searching the clouds. I hurried to where he was, ready to drag him away if necessary.

"STOP!" Mathias shouted.

I stumbled back at the force of his yell, but he wasn't talking to me. He was hollering at the people behind me.

I spun around to see a group headed across the field. They paused briefly to look at us.

"Get down! Get down!" Mathias yelled. "NOW!"

Instead of doing as Mathias said, some of the group turned and began to run toward a line of trees along the far side of the field.

For a moment, I didn't understand what was happening. Why did Mathias want them to get down and why were they running? Then I heard what sounded like ten thousand mosquitoes swarming toward us.

I glanced up to see several small, low-flying planes. In a flash, Mathias spun me around and threw me back into the ditch. I wasn't sure if I heard the screams or imagined them, but there was no escaping the rapid sound of machine-gun fire and of bullets bouncing off the ground.

My breathing quickened, to the point that I thought I'd pass out. I wanted to cover my ears, but instead I used my hands to hold on to the ditch's walls . . . afraid that somehow the world would turn upside down and I'd fall out of the hole we were hiding in. Finally, I could feel the ground around us slowly stop trembling.

"We stay here until we're absolutely sure they're gone, you hear me?" Mathias yelled.

"Don't scream at me!" I shouted back.

"I'm not!" The roar of the small planes was now fading as they headed toward Guernica. "I'm not," he said again, more softly this time.

"Why? Why are they doing this? This isn't the front lines. Guernica's not important like Bilbao."

Mathias stared at the ground, his shoulders slumped down.

A sudden realization swept over me. "Oh my God, what if they're destroying everything? Attacking all the Basque towns at once."

"They're not," Mathias answered matter-of-factly.

"How do you know? There could be planes everywhere. Here, Bilbao, San Sebastián."

Mathias shook his head. "No, this is like Durango." He closed his eyes and leaned his head against the dirt wall of the foxhole. "I overheard Father talking. This is what he feared." Mathias opened his eyes and looked at me. "I think we're just target practice for something much bigger. Something even worse."

THIRTY-ONE

I wanted it all to be over. Speed up the hands of time and have this be a distant memory. It was already growing dark, but the cool evening air wasn't the cause of my shaking.

Mathias had put his arm around me a long time ago as we waited to see if there would be another attack. We were like two statues, frozen inside the makeshift foxhole, curled up against each other . . . afraid that if either of us moved, we'd find ourselves completely alone.

"I think it's over," Mathias whispered into my hair.

"You sure?" I asked, staring up at the cloud-filled sky. I felt as if I were five again, afraid of thunderstorms and wanting Papá to tell me that everything would be all right.

"No." He stood and stretched. "But we need to see how bad things are while there's still some daylight."

"I know." I took in a long, deep breath.

"I just hope everyone made it into the bomb shelters,"

Mathias said before tossing his *makila* over the edge of the ditch.

Would Mamá have gone into a bomb shelter? She always ignored the alarms, but maybe after she saw those first planes, she would have sought refuge.

As I stood there trying to absorb the new reality around me, Mathias pushed away a stack of sandbags and pulled himself up and over onto the flat ground.

"Let's go," he said.

Thoughts of what might have happened to my home, to my mother, paralyzed me. I didn't move.

"Ani." Mathias thrust his hand back into the ditch to help pull me out. "Let's. Go." This time he spoke to me like an annoyed parent whose two-year-old wants to stay at a party for a few more minutes.

Yet something in his tone snapped me into action. I pushed his hand out of the way. "I can do it myself," I said, wanting to shake off my helpless feeling.

"Didn't say you couldn't." Mathias stood up again and looked down at me still in the hole. "Just thought you might want a little help."

"Well, I don't," I said, grabbing a fistful of grass and pulling myself over the side of the ditch.

I wanted to be angry. I needed to be angry . . . at someone, anyone.

"Hurry up!" Mathias called out. "We have to get home." He was walking faster than I'd ever seen him move.

In the distance I could see a black cloud of smoke hanging

over the entire city. The mountainside was also spotted with flames and smoke snaking its way up to the sky.

Everything I'd ever known could be gone . . . including Mamá. I shook my head. I couldn't think like that. I just needed to get down there to help whoever was hurt.

"You can't even bother to wait for me to climb out of the ditch?" I yelled, racing down the road to where Mathias was crouched next to something.

"I thought she might need help," he said, starting to stand up.

I looked and saw a woman, facedown in the dirt with arms sprawled at odd angles. The back of her dress was riddled with bullet holes, and the ground around her had taken on a dark color.

"Oh!" I quickly looked away.

"She never had a chance," Mathias muttered. "Just shot her in the back."

I could feel the bile rising in my throat. I was going to be sick. I took a few steps to the other side of the road and vomited. Closing my eyes, I tried to take a deep breath, but the air still reeked of smoke and death. I gagged and threw up again.

After a few moments, the shock of seeing a dead body wore off, and I wiped the corners of my mouth with my sleeve. I had to toughen up . . . quick.

I looked down the road toward Guernica and saw that Mathias had already resumed his fast, stumbling pace and left me behind. Our families needed us.

Catching up to Mathias required a full sprint, but once I reached him, I slowed down.

"Next time, you can wait a few seconds for me," I said, now trotting alongside him. "I was sick back there, and I'm always waiting for you."

"We have to get down there fast. Plus, I've never asked you to do that," he snapped, hobbling along with his *makila* as fast as he could.

"I didn't say you *asked* me to. How would you like it if I just ran into town right now and left you here?"

Mathias's eyes flashed with anger. "Then go! I certainly don't want to hold you back!" he said without breaking his stride.

"What if I did take off?" I said, grabbing at his shirt, causing him to momentarily stumble before stopping. "How'd you like that, huh?"

Mathias threw his hands up in the air. "Don't do me any favors."

"Fine! You're on your own." I started running . . . a slow jog, waiting for him to call me back.

"Just. Go!" he yelled. "We're all on our own now anyway!"

There was nothing else for me to say or do here. I turned to face my burning city, knowing that nothing would ever be the same again.

THIRTY-TWO

The smell of burning buildings and a gray haze of dust filled the air. It hurt to breathe. It hurt to see. Destruction was everywhere. Part of me wished that nightfall would come quickly so I wouldn't have to see it.

My welcome into Guernica was the littered streets of my neighborhood—full of bricks, rubble, broken pieces of furniture, and people digging through it all trying to reach loved ones who might be buried underneath.

I looked up at the crumbling back wall of my building. My entire apartment was gone. For a moment I thought of the things I'd lost. The radio that Papá had bought for us, Mamá's Bible in the top drawer of her dresser, the books I had in my room . . . everything had disappeared. Some of it might be in the heap of debris in front of me, but I didn't care. I wanted to find Mamá, and she wouldn't have been in the apartment. . . . She'd have been at the marketplace. There was still hope.

My feet crunched the broken glass and splinters of wood and cement that seemed to coat every path that led toward the center of town. Out of the corner of my eyes, I could see people . . . injured, bleeding, crying out, and searching for each other. None of it really filtered through to my brain. Even the sight of dismembered bodies being pulled out of the wreckage around me didn't seem to fully register. All I knew was that I had to find Mamá. Once we were together, we'd figure out what to do next. Where to go and wait for Papá. She and I would be like those homeless refugees who had been crowding Guernica. Only now we would have to be the ones invading someone else's town . . . running away from this.

But we had Mathias's family. . . . They'd help us. We'd start over somewhere else, and Papá would join us when this war finally ended.

I tried to focus. . . . I had to get to one place . . . the market in the center of town.

After a few blocks, I spun around trying to get my bearings. There was so much chaos and screaming that I wasn't sure where I was. It was like no place I could imagine or describe. The sky around me glowed with fires from burning buildings, and craters carved up the streets and sidewalks. I had slipped and fallen into hell.

Up ahead, the cupola of the church seemed to rise above all the destruction. That gave me a point of reference, so I knew which direction to run.

I couldn't tell if it took me hours or seconds to get there, but before long I was standing near the crumbling walls of the church. The market should have been right there.

I glanced at the few buildings that still stood, confirming that I was in the right place, but all that was left of the market was heaps of rubble and a huge crater in the ground. By one of the buildings there was a pile of bodies that had already been covered with a few blankets. I quickly turned my head away from it. I could not think of Mamá being there.

"Mamá! . . . MAMÁ!" I screamed, my voice joining the roar of other survivors calling out for their loved ones.

I headed toward a bomb shelter . . . the one near the school.

A young woman hastily walked toward me carrying a screaming toddler. I blocked her path.

"The bomb shelters around here, are people still in them?" I desperately asked her.

She didn't answer me, and it seemed she couldn't hear me over the child's wailing.

I asked again, this time yelling it at her.

She stood there for a moment, giving me a blank stare as if I were speaking some foreign language.

"Speak up!" she shouted. "I can't hear you!" Tears started to flow down her face. "I can't hear you! I can't hear anything!" she cried out before running down the street.

"Everyone's out of the bomb shelters, *mija*," a police officer said as he hurried past me toward one of the burning buildings. "Go see if your family's gone home," he hollered as he rounded the corner.

There was no home for me to go back to, and Mamá was certainly not there.

I stumbled along the piles of debris back toward the market. "Mamá! Mamá!" I called out, trying to pull beams and iron bars from the piles that littered the path.

Then, in a corner, thrown against a building's remaining wall, something familiar caught my eye.

Twisted metal that, even though it was covered in gray dust, still had the slight glimmer of brass.

I ran over and picked up the mangled scale. A small brass weight lay beneath it. I didn't know if I should pray for it to be the one I usually carried. I grasped the single weight, slid it into my pocket, and took a deep breath. Slowly, I flipped over the balance. My heart seemed to drop out of my chest. The truth was right there in the etched letters of our last name. This was Mamá's scale.

A hand grabbed my ankle.

I twisted around to find an old woman holding on to me. "*Lagundu iezadazu*," she mumbled. "Help me," she repeated, barely able to lift her head off the ground.

In my rush to get the scale, I hadn't even noticed her.

I looked down to see blood pooling around her and bloody streaks where she had dragged herself along the building's edge. I felt dizzy. Then I focused on her face. . . . The wrinkles of a lifetime of laughing, singing, crying, were all there. I knelt next to her, setting the broken scale down by her feet.

"I—I—I don't know what to do," I said. "I can go get someone. . . ." I began to stand.

"*Ez nazazu utzi*. I don't want to be alone," she pleaded, her eyes locking with mine.

I reached for her hand and squeezed it gently. "I'm sorry, but I have to find my mother." I gave her a sorrowful smile. "I'll get—"

But before I could finish my sentence, her eyes drifted to the side, and I felt her fingers go limp in mine. I froze, not knowing what to do next. Death was all around me, but now I was holding its hand.

A familiar voice whispered, "You've done enough. She didn't die alone."

I placed the old woman's hand on the cobblestones and inched back as Padre Iñaki bent down to close the woman's eyelids. He made the sign of the cross over her body and began to say a prayer.

"My moth—" I said as I stood up, getting ready to start my search again.

Padre Iñaki raised a finger for me to wait until he was done. "But I need . . ."

He made the sign of the cross once again, stood, and turned to me. "I'm so sorry about your mother." He put his hand on my shoulder. "The market was one of the first places they bombed. I saw—"

I jerked away. "No, she would've run. She might not have even been there." I glanced at the broken scale by the dead woman's feet and shook my head. "Maybe she was in one of the shelters. You don't know."

Padre Iñaki bit his lips. "She was there when the first bomb hit. It was one of the last things I saw before running into the church." He looked away for a moment as if trying to find the right words. "I saw the damage it did." His voice dropped to barely a whisper. "Nothing was left. No *one* was left," he muttered.

"NO!" I refused to accept what he was saying. "You saw someone else."

"It was her . . . the *sardinera*," he said softly.

"I want to see her. I want to see for myself!" I yelled.

"There's nothing left." Padre Iñaki's eyes glistened. "It wasn't like some of the others. The bomb destroyed everyone and everything in the market. The people . . . they disappeared." He took a deep breath. "The ones that were trapped in the rubble are the ones they've put over there." He pointed to the small pile covered with blankets that I'd seen earlier. "It's best to remember her as she was."

My skin became cold and I started to shiver. Yet beads of sweat formed at my temples, and I felt the world spinning under me. My knees buckled and I crumpled to the ground.

I wanted to cry, scream, pass out. Something to make this all go away. But I didn't. I sat there doing nothing.

"I'm sorry, but I have to keep going." Padre Iñaki glanced down the street. "I can't stay here." He put a hand on my shoulder as if trying to infuse me with strength. "Will you be all right?"

I nodded without knowing what he was saying, holding on to the concrete sidewalk for support.

"Come to the church. We'll find you a place to stay." He stood up, as someone was already screaming for him. "I'm so sorry for your loss. She was a fine woman."

A fine woman? She may have been many things, but I'd

never thought of her as that. Yet no matter what her faults were, she was *my* mother and I wanted her alive.

Minutes passed and I remained sitting next to the body of the old woman whose name I never knew. A few people asked if I was hurt as they ran up the street to help put out the raging fires, but I only shrugged. No one really stopped. I was alone.

Then I remembered. I wasn't alone. Standing up, my arms and legs trembling with my own weight, I took a deep breath and I ran.

THIRTY-THREE

Night fully cloaked the remains of the city as I made my way through the streets. Burning buildings cast a strange glow upon the faces of those trying to make sense of it all. I no longer noticed the smell. It felt as if my nose had rejected the entire situation. But my eyes still worked, and they took in sights I could barely describe.

I had survived, but so many had not. Bodies and body parts were scattered with the debris from what were once quiet neighborhoods. Most of the streets were blocked by mounds of brick, cement, and splintered beams. I had to constantly take detours to make my way to the theater . . . and then I saw it.

The Guernica Tree. It still stood!

The greatest symbol of Basque culture had come through the bombing unscathed. It had to be a sign.

Rushing ahead and rounding the next corner, I saw

the devastation on Mathias's street. Half the buildings were piles of rubble, and the few that stood looked as if they would collapse from a light gust of wind. It didn't seem as if anyone could have survived, but of course, some people had. I hoped Mathias's parents were among the lucky ones.

I weaved around bodies already covered by sheets or curtains, a few with their heads visible so that they could be identified by their families. I needed to find Mathias. . . . He was the one person who could help me make sense of everything.

The *makila* was what I first noticed. Mathias himself was curled up in a ball, sitting on the edge of the sidewalk, his face buried in his hands. A row of sheet-covered bodies lay in front of him.

My heart sank.

"Mathias?" I put my hand on his shoulder.

He didn't look up.

"Oh, Mati," I said softly, sitting down next to him.

Not even the slightest movement came from him.

"I'm sorry," I whispered. I could feel the tears welling up in my eyes, but I would not let them out.

Mathias lifted his head ever so slightly, and I could see the tears flowing out of him like a dripping faucet someone forgot to shut off.

"The whole stupid shelter collapsed," he muttered. "Everyone inside . . . they didn't have a chance."

I sat next to him, wrapping my arm around him.

He took a deep, shaky breath. "Your mother, is she . . . ? Did she make it?" he asked.

I shook my head, not able to speak.

"I'm sorry too," he whispered.

I crumpled against him, and we sat there on the sidewalk as the smoke of our city and the ashes of our lives drifted into the sky.

THIRTY-FOUR

The rumbling sound of a wagon and the sensation of things moving drew me out of the blackness of exhausted sleep. Mathias and I were balanced against each other, each one keeping the other from falling. As I lifted my head off his shoulder, Mathias opened his eyes. The soft light of dawn cast a glow over what used to be Guernica.

Mathias stumbled as he sprang to his feet. "What are you doing? Don't touch them!" he yelled at the two men bending down to pick up the bodies of his parents.

"*Cálmate.*" A short man, covered in dirt but still wearing his beret, walked around the wagon and came toward us. I knew he was the town's undertaker.

"I said don't touch them!" Mathias raised his *makila*, ready to strike anyone who dared lift the bodies. The men took a few steps back.

"Son, were they your parents? You know we can't leave them in the streets. . . . They need to be identified and buried." The undertaker pulled out a pen to write down the information and motioned for the men to start with the other bodies. "Tell me your parents' names."

"No! I'll bury them myself! Just go!" Mathias pushed the short man back a few steps.

"Mathias, you need to . . . ," I said, placing my hand on his back.

He turned to face me. "I need my parents. That's what I need."

I looked at the undertaker. "Can't you come back later?" I asked.

He shook his head. "I'm sorry. We need to do this now, before the day gets any warmer." Gently, with all the patience of someone who had done this too many times, he guided Mathias back to the sidewalk. "Tell me about them. Their names, addresses."

Mathias said nothing.

"García is the last name," I said. "Joaquín and Ingrid, right?" I glanced at Mathias, who nodded and sat down as the men continued to put all the bodies in the wagon.

"Are you related?" the undertaker asked me.

"No, just a friend."

He wrote something in his book. "And did they live in Guernica, or were they—?"

"No, they lived here above the theater." I gestured behind me as one of the men walked toward us and handed something to the undertaker.

"My mother. She's Jewish," Mathias muttered.

"I'll make a note of it. Here." He placed a thin gold chain with a star dangling from the end and two wedding rings into

Mathias's hand. The undertaker then took off his beret and bowed his head slightly. "I'm very sorry for your loss."

As the wagon pulled away, we saw it stop down the street. More victims. More sadness.

After a few minutes, I ached to do something . . . anything.

"Mathias, we should go. Help if we can."

He looked down at his hands, at the pieces of jewelry lying in his palm, and shrugged.

I stood up. "We have to do something," I said.

He kept staring at the jewelry, then he balled his hand into a fist . . . clenching the chain and rings tightly. "You're right," he answered, looking up at me. "We can't just let them win."

I nodded. The old Mathias was returning.

"We'll figure out how to make a difference . . . even in a small way," I said, wiping off some of the dirt and dust from my arms.

Mathias had his eyes fixed on something on the horizon. "They won't get away with this. I won't let them," he said, but I knew he wasn't really talking to me.

I pulled on his torn shirtsleeve, wanting to leave the area. "We should check the church and see if we can help over there."

"I'll need a gun. Find a place to stay, get supplies before heading out," he muttered.

"Gun? Head out? What are you talking about?"

Mathias looked at me as if he suddenly realized that I was standing next to him.

"Ani." He shook his head. "I have to go."

"No." I had lost Mamá, but I was not going to lose Mathias too. "You can't leave me. We'll wait for Papá to come back, and we'll help rebuild the city."

"Papá? Rebuild? Ani, you don't even know if he's alive!"

I staggered backward as if he had punched me in the gut. It was the one thing I had refused to think about. The idea that I might have already lost both my parents . . . just like he had.

Mathias put a hand on my shoulder. "Listen, I didn't mean it like that. Your father might be on his way back right now. It's just . . . we need to figure things out for ourselves . . . at least for now."

I glanced around at the people slowly walking by. Everyone coming to terms with the reality of having lost so much. "Yeah, I know."

"We can go up to Garza's farm. I'm sure they'll let us stay there for a couple of days."

"Garza's farm," I repeated, watching as a woman whose head had been bandaged entered one of the few buildings that were still standing.

"We can plan what to do from there." Mathias strung his parents' rings onto the chain, slipped his mother's necklace over his head, and then looked back at the rubble of what had been the theater and his apartment. "But they *will* pay for this."

THIRTY-FIVE

The trail up the mountain toward my tree looked surprisingly the same. Birds chirped in the distance. The early-morning sun reflected off white puffy clouds that lingered overhead, and a gentle breeze ruffled the long grass that lined the road. It was as if nature had forgotten what had happened the day before.

Glancing back toward the valley, at my broken town, with fires still smoldering and rubble evident even from a distance, I knew I could never forget. Nothing was ever going to be the same.

"Why are you slowing down?" Mathias asked me.

I stopped walking. "I think we should've stayed and helped the people in town." I reached forward and pulled the back of his shirt. "Mathias, can you just stop and listen for a minute?"

He paused, but only for a moment to tuck the back of his shirt into his pants again. "We can help more people by stopping Hitler from doing this anywhere else."

I rolled my eyes and trotted next to him. "Seriously, Mathias. What do you expect us to do? Go kill him ourselves?"

Mathias didn't react. In an even tone, he said, "If we get the chance."

I shook my head at the ridiculousness of his idea. "Sure, that'll work. Because Hitler doesn't have a million guards protecting him."

Mathias threw his hands in the air. "Fine. You stay quiet and do nothing."

"*Oye.*" I grabbed his shoulder. "That's *not* what I said."

"Then stop wasting time. Let's get up there"—Mathias pointed to the speck of a house on the mountainside—"and start making some real plans."

From afar, the stone and rock walls of the Garza house looked almost as if they were part of the mountain itself, and as we got closer, I couldn't help thinking how much safer I'd feel once we were inside with a solid roof overhead. There, in the quiet of that house, I'd be able to gather my thoughts. I'd be able to survive until Papá returned. I had to believe he would come back.

I walked up to the large front door and gently knocked.

No answer.

Mathias reached over my shoulder and knocked harder. "Garza? Señora Garza?" he called.

"Shhh! *¡Entra!*" a woman's voice called out in a loud whisper. "*¡Está abierto!*"

I turned the doorknob and entered a small, dimly lit room. The shutters were all closed, and the sunlight that streamed in came from a single missing panel. As my eyes quickly adjusted to the darkness, I saw a large woman crouched down in the center of the room wrapping a bandage around an unconscious boy's eyes. Several people lay strewn around the room, resting on blankets and pillows.

The woman lifted her head to look at me, and then her eyes went to Mathias. "Oh!" She drew in a sharp breath before covering her mouth.

In an instant she leapt over two people and ran around a group of sleeping children to reach Mathias. "You're alive! Alive!" she said, kissing his cheeks. She pushed him back as if to make sure it was really him, then pulled him into a hug.

Mathias couldn't help but smile.

"We heard the theater was destroyed. We feared that you . . . that you . . ."

Mathias nodded.

She glanced back at me and then noticed no one else with us. "But . . . your parents?"

I shook my head as Mathias looked away.

"¡Ay, Dios mío!" She quickly made the sign of the cross over her chest. "I'm so very sorry." She pulled Mathias close to her again and hugged him even tighter.

I could see Mathias's shoulders drop a little as she held him.

"Are you Ani?" she asked. "Mathias has told us all about you," she said, still holding on to Mathias.

I nodded and then felt something squeeze my legs.

"Ani! Ani!" a little voice exclaimed. I looked down to find Carmita wrapping her small hands around me.

"Carmita!" I knelt next to her. "¿Qué tú haces aquí?" I asked, wondering why she was so far from the church.

"Where's your mother?" I glanced around the room, not seeing Lupe.

Carmita's lips quivered. "Mami! MAMI!" she called out, running to the door.

Señora Garza released Mathias and ran to Carmita, scooping her up in her arms as the little girl kicked and struggled to get free. "Shhh," the woman said, "*tranquila.* It'll be all right."

Mathias and I exchanged a look. Lupe would not have left Carmita unless . . .

"MAMI-I-I-I!" Carmita screamed again, kicking and fighting to be let go.

Everyone around us started to wake up.

"MAMI-I-I-I!" she yelled at the top of her lungs.

The other children in the room began to join her cries. The anguished sound of their little voices felt like the same pain I had in my heart.

"*Shhh, niñita.*" Señora Garza rocked the wriggling little girl.

"Carmita," I said softly, touching her back.

The little girl paused for a moment.

"Carmita, do you want to come with me?" I held out my arms.

She dove into them and buried her head in my neck.

Mathias looked around the room and then at Señora Garza, who was already sitting on the floor cradling two other small children. "How? What happened to—?"

Señora Garza shook her head and whispered, "They were trying to escape the bombing." She pointed to Carmita, who was now crying softly on my shoulder. "Garza found her near the outskirts of town, next to her mother. Asking her to wake up."

I held on tighter to the little girl, wanting to take away the horrors she'd witnessed.

"Was she . . . ?" I asked, already knowing the answer.

Señora Garza nodded. "Garza and a few of the other farmers picked up as many survivors as they could. I've been taking care of the ones brought here, but Garza took some to town already."

"So Garza's not here?" Mathias asked, disappointment in his voice.

"No. He should be back soon, though." She stood up, leaving the two children huddled together on the floor. "Hopefully, he'll bring a doctor with him." She glanced over at the children, who were eyeing us carefully. "Watch them for a minute," she told us before going toward one of the back rooms.

I scanned the room, not recognizing any of the sleeping or dazed faces. It didn't matter. I felt a connection to them all. We had survived, but now what? What lay ahead?

"Julián, look who's here," Señora Garza said. In her arms was a boy who looked much too old to be carried and who still had sheet marks on his cheeks.

"*Hola*, Mathias," the boy answered in a scraggly voice. He glanced around at all the people. "Abuela, I think there are more people here than when I went to bed. . . . Who are they?"

"Friends. And I need you to help keep an eye on these little ones." Señora Garza strapped him into a wooden wheelchair and pushed him toward the corner where the children now sat quietly, apparently tired of screaming.

"What should we do?" I asked, with Carmita still clinging to my shoulder.

"Well, I need to feed everyone, and it goes without saying that the two of you will be staying here with us." She looked at me, waiting for my response.

Since I had nowhere else to go, I gave her a slight nod.

Señora Garza was now back to the business of running her makeshift hotel and hospital. "Mathias, why don't you go out and gather some eggs and vegetables. Ani, can you help Julián watch the little ones? . . . Make sure they stay out of trouble while I change the dressings on some of these wounds."

"C'mon, Carmita," I said, walking over to Julián. "Let's sit with your new friends."

"No! No friends!" The little girl buried her head in the crook of my neck.

"Yes," I responded. "Friends are important." I glanced over and caught Mathias's eye. "Sometimes they're all we've got."

THIRTY-SIX

By early afternoon, I was exhausted. Whether it was the lack of sleep, the constant sadness in my heart, or the fact that I'd spent all morning helping take care of the children, the truth was that all I wanted to do was sit down and be left alone. Finding a chair in a quiet corner, I leaned my head against the wall and listened to the rhythmic pounding of Mathias chopping wood outside. The sound of the ax striking the log followed by the crack as it splintered in two was like a steady, lulling drumbeat. My eyelids grew heavy.

"Ani, let's take them outside again," Julián said, staring out the window. "I'm tired of being inside."

I did a long, slow blink and glanced up at the gathering dark clouds. "I don't think that's a good idea," I said. "Looks like a storm is coming."

"Aw, c'mon," Julián pleaded.

It was all I could do to keep my eyes open, my mind finally wanting to shut down and escape everything that had happened in the last day. "Why don't we all take a nap?"

I suggested, getting off the chair and sitting on the floor, where some of the children were playing with old spools of thread.

Through a yawn, one of the little girls, Mirentxu, replied, "But I'm not sleepy."

I looked at the three children, all younger than Julián, who were probably now orphans. Most still had slightly puffy eyes from sporadic bouts of crying and a night of not sleeping. I could only imagine what shape I was in.

"How about if I tell a story?" I pulled over a little boy who had not said a word, even though he was definitely old enough to talk. "You've all heard of the *jentillak*, right? The magical people who live deep in the woods?"

The quiet boy shrugged, but sat down on the floor next to me and leaned back on his arms . . . waiting. The others joined him, all sitting close to me.

"Once upon a time, there was a beautiful princess—"

"Princess?" Julián sighed before rolling his wheelchair back against the wall. "I thought you said this was about the *jentillak*."

"It is. Just close your eyes and listen." I paused, waiting for him to do as I said. "I want all of you to imagine the story."

Carmita nestled her head into my lap, and I started again. "Once there was a beautiful princess who lived in a magical land surrounded by the sea, but she was never allowed to go too far into the water."

"My grandfather lives by the sea," Mirentxu exclaimed, sitting up in excitement.

"Shhh." I gently covered her eyes with my hand before continuing.

"You see, the princess wanted to explore new lands and have adventures, but just like everyone else on the island, she was trapped by an evil sea serpent that lived in the waves just past the horizon. Anyone who dared go out in a boat would get . . . *eaten by the monster!*"

The children all flinched, so I quickly added, "But that rarely happened because no one ever left their island home." The little shoulders around me relaxed again. "It was a beautiful place to live. It had rolling hills, and everyone always had enough food to eat because so many different plants grew there. They would have celebrations and parties every week. Keep your eyes closed, but can you imagine such a wonderful place?"

I watched as the round faces beside me nodded. The children were all starting to curl up on the floor, and I stroked Carmita's hair, her breathing already even.

"So, one day, while walking along the shoreline and dreaming of traveling across the sea, the princess heard a tiny noise from under a large shell that was covered with seaweed. Curious to see what kind of animal might be trapped underneath, she slowly reached down and lifted the shell, and"—I dropped my voice to barely a whisper—"do you know what she saw?"

The little boy, whose name no one knew because he hadn't spoken, shook his head.

"She saw a tiny winged fairy that sparkled like rays of

sunlight glimmering on the ocean's waves. The princess jumped back and started to run away because she had never seen a fairy before. But the fairy flew and caught up to her, saying, 'Thank you, thank you. I've been trapped under that shell for days and thought that I would most certainly die there.' The fairy then surprised the princess by giving her a most magical gift. Can you guess what that was?"

Silence. None of the children said anything.

I looked over at Julián, slumped sideways, his head propped against the back of his wheelchair.

Slowly I moved Carmita to the floor and curled up next to her, closing my own eyes. The only remaining noise was coming from Mathias's wood chopping outside.

"Why don't you keep going? You have a nice voice," someone from across the room said.

I opened my eyes to see the boy with bandaged eyes sitting up.

"*Gracias*," I whispered back.

"Are the kids asleep?" he asked in a hushed voice.

I nodded, not wanting to wake them up.

"Are you still there?" he said a little louder.

"Yes," I whispered again, realizing that he couldn't see me nod.

"Oh, good. Do you mind keeping me company for a while?"

I looked at him sitting next to the cold fireplace. His head was wrapped with white gauze that stretched across his eyes and covered most of his light brown hair. Even though

I couldn't see his whole face, he looked somewhat familiar. I had the sinking feeling that he was one of the older boys who went to my school.

"*¿Por favor?*" he asked.

I stood and moved closer to him. "Are you in a lot of pain? Should I go get someone?"

"No. I'm a little groggy. Must be the stuff they've been giving me." He tilted his head slightly toward me. "Am I in a hospital?"

"No, you're at the Garza farmhouse. It's about a fifteen-minute walk up the mountain." I looked around the room at the sleeping children. "There are a few injured people here and some children they found in the field farther down the mountain. Is that where you were?"

The boy nodded. "Can you go get my mother? We were running toward the mountains when a bomb exploded in front of us."

"I don't know where she is. I think—"

"Wait, you haven't seen her? She's not here?" His voice started to get louder as he threw off the wool blanket that covered his legs. "Mamá!" he called out in a loud voice, his hands fumbling to remove the bandage around his head.

"Shh!" I covered his mouth with my hand and stopped him from untying the bandage. "There are a couple of women in the bedroom. She's probably there. If not, she was taken with some of the others who—"

"Can you check?" he asked. "She has short dark brown

hair, and she's a few inches shorter than me. And she's really thin." I could hear the panic rising in his voice as he tried to whisper. "Tell her I'm here. That Diego is here."

"Okay," I said, touching his shoulder. "I'll be right back. Just leave your bandages alone."

Walking past Julián's room, I headed toward the back bedroom, which had been kept closed so that the children wouldn't run in. I opened the door and saw two bodies on the floor covered by bedsheets. I fixed my gaze on the people in the beds, not wanting to think about the people under the flowered sheets and if I might know them.

The bed by the window held an old woman, much older than Señora Garza, who had wooden splints wrapped around her legs. In the other bed, a thin, pretty woman with short hair lay quietly sleeping. It didn't seem as if she was even hurt, although I couldn't imagine anyone just resting knowing everything that was going on.

"If I'd known you were feeling better, I would have brought you in to be with her. But remember, *está inconsciente*," Señora Garza said from behind me.

I turned to see her leading the boy, who, when standing, was several inches taller than me, probably as tall as Mathias.

"She's unconscious?" I asked.

Señora Garza nodded and brought the boy to the edge of the bed, turning him around so he could sit by his mother.

"They were both unconscious when Garza found them. A bomb had left a huge crater just a couple of feet from where they were." She tapped the boy's hand. "*Son bien dichosos*," she said.

"Yeah, lucky. Right," he answered, thrusting his hand forward and then tapping his way up to find his mother's face. His touch changed once he felt her nose, and soon he was caressing her cheek. "*Despiértate*, Mami," he said, gently stroking her hair. "Please, please . . . wake up."

Señora Garza pressed my arm and whispered, "Call me if anything changes. I'll be outside."

I nodded as she left the room. The old woman in the other bed stared at me for a moment before turning to face out the window. She was awake, but obviously didn't want to talk.

"Is someone still there?" Diego held his mother's hand and turned his head toward me.

"I'm here. Should I go?" I asked, not wanting to intrude.

"No. Can you tell me how she looks? Is she hurt?" he asked.

I stared at the woman. She had a small cut on the bridge of her nose, and her clothes were torn and dirty . . . but otherwise she seemed normal.

"She just looks like she's sleeping," I said, drawing closer to the bed.

"That's good," he muttered. "Is anyone else in here with us? I hear breathing."

The old woman in the other bed groaned as she tried in vain to roll on her side, the splints forcing her to stay still.

"Um, yeah," I said. "There's someone who—"

"My name is Diego, and this is my mother, Marielena," Diego called out.

"Hmph," the woman muttered, not bothering to look our way.

"She doesn't seem to want to talk," I whispered, sitting next to him on the edge of the bed.

"Oh." Diego moved his head from side to side as if his other senses were trying to fill him in on his surroundings. "Anyone else here?"

My eyes fell on the two bodies covered by the flowered sheets. "Um, no, well . . . there are two . . . um . . . you know . . ."

"Bodies? It's okay." His right hand reached out and accidentally touched my thigh. Immediately he pulled it back, his cheeks turning red.

"S-s-sorry," he stammered. "I didn't mean to . . ."

I nodded, words trapped inside me until I remembered he couldn't see how flustered I was. "It's okay," I managed to get out.

We sat there not saying anything for a few moments.

"It was really bad out there, you know," Diego said, rubbing his mother's hand again. "We tried to escape by running toward the mountains, and that's when we got hit. But the things I saw before that . . ." He shook his head. "I'll never forget. Friends of mine . . . gone. Their bodies all mangled."

I looked down, my own memories bringing tears to my eyes, but I refused to give in to them. Mamá would never have tolerated such weakness. She used to say that things could always get worse, although I wasn't sure that was the case anymore.

Diego kept talking, unaware that I was barely paying attention. "Just be glad you weren't there." He cupped his mother's hand around his lips and kissed her palm. "I was late to my jai alai match because of her. That's the only reason I'm still here."

"Mm-hm," I muttered, a single tear silently rolling off my cheek before my fingers quickly wiped it away. I would not cry.

"All I remember is running across the field, pulling Mamá along, and then there was a high-pitched whistling noise and a flash of light. Then I heard more bombs and gunfire. I tried to move, find my mother, but I must've blacked out. After that, the next thing I knew, my head was being bandaged up and I was given some *patxaran*."

"They gave you liquor?" I asked.

"To dull the pain, I guess . . . but it doesn't hurt that much. What I remember hurts more."

"I know," I said, mindlessly answering him.

"No"—he shook his head—"you don't know." His voice had a harder edge to it now. "You have no idea living up here what it was like yesterday down in the city."

"Living here? What do you—"

"Don't get me wrong." He placed his mother's hand back on the bed. "I'm grateful to your parents for everything, but when I think of some of the things I saw . . . I . . . I want to throw up."

"What? You think the Garzas are my *parents*?"

"Parents, grandparents, whatever. You just can't understand what it was like in Guernica." His voice started to get louder. "So tell them not to call me *dichoso*. No one who was there is lucky. The only lucky one here is you."

I stood up, knocking over the chair. "I understand plenty, and believe me, I wish my mother were lying here next to me in one piece and not—" I couldn't finish the sentence. A tear ran down my cheek. I kicked the chair out of the way. "You're *un idiota!*" I said as another tear rolled down my face, and I ran out of the room.

"Wait!" Diego called out, but it was too late.

THIRTY-SEVEN

Walking outside, I felt a sudden cold wind whip through my hair. The day had turned dark, and I could smell the threat of rain in the air. A storm was blowing in from the sea . . . a big one.

I wanted to go to the field and sit under my tree, but the rumble of thunder in the distance warned against it. Standing still, I tried my best to breathe in the familiar smells of the land, to gain control of the emotions rising up inside me. I could still hear Mathias chopping wood in the backyard, but I didn't want to be with him. . . . I didn't want to be with anyone.

Drawing in a long, shaky breath, I saw what seemed like two raindrops hit my dust-covered black leather shoes. I glanced up at the sky, then realized that the drops were coming from me and not the sky. The two tears were quickly followed by two more, and then, like a flood breaking through a dam, I crumpled to the ground sobbing. Never had I felt so alone. I missed my mother.

My mother. I covered my face and cried.

"Graciela! Graciela!" I lifted my head to see Garza jump off his wagon, wrap the horse's reins around a post, and rush toward the house.

"*Aquí. ¡Estoy aquí!*" Señora Garza came running outside.

The old man immediately took his wife by the hand. "Come," he said, walking back to the wagon.

"You know who showed up here? Wait." She looked around. "You didn't bring back a doctor?"

Garza shook his head. "Graciela, the town is in ruins. There are so many people hurt." He looked up as a thick raindrop hit his shoulder. "They can't spare anyone. After the storm passes, I'll take those with the worst injuries to one of the makeshift hospitals they've set up." He reached into one of the baskets in the back of the wagon. "But first, look at this."

I watched as he pulled out a bundle wrapped in a blanket.

"*¡Ay, Dios mío!*" Señora Garza clasped her hands before taking the bundle and cradling it in her arms. A tiny hand poked up. "But why did you bring him here?"

Garza pointed to the baskets in the wagon. "Padre Iñaki asked me to care for these four. He's trying to find their families, but they need a place to stay for now. He sent a few others to the Eguiguren farm too. I told him the names of the other children we have, and he'll try to find their relatives as well."

The raindrops splattered against the ground, one drop landing on my forehead and then another on my hand. I barely noticed. The wagon felt like a magnet, lifting me off the ground and pulling me closer. Seconds later, I was standing next to the wagon, peering over the side.

Garza gave me a strange look, then a flash of recognition crossed his face when he realized who I was.

"*Espérate*, aren't you . . . Mathias's friend?"

"*Sí*. I'm—"

"Is Mathias . . . ," he asked just as Mathias came around the corner of the house, still carrying the ax.

"Mathias!" he yelled, running toward him. "Mathias! I can't believe . . . Are you . . . you look . . . *¿y tus padres?*"

Mathias looked away, not wanting to meet the old man's eyes. He didn't have to answer his question. The look on his face said what had happened to his parents.

Garza stopped in his tracks and took off his beret, momentarily closing his eyes. "*Maldita guerra*," he muttered.

"We have to end this war . . . once and for all," Mathias told him. "You'll help me, right?"

Garza put an arm around Mathias and walked back toward us as the fat raindrops continued to slowly fall. "The way things are going for us, I fear the end will be here soon enough."

Mathias stopped. "Fear? Now's not the time to be afraid. You fought with the French in the Great War. You weren't afraid twenty years ago! You know there's only one thing left to do." His eyes met mine as he said, "I need to join the fight!"

Garza sighed. "Ay, Mati, you don't even know what you'd be getting yourself into. You're so young. . . . War is not what you imagine it to be."

"Imagine?" Mathias pulled away from the old man. "I

don't need to imagine it. . . . I've seen it up close. It was there on my parents' faces when they were lying under a pile of rubble." His eyes darted from Garza to Garza's wife, then to me. "If you won't help me, then I'll do it myself. You'll see. I *will* make them pay!"

He slammed the ax into the ground.

"And if you won't help me, then you can all go to hell!" he yelled as he stomped back to the house before any of us could react.

I was frozen. I'd never seen so much hatred in someone's eyes.

"Mathias!" Señora Garza called out.

Garza shook his head, looking over at his wife and me. "Leave him alone for now. He's hurt and angry. I'll talk to him later. Reason with him."

The loud crackling sound of lightning followed by the powerful boom of thunder startled me and the babies. Instantly, they all began to cry as the heavens opened up and shed their own tears.

"Help me get them inside!" Señora Garza commanded, placing the baby she held into a basket and racing toward the house.

"*¡Apúrate!*" Garza yelled over the now-pouring rain.

I felt my hair begin to drip with water.

"*Niña*"—he grabbed me by the shoulders—"it'll be fine. Everything will be fine. Now get the babies." He picked up two of the baskets, one in each arm.

Slowly, as if lead filled my entire body, I reached for the last basket, looking down at the tiny crying baby inside. It had a few small scrapes on its nose and cheek, but otherwise it looked . . . *fine.*

"No," I muttered, watching Garza run into the house, "it's not fine."

As if responding, the wind whipped up the rain and smacked me in the face.

I looked up at the storm clouds above me and yelled, "Did you hear me? NOTHING will EVER be fine again!" Then I bolted toward the house with the basket in my arms, not waiting for the storm to answer.

THIRTY-EIGHT

By early evening, the damp, musty odors left by the afternoon storm had faded and were being replaced by the smells of Señora Garza's cooking. *Marmitako* was being prepared, and the smell of onions, potatoes, and fish filled the air, comforting me more than anyone's words ever could.

I had hoped that while we were all trapped inside the house, Mathias would have had a change of heart and reconsidered his plan to join the war. But that didn't happen.

In fact, nothing much happened during the entire afternoon. Diego stayed in the back room with his mother, the children played with each other or the babies, and I helped Señora Garza in any way I could. The only one who barely moved was Mathias.

I knew he must be tired from chopping all the wood, but it was more than that. He wasn't sleeping or resting, but instead he sat upright with his back against a corner, his eyes focused on some distant unseen horizon and a scowl on his face. He didn't move or twitch, barely even blinked. He would probably have stayed there all afternoon if Garza had not enlisted his help in taking the severely injured back to town to be treated and the dead to be buried.

As I walked toward the back bedroom, I passed Carmita, who was now playing a game of hide-and-seek with Julián. She was crouching underneath a table, giggling, hands covering her eyes, while Julián rolled his wheelchair past her.

How quickly they had adapted to their new life! Or maybe they were too young to understand that their old life was over . . . that there would be no going back to their families or homes.

I gently knocked on the bedroom door before walking in.

Diego sat in a wooden chair next to the bed, his head resting on the edge of the mattress by his mother's arm.

"Who's there?" he asked, with a start.

"It's me," I answered, taking a cautious step closer. "I thought you might want something to drink."

"Ah, the storyteller." He smiled and lifted his head. "I'm sorry for what I said earlier. I didn't realize . . . I mean, I thought you were . . . um, well, Señora Garza told me what happened to you, to your mother."

"Oh." I looked down at the glass of water I'd brought for him.

"I'm really sorry . . . about everything." He stood and offered me his chair, not knowing that there was another one a few feet away. "Are you okay?" he asked, fumbling to take a seat on the bed.

"No." I looked at the floor where the two bodies had lain. . . . It looked strangely bare, as if nothing wanted to be where death had been. "But I'll survive," I said, sitting in the wooden chair by the bed.

"Yeah," Diego muttered.

An awkward silence followed.

"Oh, here's some water." I took his hand and wrapped it around the glass.

"*Gracias.*" He gulped it down, and then, leaning over, he reached out, searching for the night table.

I put my hand on his arm. "Here, I'll get it," I said, taking the glass from him and placing it on the table.

"Thanks." He gave me a small smile. "I wish I could see. . . . I'd be more help to everyone."

"You'll get better soon," I said, staring at him. It was a curious thing to be able to look at someone so intently and not have them notice. With his light brown hair, tan skin, and strong jaw, he was actually very handsome.

"I'm not so sure about that," Diego answered.

"Um, what? What do you mean?" I asked, flustered at the thought that he somehow knew what I was thinking.

"About my seeing again." He touched the bandage that covered his eyes. "I have a feeling I won't."

"Oh, you shouldn't say that."

He shrugged. "It's okay. I think I knew the moment the bomb exploded."

I reached out and touched his knee. "I'm sorry."

Diego covered my hand with his. "I made a deal with God not to complain if we got out of there alive, and I'm sticking to it." He squeezed my hand. "I am sorry for everything you're going through, though."

A little bit of the heaviness that sat on my chest seemed to lift. Sharing my grief with someone helped. Now, unlike a few minutes earlier, we sat together in a comforting stillness.

"I've got to ask you . . . do I know you from school?" Diego shifted his weight and scooted back against his mother's hip. "I heard the kids call you Ani, but I just can't place you."

I gazed down at his hand still holding mine and slowly pulled away. I thought of Sardine Girl. Would he have heard of her? I glanced at the door.

I could see his eyebrows scrunch together under the bandages. "Are you okay? Did I say something wrong?"

"No." I paused, not sure if I wanted him to know who I was—or at least, who I used to be. "I don't think we're in the same grade."

"How old are you?" he asked.

"Twelve . . . I'll be thirteen in a couple of weeks. And you?"

"Fifteen." Diego tilted his head as if trying to recall all the younger girls he knew. "Hmm, I didn't know that many of the seventh graders. . . . Guess that's why I don't remember an Ani."

"Yeah . . . Ani," I muttered.

"Hold on, isn't that your name? I didn't get you confused with someone else here? It's kinda hard not being able to see who people are talking to."

"No, I mean, yes . . . that's what they call me now."

Diego paused, listening to the stillness in the air. "You don't like having all your friends call you that?"

"All my friends?" I almost laughed at the thought. Sardine Girl had no friends and I wasn't so sure if Ani still did.

"Yeah, from school or whatever."

I didn't want to think about Sardine Girl anymore. "Ani is fine. I like it." I nodded to emphasize my point, even though he couldn't see me.

"Hmm," he muttered, unsure whether to believe me or not. "So, maybe I should call you something else."

I shrugged. "It doesn't matter."

"Of course it does. What do you want to be called?" Diego felt around the bed until he found his mother's hand. He mindlessly started to rub it while waiting for me to answer. "Names are important. My mother always quotes an old Basque proverb that says, 'Izena duen guztiak izatea ere badauke.' Which means—"

"'Everything with a name exists.' I know."

Diego and I stayed quiet for a moment.

"Well." He grinned and a long dimple appeared. "How about if I call you Storyteller . . . until you decide what I should call you?"

"Her name is Ani," a very matter-of-fact voice answered.

I glanced over to the doorway to see Mathias standing there with his arms crossed.

"Sorry if I'm interrupting, but Señora Garza says we're eating. Bring him with you . . . if you want," he said before walking away.

Diego leaned closer to me and whispered, "Who was that?"

"Oh, that's Mathias." I reached over to help Diego stand up.

"Boyfriend?" I could see Diego's eyebrows arch up over his bandages.

My cheeks began to burn. "Oh no. Not at all. We're friends, at least I think we still are. He's just been through a lot."

"Hmph. We all have. Sounds like a really nice guy." The sarcasm of his words was obvious.

"He actually is," I said, looking back at the empty doorway.

"Well, then I guess he just doesn't like me," Diego said, holding on to my arm so I could guide him out of the room.

"Don't take it personally," I said.

Diego paused in the doorway. "I won't. But he should know the feeling is mutual."

THIRTY-NINE

Lightning flashed, temporarily lifting the darkness from the room and casting strange shadows on the wall. I pulled a few strands of my wet hair across my nose and breathed in the clean, soapy smell. It helped me forget the odor of war, which was forever engraved in my memory.

I was glad Señora Garza had insisted that I bathe and put on some of her clothes before going to sleep. Not that sleep was coming easily to me. Even my old clothes, crumpled in the corner and waiting to be washed in the morning, reminded me of the bodies buried beneath the rubble. I closed my eyes to block out the image, but that only made me think of more heinous things.

Thunder echoed in the distance.

Sitting on a red blanket on the bedroom floor, I stared out the window at the black sky, which rippled with another lightning flash. The slow rumble of thunder shook the wooden floorboards beneath me. A slight shiver ran up and down my spine. I pulled my legs close to my chest and tucked them under the large yellow-flowered dress that Señora Garza had let me borrow.

I thought about the children in Julián's room and whether they'd be able to sleep. Could they still have sweet dreams, or had those been taken from them as well?

Earlier in the night the Garzas had decided that the little ones should sleep in Julián's room, the women would stay in the Garzas' bedroom with the babies, and the men would sleep in the living room in case there was some sort of ground attack. After a few hours of feeding the babies and changing diapers, I was thinking I'd rather take my chances with the ground attack.

"*¿Todo bien?*" Señora Garza asked, rolling to her side. She was sleeping on the floor next to me since the beds were being used by Diego's mother and the old lady.

"I'm all right. Just thinking," I said, falling back against the faded red blanket.

"*¿Seguro?* Sometimes just giving a voice to your thoughts helps."

"I wouldn't even know where to start," I said, fearing that if I did talk about things, the tears would flow again. One big cry was enough.

"Hmm. Well, if not me, maybe a friend?"

I shook my head while staring up at the ceiling. "Mathias isn't in a listening mood. I don't think he even wants me around anymore."

Señora Garza reached over and tapped my hand. "That can't be true. He's just lost and grieving. He'll find his way again."

"But part of me wishes I could be like him," I whispered as a strong flash of lightning lit up the entire room.

"*¿Por qué?*" she asked as the thunder boomed overhead and shook the small house from top to bottom.

"Because he at least has a plan. . . . He's going to do something. I thought when we became friends that I'd do something too. That I'd—"

The windows rattled one last time before falling silent, waiting for the next thunderclap.

I took a deep breath. "*No importa.* I was never the type to make a difference anyway. Mamá always said we're just whispers in a loud world, and I'm pretty sure the whole planet is shouting at the top of its lungs."

Señora Garza propped herself up on an elbow. "Don't sell yourself short, *niñita*. There are many ways you can make a difference in this world. Not just how Mathias wants to do it."

"I guess."

"Listen, I'm sure your mother was a wonderful woman, but I think she was completely wrong about being a whisper. No matter how loud the world gets, sometimes a single voice can be heard."

Lightning flashed again in the distance, and thunder rocked the house with a slow quake that seemed to come in like a long wave from the ocean.

Señora Garza continued, "You see, I think people can be like that storm outside. Some people seek to do magnificent things, inspired acts that stand out like bolts of lightning. That would be our Mathias. Others move the world like the strong, and sometimes slow, rumbles of thunder."

I was neither of those things. She didn't know me.

"And I suppose, if you think about it, most people are like the rain. They follow the lightning and thunder . . . either nourishing the earth or drowning it."

I stayed silent, not quite sure what she meant by all this.

Señora Garza lay back down on her blanket. "Or perhaps I'm just an old woman who is overly tired and rambling. But I hope you understand what I'm trying to tell you."

"I think so," I muttered, exhaustion finally overtaking my body.

Just before I felt myself drift away to the blackness of sleep, I heard Señora Garza say, "You can be the thunder to Mathias's lightning."

FORTY

A piercing scream shattered the quiet of the night. For a moment, I was confused, thinking it was part of my own nightmare or that I was the one who'd yelled. A split second later, the wailing from the other room confirmed that it had not been my imagination. I covered my head with the pillow, wanting it all to go away.

"Ugh," Señora Garza moaned as she threw off her blanket and tried to get up from the floor.

The babies lying in their baskets near us began to whimper and complain about the continuing shrieks coming from Julián's room.

"Ani, can you see what the problem is over there while I deal with the babies?" Señora Garza was already by the baskets, rocking each one for a moment before going to the next.

I jumped up, almost losing my balance, and rushed over to Julián's room. Even though the house was dark, a sliver of moonlight coming in through the unshuttered window created enough light for me to see Julián, sitting up in his bed, hands covering his ears.

"Make them stop!" he yelled.

I bent down and picked up Carmita, who was crying so hard that she could barely breathe. "Shhh. *Ya, ya,*" I cooed, bouncing her on my hip while scooping up Mirentxu and rocking both of them back and forth. The two girls clung to my neck so tightly that I thought they might choke me. They were much too heavy for me to stay standing, so I sat on the floor, where a bed of blankets had been made for them.

As the girls' loud cries subsided into gentle sobs, I noticed that the boy with no name was standing silently in a corner of the room just staring at me.

"Do you want to come over here?" I asked, waving him closer.

He shook his head.

"Can we just go back to sleep?" Julián asked, flipping his pillow over and punching it.

"Sure," I said, tucking in the two girls under their covers.

I looked back at the quiet boy in the corner, who still hadn't moved. "Do you want me to tell you some more about the princess and the *jentillak?*"

The little boy shrugged, but slid down against the wall, never looking away. He curled his arms around his legs and waited.

I took a blanket balled up near Julián's bed and draped it over the little boy. "You sure you don't want to tell me your name?" I asked.

He sat still, his eyes wide open.

"All right, then, how about if I call you José, since that's my father's name?"

A slight tilt of his head was all the response I got, but it was enough for me to start calling him by his new name.

"Well, José, the last time I was telling you the story, I said that there was a beautiful princess who was trapped on her island home by a horrible sea serpent, but that the princess had rescued a fairy that was caught under a heavy seashell. Do you remember?"

"I don't remember a fairy," said Mirentxu.

"Me neither," added Carmita, lifting her head off the floor.

"Well, I'll go back to that part, then. But first, let's do the same thing we did last time and close our eyes and imagine the story." I waited a few moments and only when all their eyes were shut did I begin.

"The beautiful princess heard a strange noise coming from underneath a large seashell that was covered in seaweed. Carefully, she walked toward the shell and realized that what she heard was crying."

A shuffling sound made me pause.

"The fairy was crying?" Mirentxu asked in a groggy voice.

I strained to hear what the noise could be, but there was only silence.

"Yes," I said in a slow, whispery voice, "the fairy was crying because she thought no one would ever rescue her." Combing back José's silky hair with my fingers, I continued, "When the princess released her from the shell, the fairy was so happy that she danced and flew around like a sparkling butterfly.

The fairy wanted to thank the princess for her kindness, and so she gave her something that no one else could"—I dropped my voice even further—"a way *off* the island."

I paused. Even breathing filled the room.

Quietly I stood up and tiptoed out of the room. As I turned to close the door behind me, a shadow popped out from the hallway. I stifled the scream that was about to escape from my throat when I heard a voice say, "The storyteller strikes again."

It was Diego.

"You startled me," I said, my heart pounding from the scare.

"Sorry. I thought you saw me standing here."

"How could I? It's pitch-dark in this hallway."

"Oh. I didn't know."

I closed my eyes, feeling like an idiot. Of course he didn't know.

"I just heard you talking and wanted to listen too."

"Aren't you a little old for fairy tales?" I teased.

"Yeah, maybe." Even in the shadows, I could hear the smile in his voice, and I imagined the long dimple showing up again. "But there's something about your voice, the way you tell stories. . . . It's special."

I blushed, thankful he couldn't see me.

"And the best part is I can put a face with the voice because I finally remembered you from school."

"What?" I took a small step back. He couldn't possibly know, could he?

"Yeah," he said, "you're the *sardinera*'s daughter, right?"

"Uh . . . um . . . well . . . ," I stammered.

"It took me a while, but I knew I'd piece it together."

"I have to go," I said, my voice cracking. Sardine Girl was back . . . assuming she'd ever left.

"No, wait." Diego reached out and touched my arm. "Did I say something wrong again?" He slapped the side of his head. "Of course, I did. I'm so stupid. It must hurt to think of your mother."

I stayed silent.

"Forgive me? I didn't mean to make you upset. You were right earlier today . . . I can be *un idiota*." He took a step toward me. "I'm leaving in the morning and I just thought it'd be good if you knew that I remembered seeing you with your mother whenever I'd go play jai alai. You probably don't remember me but—"

"You're leaving?" I asked, surprised at the disappointment I suddenly felt. "In a couple of hours?"

Diego nodded. "Señor Garza said he'd take us to Bilbao . . . to a hospital."

"Oh, that's good," I said.

We stood there in the dark hallway for a few seconds, neither one of us saying anything else.

"Guess we should get some rest," Diego mumbled.

"Uh-huh." I took him by the elbow and guided him back to the family room, where Señor Garza lay snoring on the sofa.

As we approached the makeshift bed on the floor, Diego stopped. "One more thing," he said as I let go of his arm. "I'm not sure if I'll get a chance to say it before I leave . . . but, um, I just wanted to thank you for being so nice to me . . . and my mother. It made a difference."

"You're welcome," I said. "Good night."

As I walked away, I heard him say in a loud whisper, "Good night, Storyteller."

By the time I was back in the Garzas' bedroom, I had a smile from ear to ear. Even though Diego knew who I was, to him I was Storyteller, not Sardine Girl.

I really hoped our paths would cross again.

❖   ❖   ❖

The sound of whispers and giggles woke me up. The sun was already shining strongly through the bedroom window, and it took a few seconds for my eyes to adjust to the brightness.

"*¡Está despierta!*" a little voice squealed before several arms wrapped themselves around me in a big group hug.

"*Sí, sí.* I'm most definitely awake now," I said from beneath the pileup of small bodies.

"About time you got up," Julián said from the doorway. "Abuela wouldn't let anyone get near you for the past hour."

"We thought you were going to leave too," Mirentxu said breathlessly, squeezing me even tighter.

"Leave?" I sat up, knocking over Carmita and Mirentxu. "Did Diego go already?" I didn't think I'd sleep through the noise of everyone leaving.

Julián nodded from the doorway. "And his mother too. Everyone's gone except Abuela, us, and the babies."

"Mathias too?" I looked around. Would Mathias run off to fight in the war without saying goodbye?

"Yep. Abuelo asked him to go to Bilbao with him, even though I said I wanted to go." Julián rolled into the room.

"It's not fair. All morning, I've been the one taking care of these pip-squeaks." He pointed a finger at me. "Now it's your turn."

"Julián." Señora Garza was at the door, her fists at her hips. "*No hables así.* I don't like that attitude. Your grandfather needed to spend some time speaking with Mathias alone. . . . These are very difficult days for him. And for Ani. We all have to help." She walked in and pulled Mirentxu off me. "*¿Dormistes bien, niña?*"

I nodded. "*Sí, señora.* I didn't realize it was so late. I would've been up earlier to help." When I stood up, my very large yellow dress hung off my shoulders and draped to the floor. I tried smoothing out some of the wrinkles and gathered up the bottom so it wouldn't drag.

"You look funny in Abuela's dress," Julián chuckled.

"Oh, shush, Julián. She makes that dress look nicer than ever. Better than when these old bones wear it." Señora Garza smiled at me. "But your clothes are already outside drying."

I glanced over to the corner of the room where my clothes had been. I wasn't used to having anyone do things for me. It felt . . . uncomfortable. "You didn't have to do that. I would've washed them myself." I looked at the night table. The pouch and weight were gone. "My things!"

Julián raised his hands in surrender. "It wasn't me."

"Don't worry." Señora Garza tapped my shoulder. "I put them in the drawer so they wouldn't get lost." She swiveled Julián's wheelchair around and pushed him out of the room, bringing Mirentxu and Carmita with her.

"*Gracias*," I muttered, gazing down at my bare feet.

"No need for thanks, *mija*. Just wash up and come help me outside. Lots to get done before Mathias and Garza return tomorrow."

My heart dropped a little. I wanted Mathias to be here, even if he wasn't speaking to me. "Do you really think it'll take them that long? Bilbao isn't that far. They might be back tonight."

Señora Garza paused in the doorway and looked back at me. I felt as if she could read my thoughts. "Maybe, but I suspect Garza will spend the night in Bilbao and head back tomorrow. I know you want Mathias to be here, but I think Garza needs to talk to Mathias, man to man. Work some things out."

"Convince him not to leave and go fight?" My voice carried the unmistakable traces of hope.

Señora Garza's lips twitched before she muttered, "Well, something like that."

I wasn't reassured.

FORTY-ONE

The day flew by, barely giving me a moment to catch my breath, let alone think. The few minutes I'd had to myself were used to write the hardest letter I'd ever imagined. It took me several tries to come up with the right words to tell Papá that Mamá was gone. In the end, the letter was short. It simply said that I was fine and staying with the Garzas, but that Mamá had not survived. I didn't explain about our apartment being destroyed or how Mamá had died. . . . Those details would come later. I just wanted him to know.

The night didn't bring much of a reprieve from the day's hard work either. Carmita and Mirentxu had both insisted on sleeping with me on the bed formerly occupied by Diego's mother, and between their tossing and turning, my own restlessness, and baby duty, I barely slept. By the next day, even though the sun was at its peak, I was fighting a losing battle to keep my eyes open.

Then I heard it. A horse neighing loudly followed by the crackling sound of Garza's cart grinding over the gravel path. My sleepiness evaporated. Mathias was back!

My first instinct was to rush outside, but I stopped myself.

Mathias would come to me . . . when he was ready.

I stuck my hand in my left pocket, searching for the acorn, but instead my fingers found Mamá's brass weight, smooth and cold to the touch. I'd forgotten that it now shared the pocket along with the silk pouch.

The sadness I'd tried to push aside with nonstop work quickly came back. Mamá had said that everyone leaves. . . . It was something we all had to get used to. But I didn't want to ever get used to it. I wanted to expect that people would come back.

I dug deeper into the skirt pocket, feeling for the silk pouch that Papá had given me. I held both objects in my hand. An acorn and a weight, all I had left of my parents.

I gave the seed a soft squeeze, closed my eyes, and wished for the one thing I wanted most in the world . . . for Papá to be safe and to come back.

"We'll plant this seed . . . one day," I murmured.

"Ani! Ani!" Mathias yelled, plowing through the front door.

"What?" I asked, popping my eyes open and realizing that he'd woken two of the sleeping babies.

"Señora Garza!" he yelled as the old woman came out from Julián's room. "Ani and I have to go back to town! Garza has some more children that he's taking up to the Eguiguren farm, but he'll be back later." He hobbled over to me and grabbed my hand. "We have to go . . . right now!"

"*¿Qué?*" Señora Garza asked, still folding the blanket she had in her hands.

"Mathias, what are you talking about?" I asked.

He tapped his *makila* impatiently on the ground. "The Basque soldiers!" He stopped me from going toward one of the crying babies and spun me around so I'd face him. "Some of them are in town. The front seems to be breaking, and some soldiers are looking for relatives as they retreat. C'mon. We have to go!"

Mathias's words hit me like a tidal wave.

Papá. He might be back.

❖   ❖   ❖

"Just go! *¡No me esperes!*" Mathias yelled from behind me on the mountain path.

I had already slowed down twice to let him catch up a little, but I couldn't take the chance of missing Papá.

"I'll meet you at the church!" I shouted, running faster than I could have imagined. I knew that the soldiers would go there to find out about their families.

Soon I was jumping over piles of bricks, avoiding the pits and craters left by the bombs, rounding the corner of what had once been my street, and making a dash for the center of town. I tripped, fell, and got right back up. A skinned knee or elbow would not slow me down.

What had once been Guernica was gone. All that remained was a shell—a broken and shattered shell. There were no comforting smells or familiar sounds. It reeked of war, but I didn't care. I was focused on only one thing.

As I approached the church, I saw more and more soldiers. My eyes scanned each one before quickly dismissing them. There was only one face I wanted to find . . . needed to see.

Bolting into the church, I saw Padre Iñaki talking to one of the soldiers in the corner.

"Padre, Padre!" I ran to the priest, pausing only for a moment to genuflect before the altar as I crossed to the other side of the church.

The two men stopped talking and waited for me to come closer.

"*¿Qué pasó?*" Padre Iñaki asked.

I glanced at the soldier. His eyes were red and watery. I suddenly realized that he was probably getting bad news about his own family. "*Perdonen la interrupción,*" I muttered, rubbing the sides of my hands against my skirt, the feel of the bump from the acorn pushing me to continue speaking regardless of what I might be interrupting. "I heard that some of the soldiers are back. . . . I need to know if you've seen my father."

"No, *hija.*" Padre Iñaki shook his head and placed his hand on my shoulder. "I'm sorry, but I just got here a little while ago myself. He could've been by here earlier, though. Let me find out." Padre Iñaki walked over to one of the men working near the shattered stained-glass window.

I turned to the soldier standing next to me. "His name is José Largazabalaga. Do you know him?"

The soldier mulled over the name for a few moments.

"Older man? Mostly gray hair? About this tall?" He raised his hand a few inches above me.

"Yes!" I nodded.

"I met him a few weeks ago, but I haven't seen him since. Nice man, though."

I gave him a slight smile at the compliment, but I was wasting time if Papá wasn't there. "Please, if you see my father again, can you tell him that I'm staying at the Garza farmhouse?" My eyes were already darting around the church, trying to see who else to ask.

"*Claro*," the soldier said, nodding and pointing to Padre Iñaki, who was now walking back toward us. I rushed over to meet him, broken glass making a crunching sound under my feet.

"Was he here?" I asked.

"Some soldiers did come by this morning, but no one knows if your father was with them. They were headed to the hospital to try and find their families. Miguel over there"— he pointed to the man by the broken window—"wrote down your name on our children's list . . . in case your father comes to ask about you."

"The hospital? I'll go there next. ¡*Gracias!*" I turned and ran down the center aisle past several rows of people kneeling in the pews.

In one of the pews at the back of the church was a couple, hugging and smiling. A happy reunion in the middle of all the tears. There was still a chance I could have a moment like that.

FORTY-TWO

The sun was dropping, and long shadows covered the streets and rubble of Guernica. I hadn't seen Mathias all afternoon, and the guilt of not waiting for him at the church was starting to eat at me. I thought I'd run into him as I crisscrossed the streets outside the hospital, asking everyone if they'd seen Papá and leaving word that I was staying with the Garzas.

As I trudged up the mountain path, resigned to the fact that I'd looked everywhere and asked everyone, I saw the familiar silhouette of a tall boy wearing a beret, leaning on a *makila*, standing by my tree.

I darted across the field toward him.

"How long have you been here?" I asked, slightly out of breath.

"For a while. I figured I'd just meet up with you on the way back." He shifted his weight from foot to foot. "You want to stay here for a while and talk?"

I looked around. The memories of the bombing and hiding

in the foxhole were so vivid. I shook my head. "No. It doesn't feel the same anymore."

We started walking back to the main road.

"Did you find out anything about your father?" he asked.

"No. I left word where I was staying, though."

"Oh, that's good."

We walked in silence for a little longer, the sun hovering over the horizon.

"He'll come back," Mathias said after a while.

"I hope so," I muttered.

"Ani." Mathias stopped for a moment.

"What?" I asked over my shoulder, still walking toward the Garza farm.

He took a deep breath and sighed. "I saw where they buried my parents."

I stopped. The entire time, I had been so focused on my own feelings and on searching for my father that I'd forgotten all about what Mathias might be going through.

Turning around, I didn't know what to say.

"They had no way of knowing where I was, so I wasn't told about the burial. It happened yesterday . . . but they showed me the grave."

"I'm sorry," I said, wanting to say or do more for him.

"Yeah." Mathias shuffled his feet.

I studied his face. He looked different from just two days ago. There was something in the way he stood, the look in his eyes, that made him seem . . . older.

"It just feels . . . final. Like they're really gone."

"Do you want to go back? I'll go with you."

"No. I said my goodbyes, but, um . . . I want to give you this." He held out a torn piece of paper. "It's my grandmother's address in Germany. So you can write to me once I leave."

"Write to you? Are you still thinking of going there to kill Hitler?" I rolled my eyes and most definitely did not take the paper.

"I know that probably won't happen . . . but I believe I can make a difference." He took my hand and put the paper in my palm. "I want to continue the work my father was doing."

He was serious.

"Ani, my family's there," he said.

I listened as he now spoke plainly, without the anger he'd had before. "I need to help them. Things are getting really bad for all the Jews over there."

I closed my fingers around the piece of paper and slipped it into my pocket.

This wasn't how things were supposed to go. I thought Garza would talk him into staying and working on the farm. We started walking again.

"Why don't you have that side of your family move here? You're as much Basque as you are German."

He shook his head. "They can't just move, and why should they have to abandon their home . . . their country? People have to stand up against hatred like that or else things will get even worse."

I stared at some passing birds, doing a quick double take to make sure they were actually birds and not planes. "But from what you've told me, things are already out of control over there. It's dangerous."

Mathias used his *makila* to point back toward the city. "Um, where have you been? It's dangerous everywhere."

I sighed. Even in the dimming light of dusk, the wreckage of the bombed buildings could be seen from where we stood. "I know it's not safe here either, but there's plenty to do. We could fight what's happening here . . . together," I said.

"I can't. Germany is where I have family, where my father had his contacts. . . . It's where I belong." He paused. "I promise to write back and tell you what's going on over there. Didn't the blind boy call you Storyteller?"

"You mean Diego?" I asked, knowing exactly who he meant.

"Yeah, him." He waved off his name like an annoying bug. "You can make sure people here know what's happening. We can still work together."

I kicked a small rock toward the edge of the road. I thought about being Mathias's storyteller. "I guess. But who'd listen?"

"Kids, the Garzas, Padre Iñaki . . . you," Mathias said. "The important thing is that the stories get out."

"I guess," I muttered. "When do you plan on leaving?"

"While I was in Bilbao, I met some soldiers who—"

"Look!" I said, pointing at a pair of headlights slowly backing away from the front of the Garza farm. My heart sank as I thought these were the soldiers Mathias was just talking about. Was he going to leave *right now*?

I glanced over at him. "Are you—" I never finished my thought because the jeep's brakes screeched as it abruptly stopped in front of us, and out of the corner of my eye, I saw someone jump out of the back.

"*¡Preciosa!*"

FORTY-THREE

For a moment, time stopped. Silence filled the air, and it was all I could do to breathe. Then, as if God had restarted the movie that was our lives, noise surrounded me, and Papá had me in his arms, covering my cheeks with kisses and tears.

"I didn't think I'd get to see you," he said, squeezing me. He pushed me back and scanned me from head to toe. "You're not hurt, are you?"

"No, Papá," I said, barely able to catch my breath.

He hugged me again and whispered, "I'm so sorry that I wasn't here. To protect you . . . your mother. The Garzas told me that she—"

I wrapped my arms around his waist even tighter. I didn't want him to say it out loud.

The sound of the jeep's horn startled me.

"*¡Nos tenemos que ir!*" one of the soldiers shouted.

Papá held up his hand. "I know, I know. Give me one

minute." He looked me squarely in the eye. "I don't have much time, but—" Papá stopped speaking. His eyes welled up with tears, and he hugged me tight once again. *"Preciosa,"* he whispered into my hair. "You're all I have left." He sighed. "That's why I'm sending you somewhere safe . . . until this war is over."

I jerked back to look at him. "No, you can't."

A single tear dropped onto Papá's cheek. "Yes, I have to. You'll go to England with some other Basque children. The navy is already clearing mines and—"

"England? But I don't know anyone there. Who will I live with? How—"

"It's being taken care of. There'll be many children with you. . . . It'll be like one of the adventure stories you used to tell me."

"But—" The jeep honked again.

Papá looked back and nodded. He pulled me close and gave me a kiss on the top of my head. *"Preciosa,* I've already spoken to the Garzas and given them all the details. They'll explain it to you. The important thing is that you'll be safe. Who knows, maybe some of your friends will go too. But you'll be away from this war. It's for the best. Really. It is." He started to back away.

Though I wasn't sure if he was saying this to reassure me or himself, one of his last words got stuck in my brain. *Friends.*

"Papá, wait!" I grabbed his hand while I searched the darkness that had now surrounded us. "Mathias! Where are you?"

"Right here." He stepped in front of the jeep's headlights.

"Papá, this is my friend Mathias. He helped keep me safe during the bombing."

"We kept each other safe," he corrected. "Nice to meet you, Señor Largazabalaga." He shook hands with Papá.

"Thank you for helping my daughter. I'm forever in your debt." Papá glanced at the *makila*. "Are you hurt?"

"Oh, this isn't from the bombing." Mathias tapped his leg with the *makila*.

"Papá, how about Mathias? Can you arrange for him to go to England?" My voice betrayed my feelings. "Please."

"I'm not sure." Papá cocked his head to the side and looked at Mathias. "It would have to be his parents' decision. Padre Iñaki has a list at the church where—"

"His parents died in the bombing," I interrupted.

"Oh, I'm sorry. In that case, I . . . well, you . . ." Papá scratched his head, a clear sign that he was thinking.

"*Gracias*, Señor Largazabalaga, but I'll be leaving for Germany soon."

Papá's eyes grew larger. "*¿Alemania?*" he said in a loud voice, then quickly glanced back at the soldiers. "Germany?" he whispered.

I was thankful that the jeep's engine had drowned out his voice.

"It's not what you think," I blurted out, although I had no real idea what Papá thought. "His family is there. . . . They're Jewish. And things have been getting really bad for them. They—"

Papá raised his hand as if he already knew the story. "I know what's been happening over there."

"So, don't you think he should go to England instead?" I asked, but I could see Mathias shaking his head.

"I'm going to Germany, Ani." Mathias's voice was flat, and I knew he'd made his decision.

Over Papá's shoulder I spotted a soldier approaching. Our time was up.

Papá glanced back, then faced us again.

He gave Mathias a quick nod and said, "Good luck to you, son." Then he looked at me. His eyes seemed to be trying to memorize everything about me.

We had only a moment left to say goodbye.

"*Te quiero mucho*, Papá," I said, hugging him.

"And I love you, *mi preciosa*." He kissed the top of my head, and I could feel his arms gripping me tightly. "*Que Dios te bendiga*."

My voice cracked as I said, "God bless you too, Papá."

"José, I'm sorry, but it's time." The soldier was standing right next to us.

Papá nodded and let me go.

I watched as Papá and the other soldier walked back to the jeep and climbed in. For a second I thought of running after them and throwing myself against Papá, begging him not to leave. But I knew better. Growing up, I'd never considered myself very brave . . . but I had to be. For Papá's sake. For my own.

As the soldiers drove off, Mathias put his hand on my shoulder. It gave me added strength. I could do this.

Then, from the darkness, I heard Papá yell, "*¡Adiós, Preciosa!* Write to me from England!"

With silent tears rolling down my cheeks, I muttered, "I will."

FORTY-FOUR

"It'll be all right," Mathias said as we knocked on the door of the Garza house. "You'll be safe there. No one messes with England."

I shrugged, still trying to get my head around the fact that I'd be leaving Guernica. It seemed that there would be a lot of letter writing in my future.

As the door flung open, Señora Garza ran past us and out into the darkness. "Oh, I can't believe this!" She spun around. "You're here and they just left! Bernardo!" she called out to Garza. "Bernardo, try to see if you can stop the soldiers!"

"No, no. We saw them," Mathias said, putting his hand on the old woman before she became hysterical.

"You saw them?" she asked.

"Yes." I smiled. "I got to see Papá."

Señora Garza placed a hand over her chest and let out a big sigh. "*Menos mal*," she said, walking back into the house with us. "I thought for sure you'd missed them."

"What is all the shouting about?" Garza stood in the middle of the room, a pack of cigarettes in his hand.

"She thought I'd missed seeing my father, but we ran into him—"

"Why do you still have that? I thought you gave them all to the soldiers." Señora Garza pointed to the small white box Garza was holding.

Garza held up the cigarette he had just tapped out from the pack. "It's the only one I kept." He looked at Mathias as he crumpled up the empty pack and tossed it on a small table. "Did you do everything that needed to be done?"

Mathias nodded.

"Let's go talk outside." Garza put an arm around Mathias's shoulder and led him back into the darkness, where they could speak privately.

It was obvious where I was not wanted. A feeling of hurt crawled inside me. I thought Mathias and I were spy partners to the end. I guess the bombing destroyed that too. Was I back to being an invisible girl?

Without much thought, I followed Señora Garza to the kitchen to help with the dinner, which was already cooking. I wasn't sure what we'd be eating, but between the rumbling of my belly and the wonderful smells coming from the two covered pots, I knew it'd be delicious. Farm living had some definite advantages.

"Do you know what those two are talking about?" Señora Garza asked me.

I shook my head. "No, I thought you might."

"Bernardo told me he was going to talk to Mathias . . .

rechannel his anger." She handed me several mismatched plates. "I'm still waiting to find out how it all went."

"Mathias does seem less angry." I thought of how focused he was when we spoke walking back from Guernica. "But he still wants to leave."

"Maybe Bernardo is working on that right now."

"Abuela, is dinner ready?" Julián asked, rolling into the kitchen.

"Almost." Señora Garza carried one of the large pots to the table. "Tell your grandfather and Mathias to come inside and then go back with the children. I'll call you when it's ready."

"What about Ani? Why can't—"

Señora Garza cut him off by raising her finger. "Not now, Julián." She had a look that meant there was no discussing this. "Go do as you're told."

"Sí, Abuela." Julián wheeled his chair around. I could hear him muttering under his breath about how it wasn't fair and why did he have to do so much.

"We need to talk about what your father wants for you, Ani. But not in front of the kids."

My leaving Guernica. I still couldn't believe it.

As Garza and Mathias both walked into the small kitchen, Señora Garza turned off the stove and faced her husband.

"We need to explain things to Ani, but not in front of you-know-who."

Garza nodded, his cigarette dangling from the corner of his lips.

"Did your father get a chance to talk to you?" Garza asked.

I nodded. "He mentioned I was supposed to go to England

with some other children, but that's all. We didn't have time for much else. He said he'd explained it to you."

Garza took a long drag from the cigarette and slowly exhaled. "The plan's been in the works for a while. An evacuation of sorts," he said, the smoke rising in front of him like a cloud. "A few thousand will be going with you."

"A few thousand?" I repeated, certain I couldn't have heard correctly.

"Yes. Many parents believe that this is the only way to protect their children . . . especially now with these bombings."

"Can't you put that thing out?" Señora Garza complained, pointing to the small cigarette stub in between Garza's fingers. "We're about to eat."

"It's my last one. . . . I'll enjoy it to the end. Who knows when I'll get more?" He sucked on it again.

"Ha! You'll just buy more when you take Ani to the port in a few days," Señora Garza huffed.

"A few days? So soon?" I asked. I hadn't realized that I'd be leaving everything so quickly.

Garza nodded. "We'll head to Bilbao by Saturday or Sunday. Depends on how fast they clear the mines in the bay and what's happening with the roads."

"Wait, if that's the case, can't I just leave with Ani?" Mathias looked at Garza. "Wouldn't that work?"

My heart raced with the possibility that Mathias had decided to join me. Leaving wouldn't be so bad if I wasn't doing it alone.

Garza dropped what remained of the cigarette in a nearby

ashtray. "I suppose we could do that. It would require some extra effort, but I think it can be done."

I grabbed Mathias's shirt so he'd look at me. "Does that mean you've changed your mind? You'll go to England with me?"

Mathias let out an exasperated sigh and shook his head. "I already told you. I'm leaving, but not to England. Garza is helping me get to Germany."

My shoulders slumped. "I thought—"

"What do you mean Garza is helping?" Señora Garza grabbed a kitchen towel and hit her husband with it before Mathias could answer. "Bernardo, what have you done?"

"Graciela," Garza began to explain, "I helped Mathias develop a plan. He was going to go anyway, but at least now he's approaching things with a cool head. My contacts are working it out for him. Getting things . . . *coordinated*."

"*Ay, Bernardo!*" Señora Garza exclaimed, a scowl on her face. "Don't tell me you've dug up your old contacts from twenty years ago? Do you think you can still be a war hero by sending this boy on a fool's errand?"

"I have old *and* new contacts, I'll have you know." Garza reached for the still-smoldering cigarette stub, but the tip crumbled into ashes as he picked it up. He tossed it back into the ashtray. "And no one here is being a fool."

"Señora Garza, please don't get upset," Mathias pleaded. "I have to do this. I *need* to do this . . . for my parents . . . for myself."

Señora Garza opened her mouth to say something, but as she looked at Mathias, she thought better of it.

I knew why she had changed her mind, because I'd noticed it too. There was a new sense of purpose, a determined focus, to Mathias's demeanor. It was something that hadn't been there before. It bothered me, although I wasn't sure why.

No one else interrupted Garza as he briefly explained how his contacts would get a Spanish passport for Mathias and how he'd then travel to France on a merchant ship before continuing on to Germany.

"None of this is fair," I muttered.

"¿Qué?" Garza asked, looking at me as if he'd almost forgotten I was there.

"All of this. The war, people dying, having to leave Spain." I knew I sounded like Julián, but I didn't care. "It's just not right."

Mathias nodded, but said, "Life isn't always fair."

I wasn't sure if I liked this more mature version of my friend.

He took my hand and gave it a squeeze. "But it's what you do about the unfairness that counts."

FORTY-FIVE

I wish I could say that the next morning I woke up having had some huge epiphany about how I could make my life meaningful . . . but I didn't. Nothing had changed. I didn't know how to be like Mathias.

Even when we decided to go back into town to help with the cleanup, the men seemed to accept Mathias's assistance, but shunned mine. I knew it was probably due to our difference in size and the fact that he was a boy, but it was all too familiar. I was becoming invisible again.

Realizing that I wasn't accomplishing anything by standing around watching Mathias work, I decided to wander the streets of my once-beautiful city. Much of the rubble had been cleared, and I could see the skeletal remains of so many people's lives. I paused at an apartment building missing its entire facade. The front wall had crumbled, leaving every apartment exposed. The furniture and belongings of each family that had once lived there were frozen in time, giving me a peek into their lives. I wondered how many of them would never return.

A thud and a flash of light made me quickly turn around. A man holding a large camera was a few feet away.

I'd seen a couple of unfamiliar faces on the street asking questions about the bombing. I figured they were either reporters or spies.

Our eyes met for a moment, and that was enough for the man to smile and walk toward me. He asked me something in a language I couldn't understand and pointed to the building. He seemed to want to know if I lived there.

I shook my head.

He paused, and with a very heavy accent, he said, "*Tú. Ver. ¿Bombas?*" He pointed to the sky and gestured as if his fist were falling through the air.

This photographer-reporter was asking if I'd seen the bombs fall from the planes. . . . What a stupid question! Of course I'd seen them, just like everyone else who now roamed the streets. I wanted to tell him all about what I'd seen, what I didn't want to remember, but there was no way he'd really understand . . . even if we spoke the same language.

My gaze slipped away from him and onto some point in the distance. I just nodded and said, "*Muchas bombas.*" There was a larger story to be told, but someone else would have to tell him.

He stepped back and took another picture, this time of me.

The flash from the camera caught me by surprise and made me see spots everywhere. By the time my eyesight returned to normal, the photographer was saying "*gracias*" and moving on to another image down the street.

Perhaps a picture could be worth a thousand words.

Late that afternoon, while walking back to Garza's farm, Mathias mentioned all the people he'd seen who had survived. There were more than I expected, especially considering that most of the city had been destroyed.

I told him about the photographer, and he wasn't surprised. A couple of men had been asking questions around where he was working . . . although he wasn't sure if they were reporters or spies for Franco. Either way, he'd chosen not to talk to them.

"I'd rather you tell the story," Mathias explained. "Aren't you going to be my storyteller anyway?"

I smiled. He'd taken Diego's nickname for me to heart. "I guess. But who am I supposed to tell exactly?"

"I don't know." He shrugged, his eyes still on the road ahead of us. "England's a pretty big country. . . . You'll find someone who'll listen."

I wasn't so sure.

❖ ❖ ❖

The next day everyone from town gathered at the church for a special Mass to mourn those who had died in the bombing—including those who would never be buried because their bodies couldn't be found. For all of us who had lost family, this would be our final goodbye.

The service was exactly as I expected. Cleared of the broken glass and fallen plaster, the damaged church was filled to capacity with people mourning their fathers, mothers, children, and friends. I stood in the back, silently praying for Mamá and clutching the brass weight I still kept in my pocket.

Even though all around me stood a sea of familiar faces, I somehow felt more isolated than I had for several days. It was as if the sadness I'd been carrying around had finally surrounded me and separated me from everyone else.

"You're not alone," Mathias whispered as we exited the church.

"What?" I asked, watching as Garza went to talk to Padre Iñaki.

"You just had this look on your face. It reminded me of that day when we first met . . . under the tree. But you're not the same person you were back then. You've got me. . . . You've got friends."

I stayed quiet, thinking about how much my life had changed in the last few weeks . . . for the better and for the worse.

I was about to say something about my always being there for him too when a deep voice interrupted us.

"*Permiso, niños.*"

Mathias and I turned around to see Padre Iñaki standing behind us. He glanced at the crowd of people still waiting for him by the church's doorway.

He got closer to Mathias and whispered, "I have only a moment to speak with you in private, but Garza tells me you're still planning to go to Germany."

Mathias nodded.

"Here, shake my hand." Padre Iñaki stretched out his hand. Mathias gave me a puzzled look, but did as he was told.

I saw the priest slip a piece of green paper into Mathias's palm.

"It's the name of someone you can contact," he said. "In case you get into trouble." He leaned closer to us. "Or if you find out some valuable information that we should know about. We don't want to be caught by surprise again." He held Mathias's hand a second longer. "We have to be careful who we trust."

Mathias gave him a slight nod, understanding the meaning behind his words.

"*¡Bien! ¡Bien!*" The priest looked over his shoulder at some of the people waiting for him. "You'll stay strong for your family," he said in a voice loud enough that others could hear.

Trust was something relative during a war.

"No! No!" Carmita yelled as she ran toward us. A tall man in a dark suit chased after her. "I want Ani and Mathias to come too," she cried as she wrapped herself around my legs.

The man looked at us and tried to pry Carmita's arms away from me.

"*¿Lo puedo ayudar?*" I asked, protectively putting my arms on Carmita's back.

"Oh. Excuse me, I'm sorry." He took a step back, and Carmita relaxed her grip ever so slightly. "My name is Fernando Goizuela. I'm Carmita's uncle . . . Lupe's brother."

Mathias crouched down to talk to Carmita. "Is that true? *¿El es tu tío?*"

Carmita nodded.

"I'm sorry about Lupe," I said. "She was a very nice woman."

"Yes, yes she was." Señor Goizuela quickly made the sign of the cross over his chest. "God bless her soul."

Carmita looked up at me. "Ani, I don't want to leave you. Come with me."

"Go with you? Where?"

"I'm taking Carmita back with me to Madrid," Señor Goizuela explained, bending down on one knee to look at Carmita. "Your two cousins, María José and Enrique, will be there. Do you remember them from the time you visited us last year?"

Carmita shook her head. "I want Ani and Mathias!" she demanded.

I stooped down to join Mathias and Señor Goizuela at Carmita's eye level. "Carmita, Mathias and I can't go with you, but we'll all still be friends."

"You need to go with your uncle. It's what your mother would want," Mathias said.

Carmita perked up. "Will Mamá be there?" she asked, looking at each of us for the answer she wanted to hear.

Señor Goizuela stroked his niece's hair. "No. Lupe, your mother, won't be there, but we'll think about her often . . . ¿está bien? I'll even show you a few pictures of how she looked when she was little . . . just like you."

Carmita seemed to like the idea and slowly unclenched her grip on my skirt.

"Adiós, Carmita," I said as the little girl took hold of her uncle's hand. "Be good."

"You too," she said, giving me a kiss on the cheek. She then gave Mathias a quick peck.

Carmita's uncle gave Mathias and me a slight nod of appreciation, then he and Carmita walked away, hand in hand.

Mathias sighed. "Sometimes I wish I could be that young and not understand what's really happening."

"Me too," I said. "But those days are gone."

As I watched Carmita round the corner with her uncle, it seemed as if I could feel another tie to my past unravel. There wasn't much keeping me in Guernica.

An unknown path lay ahead, yet I didn't know how to take the first step.

FORTY-SIX

The rest of the day, Mathias and I kept busy helping with the cleanup efforts. We saw Señor Beltran briefly, but he quickly turned away from us, not even acknowledging that he knew us or asking how we were. Not that I could blame him. Everyone was wary about what might happen next. Rumors were already flying that the front lines were faltering and that Guernica might fall to the Franco forces within a few days. People were streaming out, in search of a new place of refuge, while those who remained tried to piece together the broken town.

But through it all, I kept thinking of what would come next. It was as if I'd already said goodbye to my old life. Perhaps that's the reason I'd been so quiet at dinner and why, even now, I stayed quiet as Señora Garza talked about England.

She had insisted I wear something nice on my trip, so she'd given me her favorite flowery dress and was in the process of trying to pin it and make it at least eight sizes smaller. I dropped my arms a bit from their outstretched position.

"*No, todavía.* I haven't finished taking in the other side," she said.

I lifted my arms again as if I were being crucified. I wondered if it were somehow symbolic of the old me dying. If so, who was going to take the place of that invisible Sardine Girl? Who would I be now that everyone and everything I'd ever known had been taken away?

Mathias was so certain of what to do next. He was going to a place where he could do something. Fight Hitler, help the Jews, maybe even get information to the Basques. . . . He'd be important. I, on the other hand, would be off in England, where nothing really happened. It was why Papá wanted me to go there . . . to be safe. Did safe have to be insignificant?

At first light, I woke up knowing that we would be heading out to Bilbao soon. Señora Garza's flowery dress lay draped over the end of my bed, and I quickly slipped it on. It fit perfectly, and she'd even made a small pouch out of the extra fabric. It gave me an idea.

It was barely dawn, but I decided to go back to the field for one last visit.

I crossed the empty pasture and touched the gnarly bark of the old oak tree. It had been here for so long. I wondered about all the stories it could tell. The events of my life were probably only the latest it had witnessed. I hoped to one day come back here and continue my story.

Impulsively, I gave the tree a kiss before racing back up to the Garza house.

Once there, I noticed that everyone except for the babies was waiting outside for me.

"I'm sorry. I didn't think you'd be ready," I said to Garza, who was already up on the wagon, holding the horse's reins.

"*No te preocupes.* But we need to get going," he said.

I walked over to Mirentxu, who, ever since Carmita left, had become almost as quiet as the silent boy.

"I'll miss you, Mirentxu," I said. "*Pórtate bien.*"

"Why does everyone have to leave?" she asked.

I shrugged, not knowing how to answer.

"Can I go with you?" she asked, her big eyes welling up with tears.

"No." I shook my head and opened my arms for her to give me a hug. "Padre Iñaki is trying to find some of your family," I whispered into her hair as she squeezed me. "You'll get to stay with them soon."

"What if nobody wants me?" she asked, so quietly that I could barely hear her.

It was the question I'd lived with all my life.

"You already have people who want you. The Garzas, Mathias . . . me." I pushed her back so I could see her eyes. "Mirentxu, you're a special girl. Don't ever let anyone tell you different. You're important."

She gazed at me as if my words held a sort of magic.

I smiled. "Always remember that . . . okay?"

She stood motionless, just looking at my face.

"Promise me that you'll remember."

She slowly nodded, breaking her trance. "I'm special," she muttered. Then, just as suddenly, she turned around and skipped toward the house, singing, "Ani thinks I'm important, Ani thinks I'm important."

The little boy I'd named José had been standing against the wall watching the whole scene.

"You're special too," I said to him.

He shrugged and walked away.

It felt final. I had the sinking feeling that I'd never see him again or learn his real name.

"Ani!" Mathias called out. "*¡Vámonos!*"

I looked up at the brilliant blue sky. I paused to soak it all in. The feel of the cool mountain breeze on my cheeks, the clucking sound of the chickens in the henhouse, the smell of the wet earth still covered with dew. I wanted to capture every little thing about this place.

Señora Garza walked up behind me. "It's only temporary. You'll be back soon," she said.

It was the same refrain she'd been telling Julián since they'd decided yesterday to send him to England along with me.

I glanced back at the horse-drawn cart. Mathias sat next to Garza. . . . Julián was sitting in the back, and his wheelchair was tied to the left side of the wagon.

"*¡Un besote!*" Señora Garza said, giving me a big kiss on the cheek. "You're sure you don't want to take any of my other clothes to change into later? I should have fixed another one of my dresses. Maybe I can give you something else." The old woman began to search her pockets.

"No, I'm fine. *De veras.*" I gave her a hug.

"Keep an eye on Julián," she whispered. "He's a handful, but he's all we have."

I pulled away and gave her a weak smile. "I'll do my best," I said before climbing into the back of the wagon with him.

As Garza cracked the whip and the wagon started rolling forward, I was almost certain that in the distance, even though there wasn't a cloud in the sky, I heard the rumble of thunder.

FORTY-SEVEN

The port in Santurce, across the bay from Bilbao, was crowded and chaotic. It was from here that our ship would sail to England, and my body already ached with a longing to go back to Guernica.

Walking around our wagon there were people carrying suitcases, pushing and shoving each other to get by, merchant seamen yelling out instructions to their crews, and children crying as their parents hurried them along.

Garza stopped the wagon as close as he could to the ship we'd been instructed to board, the SS *Habana*. There was already a large group of children being herded together by a few nuns and priests. Garza came to the back of the wagon to unload Julián's wheelchair. I could see tears forming in the old man's crinkly eyes.

"Ani." Mathias touched my hand.

"Not yet," I pleaded, "please." I didn't want to say those dreaded words to Mathias.

He smiled and nodded. "I'll walk you and Julián as far as I can. They'll think I'm going too."

It was a small reprieve from the inevitable, but it was something.

I jumped off the wagon just as Garza helped Julián into his chair. I thought about how much Julián had already gone through in his short life—his parents dying, losing his ability to walk, and now leaving his grandparents. It was enough to devastate anyone, but the only one who was crying was Garza. Julián's face was completely blank.

"I love you, Julián. *Pórtate bien.*" Garza reached out to tousle Julián's hair, but the little boy shrank away. This didn't seem to faze Garza. "You'll come home soon . . . when it's safe. For now, think of it as an adventure."

Julián looked up at me and without a trace of emotion asked, "Can we go now? I don't want to be here anymore."

I couldn't believe this was the way he wanted to say goodbye. Obviously, Mathias didn't like it either because he smacked the little boy on the side of the head.

"Mathias!" Garza and I yelled at the same time.

"He deserved it!" Mathias answered us, then focused his attention back on Julián. "You need to grow up, little man. This is not the same world it used to be. You should be grateful to have two grandparents who love you so much that they're willing to do anything to make sure you're safe."

"Love me so much that they're getting rid of me?" Julián challenged. I could tell that if he could've jumped out of his chair, he would have tackled Mathias.

"Exactly!" Mathias leaned forward on his *makila*. "Don't you think it would be easier for them to keep you by their side? Not to have to worry about how to pay for your trip or how you'll manage in England?

"You have no idea how much I wish I could've had a real goodbye with my parents"—he paused to catch his breath— "and here you are acting like *un malcriado*!"

No one spoke or moved.

"Well?" Mathias asked. "What do you have to say?"

Julián gazed at Mathias and then slowly turned back to Garza, who, with shoulders slumped, was standing silently by the wagon. "*¿Abuelo?*"

"*Sí*, Julián?" The old man walked over toward his grandson.

The little boy's bottom lip began to tremble. "I don't want to go," he whispered.

Garza bent down and hugged him. "I know. I know."

"Can't I stay? Please?" Julián begged. "I'll be good. I promise."

"You're always good. But it's become too dangerous here." Garza brushed away the little boy's tears. "I promised your mother that I'd keep you safe. You're all we have."

"I love you," Julián said, choking back the sobs. "You and Abuela. Tell her, okay?"

"She knows, but I'll tell her." Garza gave his grandson one more embrace and then pushed the wheelchair closer to me. "We love you . . . *con todo nuestro corazón*."

Julián nodded and looked back as the old man walked to the front of the wagon.

From where I stood, I could see Garza pat Mathias on the back and mouth the word *"Gracias."* The two stood close together whispering something, then shook hands.

Garza climbed up to the driver's seat and, without looking back again, cracked the whip so the horse would begin the return trip to Guernica.

Mathias joined Julián and me, and the three of us maneuvered through the crowd gathering in front of the freighter. The sights and smells around us were mostly new to me, but I didn't want to pay attention. All I wanted to remember of this day was the glorious morning on the mountain . . . not the stagnant air of too many people crowded together or the cries of people saying goodbye.

And then we were at the ramp. Mathias would not be allowed to go any farther. Already we had been waved through by one official, but the next one had a clipboard and I knew the time had come.

"You sure you won't change your mind and come with us? We could find a way to get you on board," I said, knowing the attempt would be futile.

"You know I can't," Mathias answered. He took a step in front of the wheelchair and stuck out his hand. "You're a man now, Julián. Time to act like one, okay?"

Julián nodded and shook his hand. "I'll make you proud, Mathias," he said, then cracked a smile. "But just so you know, next time you hit me upside my head, I'm going to knock you out."

Mathias laughed. "Ooh, tough talk. We'll just have to

see how strong you are when we meet again. How about next time I challenge you to some arm wrestling?"

"You're on!" Julián said, wheeling himself back a bit. "I'm going to get these muscles strong!" He smiled, flexing his biceps.

A ship's horn rocked the pier and reminded us that we had to hurry.

Mathias and I stared at each other.

"Are you two going to get sappy? I don't want to see this." Julián turned his wheelchair around to look out at the harbor.

Mathias and I couldn't help smiling.

"You better be careful over there," I said, and gave Mathias a light punch in the arm.

"Now look who's doing the hitting!" Mathias rubbed his arm as if I had actually hurt him.

Julián glanced over his shoulder, but then quickly turned around in his chair again.

"Seriously," I said.

Mathias nodded. "I will."

We stood together, not knowing what else to say or do. A few people pushed us aside as they were going up the ramp, so we stepped out of their way and got closer to the edge of the pier.

Mathias pulled something from his pocket and put it in my hand. "Here. So you can buy some stamps."

I looked down at the money. "Where did you get this?" I asked.

"Before the bombing, Garza paid me for the work I did on the farm. He gave me a little extra before we left."

"I can't take this." I thrust it back at him. "You need it more than I do. No one on the ship expects me to have any money."

"I know. But I need you to write to me as soon as you have an address. We're still partners, right?"

"I'm going to miss you" was all I could say. Then I hugged him.

"Me too," he answered, giving me a small squeeze.

We separated and I looked up at him, trying to memorize his face. "You're my best friend," I said.

"Aren't I your only friend?" he teased.

I crossed my arms and scowled at him.

He raised his hands in surrender. "Kidding. I know that's not true . . . at least not anymore."

I thought for a moment of everyone in the Garza house and how, young and old, they all felt like my friends. "Yeah, but you're still the best one."

"Yeah? Well, good."

I could feel a lump forming in my throat, but crying was something I had been raised not to do.

"Go," Mathias said very matter-of-factly.

"What?" It was such a change of mood that I thought he was joking.

Mathias gave me a slight push. "Before I start to rethink everything. Go. *Adiós.*"

I inched backward. As much as I wanted Mathias to be with me, I knew he was destined for something else. I wasn't going to try to change his mind. "Bye, Mathias," I said, slowly turning around.

Without saying another word, I grabbed the wheelchair's handles and headed toward the ship. Every few seconds Julián glanced back at me, but wisely chose not to make any comments. As we reached the gangplank, I realized that this was it. My last time on Basque soil . . . at least for a while. I shoved the money into the skirt pocket of Señora Garza's dress and felt the small pouch. How could I have forgotten?

I spun around and searched the crowd behind us.

"Mathias!" I yelled. "Mathias!"

"What's wrong?" asked Julián.

"I forgot to give him something." I scanned the crowd.

"Over there!" Julián pointed to a group of people huddled near the end of the pier. Mathias saw us staring and waved his *makila* in the air.

I glanced down at Julián. "Can you . . . ? I'll only be gone for a minute."

He nodded and locked the wheels with his hand brake. "*Sí*. Just hurry."

"Don't go anywhere, Julián!" I shouted as I ran down the gangplank, bumping and pushing people out of the way.

Mathias met me halfway up the pier. "What's wrong?" he asked.

"Nothing." I caught my breath. "There's something I forgot to give you." I dug into my pocket.

"Give me? But . . ."

I pulled out the small pouch that Señora Garza had made with the extra dress fabric and gave it to him.

As he untied the rope around the top, I said, "It's for luck and to remind you that you're Basque too."

Mathias dug his fingers inside the pouch and took out the acorn. "Ani, I can't. Your father gave that to you."

I smiled. "No, the one Papá gave me is here." I tapped my other skirt pocket. "This one I got for you this morning from my—I mean, *our*—tree in the field."

Mathias squeezed the acorn in his hand. "It's the best gift ever." He paused for a moment, then reached into his shirt and pulled out his mother's gold necklace.

Unfastening the clasp, he slipped the two wedding bands off of the chain and put them both in the pouch, along with my acorn.

"Here." He handed me the chain. "This is for you."

"No, I—I can't." I took a step back. "It was your mother's."

"But I want you to have it." He stepped forward and fastened it around my neck. "It'll make me happy to know you have something of hers . . . of mine. Plus, it'll be safer with you . . . considering where I'm going."

I touched the star that dangled from the chain. It lay on my chest, near the third button of my dress.

"That's the Star of David . . . the Jewish star. You don't have to wear it out or anything, but I hope you'll keep it."

I slipped the chain under my dress. "I'll wear it all the time. Won't take it off at all."

"And I'll come back and plant the acorn in the field . . . after everything is over."

I smiled and we just stared at each other, not saying a word.

Then someone bumped into me and another person

jostled me backward and away from Mathias. The world around us was moving quickly, even if we had tried to make it stop.

"Friends always," I said as the crowd around us began to swell.

"Forever!" he shouted.

I turned and let the mass of people sweep me back toward the gangplank and Julián.

Mamá had been wrong. People don't always abandon you . . . even if they have to leave.

FORTY-EIGHT

As I got closer to the ship and saw the line of children standing where I'd left Julián, a feeling of panic started to grow. . . . Julián was gone. Spinning around, I looked back into the crowd. Certainly a boy in a wheelchair would be easy to spot.

My eyes scanned the pier several times, but he wasn't there. Maybe he'd already boarded. If he'd decided to just leave without me . . . I . . . I was going to murder him!

I ran toward the seaman with a clipboard.

"*Permiso, señor*," I said, cutting through the line of people. "I'm looking for a little boy."

"Hey! I was next!" A boy pushed me out of the way as the others behind him joined in his complaint, telling me to get in line.

"I'm sorry," I said, glancing at the boy before facing the seaman again. "It's just he's in a wheelchair and I can't find him. I only left him for a moment."

"Name?" the seaman asked, rolling his eyes a bit.

"Julián. Julián Garza."

The seaman didn't seem to care about everyone's complaining and flipped through a few pages. "He's on board. In the infirmary, with the other injured children. You his sister?"

"I, um, well, no . . ."

"Then end of the line. You'll have to go with everyone else," he called out.

I glanced back at the long line of people. I had promised Señora Garza that I'd keep an eye on him, and I'd told Julián I wouldn't leave him. There was no way I was going to break my promise.

A hand grabbed me by the sleeve and pulled me out of the way.

"Wait! I'm his stepsister. I need to go with him!" I shouted.

The seaman shook his head and waved me back toward him. "Why didn't you just say that? You need to speak up, girl. Last name Garza as well?" He ran his finger down the page on his clipboard.

"No, Largazabalaga. My mother remarried."

"Hmph," he muttered, turning back the pages.

I stood by him as he flipped to the list with all the *L* names. Quickly I spotted my name about halfway down the page. "There!" I pointed to it.

"I see," he muttered. Next to my name were the words *general boarding*. "The boy's your stepbrother, you say?" he asked.

Looking him right in the eyes, I nodded. "Yes, sir. My mother was a widow when she met Julián's father. He lost his wife to polio, the same awful disease that damaged Julián's legs. I promised to take care of him in England. I have—"

The seaman raised his hand to cut off my story. "*De veras, no me importa.*" He wrote my name, date of birth, and the word ENFERMERÍA on a yellow piece of paper and gave me a stickpin. "Put this on as identification and go to the room labeled INFIRMARY, one floor down. If they ask why you're not on their list, tell them Lorenzo sent you there to be with your brother." He stared at the growing line behind me. "Next!" he called out as I quickly boarded the ship and ran belowdecks.

❖   ❖   ❖

By the time I finally found the infirmary, the ship had already left port. It was no wonder I couldn't find it, considering the room was three floors down, not one, and it was really the freighter's dining hall with a paper taped to the door that read CHILDREN'S INFIRMARY.

When I walked into the room, no one questioned who I was because Julián immediately started yelling my name. The room itself was crowded, but not like the top deck, where the rest of the kids were staying. Here there was a bit more space . . . but not much. Nurses and nuns were making sure everyone got some food, and a few children were eating as if they hadn't had a meal in days. It took me a moment to realize—they probably hadn't.

I marched toward Julián. "Why did you leave? I told you I'd be right back. You scared me to death."

"What? I didn't leave. A nurse got me and wheeled me inside. I didn't have any choice." He crossed his arms over his chest. "Plus, who are you . . . my mother?"

One of the nuns lifted her head and glanced at us.

"Um, no . . . but I *am* your sister," I announced in a loud voice.

Julián scrunched up his eyebrows and looked at me as if I had gone crazy. "My sister? Are you nuts?"

I clasped my hand over his mouth. "Do you want to be left alone?" I whispered.

"Everything fine over here?" the nun asked, now standing right by us.

I peeled back my hand. "Um . . ."

"Everything's fine. My idiot sister here just likes to boss me around too much," Julián answered.

The nun looked at the two of us, unsure what to make of the situation.

"*¿Idiota?*" I pretended to be insulted. "I can't believe you just called me that!"

"Well, that's what you are, right?" Julián mocked me.

"Sounds about right for a brother and sister." The nun smiled and walked away.

"Good job," I whispered to Julián as he gave me a wink.

"Storyteller?" a voice called out. "Is that you?"

I spun around to see Diego being brought into the room.

Julián and I both shouted, "Diego!" I was about to run over when I remembered Julián and turned to bring him with me.

"Who else is here?" Diego asked.

"Just me and Julián," I said. "I mean, there are other kids in here and more up on deck . . . but just us from Garza's house."

Diego smiled, showing off his dimples. "Well, I certainly didn't think we were by ourselves on the freighter."

"Ha! Good one, Diego." Julián leaned forward and gave Diego a tap on the leg.

"Seriously, how many people are here?" Diego asked. "It sounded like a million voices when I was brought on board."

I looked around. "There are probably about a hundred in here with us, but I heard they expect more than three thousand on the ship. Basque kids from all over."

"Three thousand!" Julián exclaimed. "We'd better stick together!"

"That is a lot of people," Diego muttered. "Either of you know anyone in England?"

"No," we both replied.

Diego sighed. "Me neither."

I crouched down between Diego and Julián, not wanting to stick out as one of the few uninjured in the room.

"No parents on board either, right?" Diego asked.

"No," I answered. I knew it had to be strange for him to hear so many voices and not know who was speaking or what the surroundings looked like. "All kids, no parents."

I wondered how many of us on the freighter still had a parent.

"Your mom," I blurted out, suddenly realizing that I didn't know what had happened to her.

"She's doing better." Diego leaned back in his chair. "Well enough to regain consciousness and send me away." He crossed his arms and let his head rest against the wall behind him. "Can you believe it?"

"I'm sure she's doing what she thinks is best," I offered.

Diego shrugged. "Maybe. Or she just didn't want to deal with a son who's blind."

I thought of Mamá and how she couldn't stand people who were sick or crippled.

"I'm sure that's not it," I said, not knowing if it was true.

Diego's shoulders seemed to drop a little. "I know. I just get . . . I don't know . . . angry sometimes."

"We all do," muttered Julián. He wheeled himself around to face away from us. I saw him lock his wheels and quickly wipe a tear from his cheek.

For the first few hours, the trip was relatively quiet. The ship swayed a bit, but many of the children didn't seem to mind the rocking motion. I even spotted several eating some of the food they'd hoarded from when the nurses had first handed out the meals. More time passed, and it felt as if everyone was waiting for something to happen.

By early evening, the ship's rocking became stronger, and then suddenly the freighter seemed to tilt too far to one side. Everyone was thrown off balance, and kids tumbled into each other. Before I could recover, we were all rolling the other way.

Julián screamed as his wheelchair toppled over. I grabbed him and held on to a table that was fastened to the wall.

Had we hit a mine laid by Franco's men? Was someone trying to stop us from leaving?

As the freighter steadied itself, I peered out the porthole. A storm was howling outside, and waves smashed against the side of the ship. Behind me I could hear the commotion of everyone talking at once and several of the younger children crying out for their parents. A particularly large wave hit the ship, and sea spray doused the porthole glass, making me jump back.

We were still being swayed side to side, but I seemed to have been born with sea legs and had already found my balance. Maybe it was a family trait inherited from Papá.

But not everyone was as lucky. I watched as many of the children were quickly turning green.

"You! Girl by the window . . . *¡ayúdanos!*" a voice called out.

I looked over to see a small nurse with a booming voice shouting at me. Hesitating, I pointed to myself, unsure if she was talking to me or how she expected me to help.

"Yes, you. Go get some bowls and pass them out." She pointed toward the kitchen as she held a boy's head and he threw up everything he'd been so happy to eat a few hours earlier.

Running toward the kitchen, I jumped over a few kids on the verge of losing their lunch. There was no time to spare. I found several mixing bowls and a few pots and began to pass them out.

During the next twenty minutes or so, the room grew relatively quiet except for the occasional moans and retching noises. The stench of vomit was now making even those of us with stronger stomachs feel sick. Having emptied the kitchen of every bowl, pot, and bucket, I walked to the corner where I could see Diego holding on to the side of Julián's chair.

I thought about going to the upper deck, where most

of the other noninjured kids were. At least there I'd have fresh air.

"Ani," Julián whispered, reaching out to grab my hand. In his eyes I could see the scared little seven-year-old and not the wisecracking kid he pretended to be.

There was no way I was going to leave him behind just for some fresh air. "It'll be okay," I whispered, lying down next to his chair.

Julián looked me in the eyes. "You'll stay." It was half command, half plea.

I nodded.

The rest of the night the room remained eerily still. Eventually, everyone fell asleep, the steady swaying of the ship causing us all to regress to babies being rocked in cradles.

The murmuring of voices woke me up. As I lifted my head off the floor and got my bearings, I noticed that sunlight was already pouring in through the porthole nearby. It seemed that the weather would cooperate until we docked in England.

"G'morning, sleepyhead," Julián greeted me while chewing on a mouthful of bread.

I wiped the sleep out of my eyes and focused on him sitting in his wheelchair . . . a roll in each hand. How had he gotten there? He'd gone to sleep on the floor next to me, and I was pretty sure he needed help getting into the wheelchair.

"She's awake?" Diego asked.

"Yep," answered Julián. "At least I think she's awake. She still looks kinda groggy."

I sat up and rubbed my eyes. "I'm fine. Just tired."

Julián smirked. "We should be the ones complaining. . . . You snored really loud all night."

"Liar!" I said. . . . But what if it was true?

Julián laughed.

"It's not true. I slept right here, and you were as quiet as a mouse," Diego said, smiling.

"Ah, but you should see the look on her face, Diego." Julián slapped the side of his chair. "I got her good."

Rolling my eyes, I stuck my tongue out at Julián.

"Hey, don't stick your tongue out at me," he said.

Glancing at Diego with his bandaged eyes, I smiled and said, "I did no such thing."

"Ugh, now she really is a liar," Julián complained.

"Do you want something to eat?" Diego asked. "They've been passing out breakfast rolls."

I smoothed my hair, immediately realizing that Diego couldn't see whether I looked presentable or not. "Um, no. I'm okay. What have you two been doing besides eating?"

"Oh, just talking. Tried to tell Julián a story, but I'm no good at that kind of thing. Best I leave that to you."

"Not if it's the story Ani was telling before. That one has too much about some silly princess."

At the sound of the word *princess*, a little girl with straight blond hair who sat only a few feet away from us turned her head.

"So you don't want to find out what happens next?" I asked.

"Well"—Julián crossed his arms—"I did like the part about the sea monster." He paused for a moment. "I guess since we're in the middle of the sea with nothing better to do . . . might as well hear about the dumb princess getting eaten—"

"The princess does *not* get eaten," I answered, watching the little blond girl out of the corner of my eye.

"What was the princess's name?" Another little girl, this one with big brown curls, scooted toward us.

"Her name?" I thought for a moment as both girls sat closer to me.

"Who cares?" Julián said, rolling his eyes. "Just listen to the story. Her name doesn't matter."

The little girl crossed her arms. "Of *course* it matters!"

"Um. Well, her name was"—I glanced at Julián and smiled—"Juliana."

Diego chuckled, and the little girl nodded. "Princess Juliana is a pretty name," she said.

"Ugh," Julián groaned.

I retold the story from the very beginning, making sure to dwell a little longer on my description of the beautiful Princess Juliana. As I got to the part about the fairy granting the princess her wish to get off the island, all the children were mesmerized, hanging on my every word.

"So the fairy gave Princess Juliana a magical token that would let her travel the seas without being attacked by the horrible sea monster."

A little boy with dark hair and green eyes raised his hand as if we were in school.

I paused the story and pointed to him, as so many of my teachers had done to me.

"What's a token?" he asked.

"A token is something small. It can be a coin or a shell." I looked at the several new faces that had gathered around me to hear the story. "In this case, the fairy gave Princess Juliana a magic seed." I reached into my pocket, skipping over the brass weight, and pulled out my silk pouch. "This seed would protect any traveler, and it could be planted so that new seeds would be produced for more people to travel the seas." I opened the pouch and pulled out my acorn. "It was just like this one."

A chorus of oohs and aahs erupted.

"Can I hold it?" A little hand reached out to me.

I clasped the acorn. "No, because . . ." I glanced around and curled my finger to bring the children even closer, then whispered, "It has to stay a secret, just between us, but I think this acorn might be one of the magical seeds."

"Will it help us avoid the sea monster?" one little boy exclaimed.

"Of course," I replied, putting the acorn into its pouch and slipping it back into my skirt pocket.

"Are you the princess from the story?" a little girl asked, her eyes wide as could be.

I shook my head. "That princess lived a long time ago, and when she crossed the sea and arrived in the new land, she planted the magic seed. After many years that seed grew into a tall, strong tree. It was a tree so great and so magical that kings and queens would use it as a place to meet with other leaders."

"Hey, was that the oak in Guernica? Did it come from the magic acorn?" Julián asked, caught up in the story like the other children.

"No one knows for sure. But legend has it that the *jentillak*, those mythical creatures that live in the Basque forest, would gather up the acorns of the magic tree and plant them in different cities."

"Why?" Julián asked.

"Because each tree would produce acorns that carried a special magic for those who knew the secret."

"What secret?" several voices said at the same time.

I smiled. "Well"—I paused—"are you sure you want to know?"

"*¡Sí!*" they all shouted.

"The secret is . . . those magic seeds help you to always find your way home."

"That's good because I want to go home soon," a little girl announced, with many of the children responding with strong "Me toos!"

"And so, *colorín, colorado, este cuento se ha acabado,*" I said, signaling the end of the story.

"*¡Otro!*" shouted the blond girl.

"Yes, another one . . . pleeease!" said the one with big brown curls.

Julián nodded and smiled. "Pretty good story."

"Pretty good storyteller," Diego corrected.

"I'd have to agree with that," a voice said from behind me. I turned to see the small nurse who'd ordered me to pass out the bowls the night before. "You have a real gift."

I could feel my cheeks turning red from the attention. Instinctively, my hand dug into my pocket, bypassing the silk pouch with the acorn and grasping the brass weight. "It's nothing, really," I mumbled.

"It most certainly is something," she said, smiling down at me.

In the morning light, the nurse, wearing her crisp white outfit and small white cap, didn't seem as fierce as she did when everyone was sick. She actually looked sweet.

"I'd say you've got a real blessing there . . . to be able to tell stories like that. Not many people have the gift of getting others to listen to them." She bit at her fingernail. "Maybe we can have you do something at the camp. What do you think?"

My eyes darted toward the window. In the distance, I could already see what seemed to be land.

England. A new country, a new life, was just on the horizon.

Could this be my chance? I wanted to be able to share Mathias's stories and tell everyone there what was happening back home.

"I'd like that," I replied. "Maybe I could be a reporter . . . or something."

The nurse chuckled a bit. "Well, you certainly dream big!"

I tightened my grip on the brass weight in my pocket—so much that I could feel it leaving an imprint on the palm of my hand.

"I was thinking more along the lines of you telling the children stories . . . to keep them from being so lonely." She gave me a wink. "We'll see how it goes from there. Who knows what else you might do."

I gave her a slight nod.

"Good." She began to walk away when she suddenly turned on her heels and quickly came back. "I almost forgot.

I'm Nurse Estévez." She looked down at the yellow paper pinned to my shirt. It had become slightly crumpled over the course of the night, and one of the corners was folded over, hiding part of what was written. "And what's your name?" she asked.

It was such a simple question, but so many things flashed through my head.

Everything with a name exists. That was the old Basque saying, but who was it that existed? Mamá's *neska*? Papá's *preciosa*? How about Sardine Girl, who had no friends? Or Mathias's princess? Maybe it was Diego's storyteller?

Perhaps Mamá had been right about something—it *was* time for me to make a choice. I could choose to be a whisper, or I could make myself heard.

In my pocket, I unclenched my fist and let go of the brass weight.

A new girl existed. One who would thunder . . . who would matter.

I straightened up and smiled at Nurse Estévez. "My name is Anetxu," I said. "But my friends call me Ani."

EPILOGUE

The trip from London to Guernica had been planned for weeks. So much had changed in the years since I'd first left Spain. I no longer resembled the twelve-year-old daughter of the *sardinera* and, after almost forty years of Basque culture being outlawed, I didn't expect Guernica to be the same either.

But the reality was worse than I'd imagined. The city no longer felt familiar. Some buildings were modern and others had been *made* to look old. In the months since Franco's death, the new Spanish government had granted the Basque people the right to speak their language and celebrate their culture, but too much had already been lost. Two generations of cultural secrecy had taken its toll. I wasn't sure if it could be recaptured.

I paused and looked through the window of a small store on the main street of Guernica. The building was similar to the one that used to stand there, but I knew the truth. It wasn't the original.

Inside the shoe store, a little girl was trying on a pair of white sandals and she twirled around in front of her mother, clearly pleased with the pretty shoes. It made me flash back to the times before the bombing when Carmita would ask to play with Mathias and me. Perhaps Carmita had children of her own by now. I wondered if she even remembered us or her time in Guernica.

The little girl in the store seemed to sense my eyes on her, so she stopped spinning, looked at me, and waved. I smiled and waved back, briefly catching my reflection in the storefront window.

I was now older than my mother was when she had been killed. The oversized sunglasses I was wearing couldn't hide the little wrinkles time had etched on my face. Yet, even after so many years, here I was, longing to feel connected to my first home.

I kept walking. The answer would not be found in the city. So I headed for the outskirts of Guernica, and a field that I hoped still remained. The Garzas had sold their land after the war, and I wasn't sure who owned it anymore.

As I walked up the mountainside, the familiar smells and feelings of my childhood returned. Memories of Papá sharing his stories and that first day when I met Mathias came flooding back. I picked up the pace as a gentle breeze urged me forward.

And then I was there, in the field, my tree within sight.

As I approached, I noticed that a skinny little tree, not more than ten feet high, had sprung up only a few yards away.

I had planned to sit in the shade of the old oak again, but something drew me to the younger tree.

It was carefully tended, with a circle of rocks surrounding the base. Then I noticed a small wooden sign.

A single tear ran down my cheek while a smile, as big as all of Spain, spread across my face. I had found the connection I most needed. I read the words that only one person could have written.

"*This* is Ani's tree."

AUTHOR'S NOTE

This story came about because of several, seemingly unrelated occurrences. It began in a brief conversation with a friend about art and Pablo Picasso's famous painting *Guernica* (in which I discovered that I knew embarrassingly little on either subject). I had a strong desire to learn more about my Basque heritage. And then a random photo of a *sardinera* sparked my imagination. It's funny how a quote from Picasso sums up what I was doing: "Inspiration exists, but it has to find us working."

Pablo Picasso's famous mural *Guernica* (*courtesy of the Estate of Pablo Picasso/Artists Rights Society [ARS], New York*)

My great-great-grandmother Justa and her daughter Bernarda in the
Basque countryside, circa 1917

While I was writing and doing research for the story, it became
evident that I needed to visit Guernica to truly appreciate the
people and atmosphere of the city. Most of the city was destroyed
during the bombing, so I had to depend on old photographs and
the lovely people of Guernica to show me what the city looked like
before that fateful day of April 26, 1937.

Guernica before the bombing—Plaza de los Fueros
*(courtesy of the Center of Documentation Regarding the Gernika Bombing,
Gernika Peace Museum Foundation)*

Guernica after the bombing *(courtesy of the Center of Documentation Regarding the Gernika Bombing, Gernika Peace Museum Foundation)*

After the devastation caused by the bombing, fear of another massive attack caused thousands of Basque parents to send their children to England to keep them out of harm's way. These children were first placed in a makeshift camp in Southampton and eventually sent to homes all over Great Britain. By the time World War II began in 1939, the Spanish Civil War was over and most of the Basque children returned to their parents. However, about four hundred Basque children remained in England because their parents either had died during the Spanish Civil War or had been imprisoned.

1937 photo of Basque children at Stoneham Camp in Eastleigh, Southampton, England (*courtesy of the Basque Children of '37 Association UK*)

My understanding of Guernica's history was brought to life by often painful retellings by those who experienced the bombing. I am truly grateful to Ana Teresa Núñez Monasterio of the Gernika Peace Museum and to José Angel "Txato" Etxaniz Ortuñez of the Historical Society of Guernica (Gernikazarra), who not only showed me what was readily available in their collections but walked the town with me, pointing out little-known facts, and even snuck me into one of the old air-raid shelters. Their hospitality strengthened my connection to my Basque heritage. *Eskerrik asko!* Thank you.

ACKNOWLEDGMENTS

As always, I am grateful to so many for giving me the opportunity to work with my ideas and allowing me to discover my inspirations.

First and foremost, I thank the Lord for all my many blessings, including my husband and my two greatest joys, my sons.

Thank you to all of the Diaz/Gonzalez/Pintado/Eguiguren/ Vazquez-Aldana/Llerena/Alcazar/Roiz/Garcia/Buigas members who make up my loving, supportive, boisterous (nice way to say loud), unique (a nicer way of saying slightly crazy) family. . . . I love you all!

For all my writer friends, who understand the roller-coaster ride of this business, thank you for keeping me sane. To those of you who gave me feedback and advice when this story was in its early stages, Adrienne Sylver, Linda Rodriguez Bernfeld, Gaby Triana, Joyce Sweeney, Bel Miranda, Liz Trotta, Mary Thorpe, Sylvia Lopez, and Kay Cassidy, *muchas gracias!* A special thank-you (and a tall peppermint mocha) to my writing cohort, Danielle

Joseph, who gives me such wonderful writing advice and always saves my favorite chair at our local Starbucks.

Thank you to all the amazing booksellers, librarians, and teachers who encourage me with their enthusiasm and love for stories, especially Debra, Becky, Jeanne, and Allison, who turn my favorite bookstore into a refuge.

Eskerrik asko to Ana Teresa Núñez Monasterio of the Gernika Peace Museum and to José Angel "Txato" Etxaniz Ortuñez of the Historical Society of Guernica (Gernikazarra), who walked the streets of Guernica with me (even in the rain) and helped me understand what it was like to live there during the Spanish Civil War. I look forward to my next visit.

Finally, I am extremely fortunate to work once again with my amazing editor, Nancy Siscoe, and the fantastic team at Random House/Knopf, which includes (but is not limited to) Katherine Harrison, Adrienne Waintraub, Dominique Cimina, and Melissa Greenberg. Thank you, thank you, thank you to my fabulous agent, Jen Rofé, for making it all happen!

GLOSSARY

Most glossary entries are Spanish,
but some Basque (*) terms are included.

abierto (ah-bee-EHR-toh): open

abuela (ah-BWEH-lah): grandmother

abuelo (ah-BWEH-loh): grandfather

adiós (ah-dee-OHS): goodbye

***agur** (ah-GOOR): goodbye

ahora (ah-OH-rah): now

Alemania (ah-lay-MAH-nee-ah): the Spanish word for Germany

alguien mas (AHL-gee-en mahs): someone else

*ama (AH-mah): mother

¡Apúrate! (ah-POO-rah-teh): Hurry!

aquí (ah-KEE): here

*arratsalde on (ah-RAHT-sahl-deh un): good evening

ay, Dios mío (ai, DEE-ohs MEE-oh): oh my God

ayúdanos (ai-YOO-dah-nohs): help us

¡Basta! (BAH-stah): Enough!

¡Bien! (bee-EN): Good!

búscame (BOO-skah-meh): look for me

¿Caballito otra vez? (kah-bah-YEE-toh OH-trah vehs):
    Horsey again?

cálmate (KAHL-mah-tay): calm down

carga (KAR-gah): carry

claro (KLAH-roh): of course

cojo (KOH-hoh): lame; crippled

colorín, colorado, este cuento se ha acabado (koh-loh-REEN,
    koh-loh-RAH-doh, ES-teh KWEN-toh seh ah ah-kah-BAH-
    doh): this story has finished

come basura (KOH-meh bah-SOO-rah): trash eater (derogatory term)

con todo nuestro corazón (kohn TOH-doh NWEH-stroh koh-rah-SOHN): with all our heart

de verás (deh vehr-AHS): really

¡Despiértate! (deh-spee-EHR-tah-teh): Wake up!

dichoso (dee-CHOH-soh): lucky

¿Dormistes bien, niña? (dor-MEE-stehs bee-EN, NEE-nyah): Did you sleep well, girl?

dulce (DOOL-seh): a sweet

el cine (el SEE-neh): the movie theater

¿Él es tu tío? (el ehs too TEE-oh): Is he your uncle?

enfermería (en-fehr-meh-REE-ah): infirmary

¿Entiendes? (en-tee-EN-dehs): Understand?

entra (EN-trah): come in

eres (EHR-ehs): you are

espérate (eh-SPEHR-ah-tay): wait

está (eh-STAH): it is

¡Está despierta! (eh-STAH deh-spee-EHR-tah): She's awake!

está inconsciente (eh-STAH een-kohn-see-EN-tay): she's
unconscious

estoy (eh-STOY): I am

estúpida (eh-STOO-pee-dah): stupid

*ez nazazu utzi (ehz nah-ZAH-zoo oot-ZEE): don't leave me

gracias (GRAH-see-ahs): thank you

¿Haciendo qué? (ah-see-EN-doh kay): Doing what?

hija (EE-hah): daughter

hola (OH-lah): hello

*izena duen guztiak izatea ere badauke (EE-zehn-ah dwehn
gooz-TEE-ack eez-AH-teh-ah eh-reh bah-DOW-keh):
everything with a name exists

*jai alai (hie AH-lie): a court game that uses a ball and a long
wicker basket strapped to the wrist: a variety of pelota vasca

*jentillak (hehn-TEE-lack): mythological race of Basque giants

*kaixo (KAI-show): hello

La Fuga de Tarzan (lah FOO-gah deh TAR-zahn): *Tarzan Escapes*

*lagundu iezadazu (lah-GOON-doo ee-eh-sah-DAH-zoo): help me

¿Lo puedo ayudar? (loh PWEH-doh ai-yoo-DAHR): Can I help you?

*makila (mah-KEE-lah): a Basque walking stick

maldita guerra (mahl-DEE-tah GWEH-rah): evil war

*marmitako (mahr-MEE-tah-koh): a Basque fish stew

me lo imagine (meh loh ee-mah-HEE-neh): I imagined that

¿Me veo bien? (meh VAY-oh bee-EN): Do I look fine?

menos mal (MEH-nohs mahl): an expression meaning "thank
  goodness"

mentirosa (mehn-tee-ROH-sah): liar

mija (MEE-hah): shortened from *mi hija*, which means "my daughter"

mira (MEE-rah): look

muchas bombas (MOO-chahs BOHM-bahs): many bombs

nada (NAH-dah): nothing

*neska (NEH-skah): girl

niña (NEE-nyah): girl

niñita (nee-NYEE-tah): little girl

niños (NEE-nyohs): children

no hables así (noh AH-blehs ah-SEE): don't speak like that

no importa (noh eem-POR-tah): doesn't matter

no me esperes (noh meh ehs-PEHR-ehs): don't wait for me

no seas tonta (noh SEH-ahs TOHN-tah): don't be stupid

no te preocupes (noh teh preh-oh-COO-pehs): don't worry

no, todavía (noh, toh-dah-VEE-ah): no, not yet

¡Nos tenemos que ir! (nohs teh-NEHM-ohs keh eer): We have to leave!

otro (OH-troh): another

oye (OY-eh): hey

*patxaran (pah-CHAH-rahn): a liqueur made from sloe berries

pelota vasca (peh-LOH-tah VAH-skah): a variety of court sports played by hitting a ball with one's hand, a racket, a wooden bat, or a basket against a wall

perdóneme (pehr-DOH-neh-meh): pardon me

perdonen la interrupción (pehr-DOH-nehn lah een-tehr-oop-see-OHN): pardon the interruption

permiso (pehr-MEE-soh): excuse me

peseta (peh-SEH-tah): money

por favor (por fah-VOR): please

¿Por qué? (por-KEH): Why?

pórtate bien (POR-tah-teh bee-EN): behave well

preciosa (preh-see-OH-sah): precious

¿Qué? (keh): What?

¡Que bueno! (keh BWAY-noh): How good / wonderful!

¡Qué cosa! (keh KOH-sah): What a thing! / Unbelievable!

qué Díos te bendiga (keh DEE-ohs teh ben-DEE-gah): may God
   bless you

¿Qué pasó? (keh pah-SOH): What happened?

¿Qué tú haces? (keh too AH-sehs): What are you doing?

¡Sardina fresca! (sahr-DEE-nah FREHS-kah): Fresh sardine!

*¡**Sardina frescue!** (sahr-DEE-nah FREHS-kweh): Fresh sardine!

sardinas (sahr-DEE-nahs): sardines

sardinera (sahr-dee-NEHR-ah): woman who sells sardines

seguro (seh-GOO-roh): sure

señor (seh-NYOR): sir

señora (seh-NYOR-ah): madam or ma'am

sí (see): yes

sombrero de copa (sohm-BREHR-oh deh KOH-pah): top hat

son bien dichosos (sohn bee-EN dee-CHOH-sohs): you are very lucky

Te quiero mucho (teh kee-EHR-oh MOO-choh): I love you very much

¿Todo bien? (TOH-doh bee-EN): Is everything good?

Todos creen que se van hacer de dinero (TOH-dohs CRAY-en
keh seh vahn ah-SEHR deh dee-NEHR-oh): You all think you
are going to make money

tranquila (trahn-KEE-lah): relax

¿Tu. Ver. Bombas? (too vehr BOHM-bas): You. See. Bombs?

¡Un besote! (oon beh-SOH-teh): A big kiss!

un idiota (oon ee-dee-OH-tah): an idiot

un malcriado (oon mahl-cree-AH-doh): a spoiled brat

un placer (oon plah-SEHR): a pleasure

¿Una bellota? (OO-nah bay-OH-tah): An acorn?

una carta (OO-nah CAR-tah): a letter

vale (VAH-leh): okay

vamos/vámonos (VAH-mohs/VAH-moh-nohs): let's go

ven (vehn): come

verdad (vehr-DAHD): truth

viejos (vee-EH-hohs): old men

¿Y tus padres? (ee toos PAH-drehs): And your parents?

ya (yah): enough

Yo soy él que va a salir de aquí (yoh soy el keh vah ah sah-LEER

    deh ah-KEE): I am the one that is going to get out of here